PERFECTIBLE ANIMALS

Thomas Norwood

Perfectible Animals

First published in 2013 by Global Activision Limited

Norwood, Thomas
    Perfectible Animals
    ISBN-10: 0992355206
    ISBN-13: 978-0-9923552-0-3

Global Activision Limited
PO Box 94
Flinders Lane
VICTORIA, 8009
Australia.

Front cover image: Hybrid Medical Animation
Back cover author photo: Erin Lee Photography

More information: www.thomasnorwood.com.au

To my parents, who made me who I am,
And Iliana, who has to put up with that.

PERFECTIBLE ANIMALS

Thomas Norwood

Thomas Norwood

Chapter One

MY ELECTRIC VEHICLE slows as it joins the line of traffic waiting to get through the gates to the regulated zone. I watch a group of poor people sitting around on the dusty ground in what used to be a park, waiting for someone from inside the fence to come out and offer them a job. It happens sometimes – someone might need a laborer or a cook, even the occasional accountant or teacher. Nobody is safe from unemployment these days.

There is a fire burning in a forty gallon drum and a man is spit-roasting the remains of what looks like a wombat. People are lining up for it. A woman collects the money while the man cuts slices directly onto plastic plates. A couple of guys with sawn-off shot guns stand nearby in case of trouble, no doubt taking their cut of the profits. A wombat must be a rare find these days – and the man and woman will probably live like royalty for a few days before returning to their pre-wombat squalor.

Behind the park, a new shipping container housing

estate is going up, surrounded by blackmerries which are rolling across the land like a floodwater. The bastard child of wild blackberries and genetically-modified blackberries, blackmerries are drought and herbicide resistant and seem to be in a race with *Homo sapiens* to take over what is left of the world.

A fight breaks out in the line of people between a man with a matted beard and a woman clutching her emaciated child. I consider getting out of the car and giving the woman a couple of hundred dollars so she can get a decent meal for a few days and feed her son, but the line of vehicles moves on and I'm up at the checkpoint having my retina scanned.

"Returning home, sir?" a guard holding a machine gun asks.

"Yes."

"Can you tell me where you've been?"

My com profile, which he has access to, contains all the information he needs to know, so I'm not sure why he's asking me questions. I wipe sweaty palms off against my trousers.

"I'm a scientist. My company has a facility in the medical exclusion zone. I've been working there," I say.

I think back to the clinic in the desert, from where we've just evacuated over one hundred genetically modified children.

"Company name?"

"Geneus."

"Have you been through quarantine?"

"Yes." Again this information is all on my profile. Why is he stalling?

"Just a moment." He walks back inside his cubicle and I see him talking to another guard. I watch my clock. Two and a half minutes go by. I try to read their expressions or gather information from their body language using an app on my visual overlay but it tells me nothing.

Finally, the guard comes out again. "Go on through, sir."

As my car takes off I breathe out with relief.

My house is located in a gated community in what was once inner Melbourne, but is now a beachside suburb. Ten years ago, one particularly hot summer, the West Antarctic Ice Sheet collapsed and caused a global sea level rise of two-point-eight meters. Melbourne, along with all the other major coastal cities in Australia, was partly destroyed. Those who had enough money took over the dry houses, and those left without jobs were forced to move to shanty towns outside the city, where crime and disease run rife.

Before long, unofficial lines were drawn between the protected enclaves and the unprotected poor, and it wasn't long after that that official lines, marked with heavily guarded fences, were erected, inside which government control still operates and outside of which they no longer bother.

It isn't only the flooding that is causing this turmoil; weather extremes in the world's key food bowls means it is now impossible to feed everyone. Democratic governments around the world, unable to adequately protect their citizens, are losing their grip and being taken over by military dictatorships, rebel groups or corporations, and even in Australia, where we were shielded from the worst of it for years thanks to the wealth generated by our large supply of coal, uranium, steel and oil, things are difficult.

Ironically, some of the poorer countries are surviving the flooding and weather extremes better than the wealthy ones. Many of their citizens have always been subsistence farmers, and they know how to grow their own crops and tend to animals, so the loss of industrial farming capabilities in centralized areas hasn't hit them so badly.

My car pulls up to the gate leading into our community and my window opens so I can identify myself to the retina scanner. I give Henry a wave and drive on through as he opens the gate.

Inside our house, I find Annie in our bedroom packing our cases. Her dark eyes look up at me. I brush her hair away from her pale face and we kiss. I hold onto her for a minute, inhaling her sweet smell.

"How are you feeling?" I say.

"A little better," she says, brushing my chin and going back to her packing. "Have you heard anything about the children?"

"No, not yet. Last I heard they'd left the compound but hadn't boarded the planes. Dylan said they were having trouble getting clearance to land, and they might have to fly in to another airstrip."

"Is our plane ready?"

"I hope so. Apparently it's waiting for us at Essendon airport."

"Which shoes do you want to take?" Annie says, squatting down in front of our closet where my shoes are neatly lined up. "I don't think we can fit all of them in."

"Here, I'll do it." I bend down to select my shoes. "Are you all ready?"

"Almost. Do you really think leaving is the right thing, Michael?"

"I'm not sure. If anyone finds out about those children and what they're capable of, though, we'll be arrested."

"Maybe you should turn them over to the government," she says.

"So they can turn them into soldiers? Create more bio-weapons?"

"Yes. You're right. Can we take these photos?" She holds up one of the framed photos we have on our dresser – the one of us on our honeymoon in Paris, smiling in front of the Eiffel tower.

"Of course."

Annie puts the photo into her suitcase and zips it up. I take my three favorite pairs of shoes – two pairs of sneakers and a pair of brown leather boots – and squeeze them into the side of one of my own cases.

Half an hour later, everything is packed into the car and Annie and I take one final walk through our house together. There are still books on the shelves, paintings on the walls, rugs on the floors. Annie's favorite cup is out on the kitchen bench. Memories of the last ten years of our life here are stored in every corner, in every room, and I take Annie's hand and squeeze it gently as we stare around for one last time.

We lock the front door on our way out. Annie has already contracted a real estate agent and the house will be put on the market next week, the money wired to us via bitcoin when it's sold.

"Well, this is it," she says.

"Yes, it is."

We climb into our car and I ask it to take us to the airport.

As we are leaving our one way street a black van pulls up in front of us. We wait for it to move but four men in dark suits climb out and surround our vehicle. A police badge flashes through my window and knuckles rap on the glass. A hand goes to the side of a jacket where I see the bulge of what I assume to be a pistol.

I consider switching the car into manual and flooring it in reverse, but that would involve running over the man in my rear-vision mirror and possibly getting shot at. Besides, there is no escape. It's a one way street.

I lower the window.

"Michael Khan?" the man says; a square-jawed, close-shaved, cropped-haired brute of a man. His gray eyes look in at me through flawless skin and I wonder if he's one of the new androids the police force is using.

"Yes?" I try to sound casual.

"You're going to have to come with us."

"Where to?"

"Just step out of the vehicle, please."

I look around me at the four solid men with guns and realize I have no choice.

"Michael, no!" Annie says. She puts her hand on my arm.

"It's okay," I say. "It's going to be okay."

I tell the engine to switch off and climb slowly out of the car. Adrenaline floods me like cold water. Everything is happening in slow motion. I can hear the men's feet on the concrete, their breathing, a siren wailing in the distance.

The first man takes out a pair of plastic handcuffs.

"Can I ask what this all about?" I keep my back to the car as if there is still a chance I might be able to return to it.

"You'll find out soon enough. This way please." He grabs me by one arm and twists it around behind my back while another of the men, slightly older with thinning hair on top, comes around and grabs my other arm. Before I know it they've got the handcuffs on me, digging into my skin.

Annie tries to open her door but one of the men leans against it and stops her.

"Please remain in the vehicle, ma'am."

"Let me out! What the hell is going on?"

The three men holding me push me in the direction of the van. What will happen if I run? Will I be shot down in the street? The one who spoke to me first has a bulky, animated, athletes body, and the other two, although shorter, look like they could easily outrun me too.

One of the men, a cold, blue-eyed, ambitious looking unit, forces me into the van and sits across from me. His jacket is forced open by his weightlifter's chest. I look back to see Annie getting out of our vehicle but the man who was holding her back jumps into the back of the van with us and we take off on autopilot.

Are they really police officers? Or am I being kidnapped?

"What is this about?" I say.

"Everything will be explained to you when we arrive," the man across from me says, no emotion in his voice.

I try to access the net on my com, a nano-tech computer built into my brain, but they've somehow put a block on it. I have heavy-grade firewalls so, whoever they are, they're very well equipped. As far as I know only the government has the technology and the authority to do that.

Without the constant stream of data about the outside world on my visual overlay I feel blinded. I try to guess where we are going by sight alone, but all the windows are blacked out except the windscreen and after a few blocks I lose track of our direction. I catch the occasional glimpse of an industrial shed or a truck with shipping containers. There is little traffic on the road. We must be down near the old port somewhere – this is not an area I've ever spent any time in, and in the last few years, since the sea level rise, it has changed dramatically.

After a long drive we pull up at a gate in a high-security, razor-wire-lined fence. Guards carrying machine guns look into the van and we are waved on through. Once inside, the man across from me opens the van door and asks me to step down. The other two follow. I find myself in the car park of a two-story, cream-brick building that looks like a mental institution. Blue bars cover small windows. I am led over to a glass entrance, past more security guards. My captors check in with another guard behind thick glass then pat me down and check the contents of my pockets. A loud buzz precedes the opening of a steel gate. I am taken to a small interrogation room, asked to sit down, then left alone.

I look around me. There is a two-way mirror. Security cameras are mounted on the ceiling. The walls are the same pale blue as the rest of the building. Time condenses and my mind goes into overdrive as I think about what to do. In the space of less than a minute, I've thought about the last ten years of my life and all the possible mistakes I could have made which led me here. I think about the genetically modified children, how the viruses they were designed to resist mutated and got out of control. I try once again to access the net, but I am still being blocked. At least my com itself is still working, and I monitor my vital signs. My heart rate is up. I breathe slowly. I must stay calm.

The door to the room opens and a tall man in a pair of suit pants and a white, pressed shirt but no jacket comes in. His hair is not short like the others, but is styled back in a thick wave. His face is angular but good-looking. He unlocks my handcuffs and offers me his hand which I shake with relief.

"I'm Don James," the man says. "Michael Khan, isn't it?"

"That's right."

"Welcome to ASIO."

The Australian Security Intelligence Organization. So they still exist.

"ASIO?"

"That's right. They didn't tell you?"

"They didn't tell me anything."

Don chuckles briefly, as if at some private joke. "Well, never mind."

"What am I doing here?"

"To be perfectly honest, Michael..." Don sits down in one of the chairs across from me, crossing one leg over the other and resting his elbow on it, cupping his chin in his hand and looking at me. "You've been involved in some fairly interesting business."

"What business is that?" Playing dumb is my only strategy until I find out what they want.

Don stares at me, then uncrosses his legs and stands up

again. He presses the tips of his fingers onto the tabletop. His knuckles start whitening. The flesh under his nails goes red.

"I think you have a pretty good idea what I'm talking about." He stares at me with an unwavering determination, as if trying to see right through my skull and directly into my thoughts. I wonder if they've come up with an app which allows him to do that. At the very least I presume he's measuring my biometrics and monitoring my gestures and facial expressions, just as I am doing to him. Although he gives away nothing.

I can feel the way my ventricles throb, opening up to draw in blood and squeezing down hard to spread it through my body. I hear a sound that I initially think are footsteps but then realize are my heartbeats. I wonder if I am going to have a heart attack. According to my com, my heart rate is over one hundred and twenty. I have to calm down. Although if they know about everything I've been involved in, a heart attack might be merciful. I imagine months if not years of solitary confinement. Torture, as they try to extract every last piece of information from me, even after I've told them everything.

Doubts open up inside my mind, threatening to tumble me into a dark, knowledge-less abyss. Who is really in charge of Gendigm, the organization I have been secretly working for? I have always considered them democratic, but there must be someone at the head, behind the scenes so they can never be implicated. There have been hints now and then that their supporters are everywhere, at every level of society. Presumably not in ASIO, or I wouldn't be here. Unless I am their scapegoat.

"I think I need to see a lawyer."

"All in good time." Don smooths his hair back with one hand. "But before you do, you might like to listen to what I have to offer."

"What's that?" I grip the sides of my chair.

"A plea bargain."

"What type of plea bargain?"

"You tell us everything you know, and we'll make sure that you get off lightly. A lot more lightly than you will if you don't tell us anything. Or if you get your lawyer involved in this." His eyes narrow and I can see the thick lines of determination scarring his face.

"I have a right to a lawyer."

"I'm afraid you don't. So far, you haven't been charged with anything."

"Well, shouldn't you charge me with something, then, before holding me?"

"In cases like yours, we can hold you for as long as we like." Don seems pretty smug.

"What do you mean, cases like mine?" I feel the sweat emerge on the top of my brow, resist the urge to wipe it away. One of the fluorescent lights flickers and buzzes. My heart rate picks up again and I can see 124BPM in the top right of my visual overlay. Don's is at a steady 60.

"Terrorism." Don sits back down in his chair, clutching his armrests.

"I'm not sure I understand you. I'm a scientist. A geneticist. I'm involved in clinical trials, specifically to do with the immune system. I've done quite a bit of work for the government even, surely you know that. As far as I know, everything we do now in the regulated zone is perfectly safe, and anything even potentially risky is carried out in the de-reg zone. I thought the government wasn't interested in what goes on there."

"We're not, unless it threatens people here."

"It's not in your jurisdiction."

"We tend to look at it the same way as we do another country," he says, as if explaining something to a child. "We have very little control over it, but if someone there starts doing something which threatens our safety here then we'll do what we can to stop them."

"And how do you think I'm doing that?"

"I think you know the answer to that question already, Michael." He stands up and heads towards the door. "So, I'll tell you what I'm going to do. I'm going to give you a night to think about it. Let's meet again in the morning and you can tell me if you're ready to cooperate or not."

He walks out and a few minutes later, a guard comes in and takes me to a small, artificially lit room where I am made to strip and change into an orange jumpsuit. I am led down another corridor lined with doors. Each door has a tiny window in it. Faces are pressed up against some. Gaunt eyes stare out at me, desperate, it seems, for even the sight of another human being. The guard presses his hand against a screen on the wall and, with a metallic click and a beep, the door to a cell opens, and I am guided inside. The guard removes my handcuffs then leaves.

The room is two meters by three, with nothing but a bed, a toilet and a basin in it. The only window is the one in the door looking back out into the corridor. The ceiling is high, nearly three meters, probably to stop people hanging themselves from the single, bare light globe that hangs down on a brown cord. The walls are made of concrete blocks, painted matte white. A tiny vent in the ceiling lets off a whiff of stale air.

After a complete inspection of the room, which takes less than ten seconds, I gulp some water from the basin, brush it over my face and through my hair, rub it against the back of my neck and sit down on the mattress. It's bare apart from a thin blanket and a pillow. They obviously don't want their prisoners getting too comfortable. I lie down on my back, pull the blanket over myself, and stare at the ceiling, but all I can see is Annie climbing out of our car and screaming after me.

CHAPTER TWO

THAT NIGHT I can't sleep. Paranoia starts playing tricks on my mind. I'm no longer even sure where I am. My breathing is heavy but I still feel as if I can't get enough oxygen into my lungs. I stand up and pace around the room and then lie down again but it does no good. All I can think about is Annie. What she's doing. If she's okay. To distract myself, I think back to the time when we met. I force myself to imagine every detail, and as I do so I feel my breathing slow, my mind start to relax.

It was the first day of Year Ten. I was sitting in class, doodling in the margins of my English exercise book, when our teacher brought her in and introduced her to the class. She stood there quietly, dark eyes to the floor. I felt myself starting to warm as I glanced over her slender body, already mature, in a summer school uniform. Between the top of her socks and the hem of her dress I caught sight of the smooth white skin of her thighs. Being virtually friendless, the only spare seat in the room was next to me and my heart pounded as I waited for her to be seated in it.

Sure enough, a moment later, her black eyes were staring at me.

"Hi," I whispered.

"Hi," she whispered back. "I'm Annie." She gave me a smile the likes of which no girl had ever given me before.

"I'm Michael."

I spent the next hour and a half of class not daring to look across at her in case she disappeared, or I caught a look on her face which told me that she had suddenly become infected with the same opinion of me that most other girls in the school seemed to have.

After class it was Annie who spoke to me. I was even less articulate with girls than usual, but somehow she managed to get out of me where the school library was and, on the way there, the fact that my parents had died ten years earlier and that I was now living with my maternal grandparents. It was this piece of information that brought us together and cemented our friendship, at least for a while.

"That makes two of us," Annie said, pawing through the novel section looking for the prescribed reading texts for English class: Robinson Crusoe and The Chocolate War.

I was just hanging around by then, not quite sure if I should stay or go.

"Your parents died too?" I said.

"No, silly." She turned to me and gave me another one of her smiles. "My Dad left. That's why we're in this shit hole, if you'll excuse my French. My grandparents live here and my mum wanted to be close to them." She spoke with a mild English accent and was sophisticated in a way other girls in town weren't. From that first day on I found myself obsessed with her in a way I'd never been obsessed with anyone else before.

By the following Friday, she was still talking to me and after school she asked me if I wanted to do something with her on the weekend. I knew that what most other kids did when they went on a date was to go to the local cinema where they could grope and kiss one another in the dark. It seemed too soon for such a daring plan, though. I wasn't at all certain of my groping and kissing abilities, and the only movie which was playing was a re-run of an old *Terminator* movie which I thought probably wouldn't interest her. Instead, I invited her to go swimming at the local lake, which was probably the single worst decision I had ever made in my life. There was a reason, I discovered, that young lovers sought the anonymity that the darkness of the cinema provided them with, rather than going to public places full of mocking rivals.

That Saturday morning, I took along an old bike, that I had found at my grandparent's house, to Annie's house, and gave it to her to ride. As it turned out, she wasn't used to riding bikes, and the ten kilometer ride to the lake, which I did quite easily, almost killed her.

Eventually we made it, but when we arrived a brown Ford was parked next to the lake; it's owners a group of boys in the year above me who often teased me for being a geek. I tried to sneak past them to the next swimming spot along, but they spotted me, and Annie by my side, and started calling out to us.

"Hey, lover boy, who's your woman?"

We ignored them and walked on. We swam together,

splashing around in the water, and I admired the water glistening and dripping off her pale skin. We sat on the bank and talked about our parents, and about Annie's life in Sydney, where she used to live.

"Hopefully, I'm only going to be here for a few months," she told me. "My mother's trying to find a private school for me in Melbourne."

After a few hours we were tired and we had forgotten to bring sunscreen and Annie, who was very pale, was starting to go red. I was afraid to walk past the boys again but there was no other way out of there.

Two of the boys stood up and approached us as we came near. One of these, Nick, was considered the most attractive guy in school.

"Hi, I'm Nick," Nick said to Annie.

"I'm Annie," she replied.

"You're not going to make her ride all the way back into town are you *Michael*?" Nick pronounced my name as if it created a sour taste in his mouth.

"I'm okay," Annie said, although I detected hesitation in her voice.

"Why don't you let us take you back?" Nick said.

Annie looked at me for a moment. I knew the ride had been difficult for her, and I felt guilty about having inflicted it on her. But I also knew that if she went off with these guys then she would be lost to me forever. They'd tell her what a geek I was, and win her over with their confidence in a way I never could. They'd probably kiss her, might even have sex with her.

"It's okay," I said. "Go on."

"What about the bike?" She looked down at the bike I

had given her.

"It won't fit in the car," Nick said.

"Don't worry about it. I'll take it," I said.

When they all left together, I sat down and stared at the lake for a long time.

As I'd suspected, Annie started hanging around with Nick's gang after that. Then, a few months later, I heard she'd moved to a private school in Melbourne.

I didn't see her for nearly four years after that. Then, one night, I was at a party, sitting down on the steps outside someone's parent's country house, staring at the star-speckled night, when a voice next to me said, "Michael?"

I turned to find Annie staring at me. Her dark eyes glowed out at me like two orbs in the night.

"Annie?" I said, my heart suddenly pounding. She was as gorgeous as ever.

"How have you been?" she said.

"Okay. How about you?"

"Pretty well. What are you doing here?"

"I'm friends with Dylan, who apparently knows the owner of this party, although with Dylan you never know. How about you?"

"I came with a friend as well. Can I sit down?"

"Of course."

We chatted for a while about how horrible secondary school had been and what we'd been up to since then. She was studying medicine and I was studying science. I felt more comfortable with Annie than I had with anyone else in a long time. Even with Dylan I always felt like I was in some kind of a test of coolness or intelligence or superiority. Not necessarily superiority over Dylan himself, but superiority over other people in general. I could never feel completely at ease. With Annie it was different.

"Here you are!" A blonde girl in a short white tennis skirt with two pony tails came out onto the terrace.

"Michael, this is Jane. Jane, Michael," Annie introduced us.

"Can I borrow her for a minute?" Jane said.

"Sure." I remembered for a moment that deep feeling of loss I'd felt that day at the lake.

"Back in a minute." Annie rested her hand on my forearm, gave me a conspiratorial smile, then stood up and went inside.

I sat there for a few minutes feeling sorry for myself, then I wandered back inside to the kitchen and glanced over at Annie and Jane who were talking excitedly to two boys.

I poured myself a glass of champagne, then saw Caroline, Dylan's girlfriend, coming towards me.

"Can I have some of that?" Caroline held out her glass.

"Sure."

"So who was that girl I saw you talking to?" Caroline said with mock jealousy.

"Annie. We went to high school together."

"She's hot," Caroline said.

"Isn't she?"

"So what happened?"

"Either her friend came and took her away from me, or she wanted her friend to come and rescue her from me, I'm not sure which."

"What did she say to you?"

"When?"

"When her friend came?"

"She said she'd be back in a minute."

"Nothing to worry about."

"What do you mean?"

"If she'd wanted to escape she would have said "nice to meet you"."

"What makes you think that?"

"That's what women say. It would get you off her back. Give you the message that she didn't want to continue talking to you. Men are pretty thick witted sometimes, so women have had to adapt fairly explicit signals. And besides, she looked like she was interested in you."

"How could you tell?" I was secretly delighted that Caroline had been keeping an eye on me.

"A girl's intuition. What did she say to you? Tell me everything." She wrapped her hand around my upper arm. "Look. I think she's looking your way. Go and take her a glass of champagne."

I looked over and Annie was looking at me. Jane and the two boys were talking amongst themselves and Annie was looking lost.

"Go on, quick," Caroline said, holding out her glass for me to take.

I walked over to Annie and held the glass out for her, hoping I could somehow sneak off with her without the other three noticing. Annie thanked me and huddled in close. Excitement made my body rush.

"Who was that girl you were just talking to? Is she your girlfriend?" Annie said.

"No, no, that's Caroline. Dylan's girlfriend. An old friend." I felt thrilled that she thought Caroline could be my girlfriend.

"Do you want to go outside again?"

"Sure."

"Those two were so boring," she said, as we walked out into the cool air. "Thank you for saving me."

I wondered if that meant she didn't find *me* boring.

"Who were they?"

"I don't know. Some guys Jane met. She always goes after those boring sporty types."

"Well, you can rest assured that I'm totally incapable of playing any type of sport at all."

Annie let out a husky laugh, which I took to mean that she liked me.

Three years later, sitting on the steps of the Natural History Museum in London, just under the statue of Darwin, I asked her to marry me.

Chapter Three

THE NEXT MORNING, after a bowl of sloppy porridge, I am taken back to the interrogation room. I haven't had a shower and I can smell my own stench.

Don is there, looking as clean and fresh as he did the day before. I imagine how he went home the night before to his loving wife and his naughty but adorable children, and how he got up this morning and picked out the gray suit he is wearing from among the many on his rack, and brushed his hair back with a comb and the blow dryer.

I wonder how to manipulate him. Praise won't work, he'll see through that too quickly. A challenge, maybe. Something to engage him and make him eager to prove himself.

"So, how are you feeling this morning?" Don says, as if he already knows the answer to the question. "Ready to tell us a little more?"

"I'll do what I can."

"How well do you know Dylan Hume?"

"What's Dylan got to do with this?"

"It's specifically the work you've been doing with Mr Hume that we're interested in," Don says. "Mr Hume is also being questioned, and he's started telling us some pretty interesting things."

My heart starts pounding. So they've got Dylan as well? I wonder if that means they've got the children, too.

"What sort of things?" I wonder if Don is just bluffing me. Maybe they haven't got Dylan at all.

"Maybe you'd like to tell me yourself?" Don says.

"If Dylan's told you already..."

"That's just the thing. We don't know if what Dylan has told us is true or not."

"Tell me what he's told you, and I'll tell you if it is." I really can't believe that they've managed to capture Dylan.

Don laughs, a brief bark that sets my nerves on edge, like someone grinding their knife too hard against their plate. "I'm afraid that's not how this game is going to work, Michael. In here, it's more about you telling us absolutely everything you know and us telling you how long we're going to lock you away for. After a trial, of course." Don crosses his arms and stares at me with pale eyes. He shows no trace of emotion at all. My com registers nothing. Nothing that I can latch onto and try to manipulate. I suddenly feel very cold, and very alone, as if I might never see the outside world again.

"Am I allowed to make a call? To tell my wife where I am?"

"I'm afraid not."

"What is it you'd like to know?" I say.

"Everything." Don sits down and clasps his hands on

the table, staring at me attentively.

"Everything about what?"

"About what you and Mr Hume have been up to. Maybe start by telling us about Dylan's involvement with the New Church."

The New Church is one of the largest new-age religious movements in the country.

"Dylan's one of the leaders, as you probably know."

"What about your own involvement with the New Church?"

"It's been very brief. I went to one of their gatherings once. Met the founder, Rowen. He died a few years ago, and Dylan took over."

"So, are they as crazy as we're told?"

"What do you mean?"

"I mean with the sex and everything?" He is referring to the orgies that the New Church gatherings are renowned for.

"Pretty much," I nod, taking a deep breath, wondering if I am finally getting to the human side of Don. Everyone has to have a human side.

"What happened after that? After Rowen died?"

"Dylan took over."

"And what are Dylan's plans for the organization?"

"I think you'd better charge me, before I answer any more of your questions. I really would like to speak to a lawyer."

"So, you like the look of this place, do you?" Don spreads his hands towards the empty room around him.

"Why's that?"

"Do you know what the penalty is for terrorism?"

I shake my head.

"Life imprisonment. Probably solitary confinement for six out of every twelve months. I'd think about it if I were you." Don makes his way towards the door.

"What is it exactly you think I've done?"

"As I've said, Michael, I think you already know the answer to that."

I picture Dylan. He could have sat in this same chair just minutes ago. I try to detect his familiar scent in the air, but all I smell is disinfectant and Don's aftershave. If he is here — is there any way for us to communicate? A note? A sign? A corrupt guard?

"I really don't know what you're referring to. What is it that Dylan has told you?"

"Uh uh," Don shakes a finger at me. "We're not going to get into that again, are we?"

"I don't think he's told you anything. I think if he had, you wouldn't have me here." I cross my arms. I'm frightened, but I'm not going to let this bully get the better of me. He's like a shark. If I hold my ground, he'll leave me alone. If I flee, he'll come after me.

"Maybe he's told us enough to convict you, but not enough to convict those you're working with," Don says, and my heart pounds. I look at Don to see if that was just a lucky bluff, but his face is inscrutable.

"How do you know I'm not working alone?"

"Tell us what you know about Gendigm."

"Gendigm?"

"Yes."

"Nothing." I shake my head, forcing myself not to look away. I try to avoid any tells: brushing my nose or face, an unnatural delay between words and expression. "Just what everyone knows. They're rumored to be trying to create a super-race, a new species of humans."

"Isn't that what you yourself are involved in?"

"I'm not trying to create a new species. I'm just making some changes to the current one."

"According to your former colleague, Anthony, the project you were working on at Geneus also included some modifications to make humans more cooperative. Is that true?"

"There's no secret there."

"And the company who took over Geneus supported this research?"

"That's no secret, either."

"One has to wonder why, given that, according to Anthony, the research had almost no economic value."

"I guess there are still some people in this world who don't base all of their decisions on economic value," I say.

"And thank God for that," Don says, which makes me warm to him a little. "The part of your project that I'm really interested in, though, is the immune system research. Tell me about that."

"What would you like to know that the government doesn't already know? A lot of our work has been done for them."

"It's the work you're doing now that interests me. I'm particularly worried about the possibility of your project creating a virus that might spread into the general population, whether by accident or on purpose."

So they do know about the recent outbreak. I have been telling myself we did the right thing. But now that I am here, locked inside a prison with the full weight of society bearing down on me, I wonder if I shouldn't be punished after all. For a moment I feel relief, as if responsibility has suddenly been taken away from me.

"We have protocols in place so that doesn't happen," I tell Don.

"If someone wanted to, though, couldn't they use this for their own purposes?"

"Yes. If they wanted to. In fact, that was part of the work I was doing for the military. Have you spoken to the Prime Minister about this? Or General Savage? They were the ones we had the most to do with."

"We have spoken to them, yes, which is partly why we're so worried. We know what this technology is capable of."

"The government helped fund this project. They knew about every detail of it."

"Not every detail, I don't think."

"Such as?"

Don suddenly goes silent and I can see his eyes going into that blank stare people get when reading something on their visual overlays.

"Who's Toby?" Don says.

"Toby? Why?" I say.

"Dylan mentioned he was involved."

Toby was a rhesus macaque who had been part of our experiments on the immune system and had shown a much higher level of empathy and cooperation than an unmodified monkey. It was an unintended side effect. Why would Dylan say Toby was involved? And why would Don think he's a person?

Then suddenly I realize. This is Dylan's way of telling me to cooperate, like Toby did. To not give anything away. The government is trying to play us off against one another, but if we both keep quiet they won't be able to.

"I have no idea. Why don't you ask Dylan?"

Don says nothing and I can see him reading again.

"I think that's enough for today," he says when he's done.

"Can I make a call? Or see a lawyer? Are you actually going to charge me with something?"

"Not yet, we're not. Not until we find out more about your case. Or until you give us more information."

I wonder if I will get to the point where I tell them everything just to get out of here.

"So you're going to keep me here, forever?" I say.

"No. Probably not. Not if you tell us what we want to know."

"I can't do that until I know what that is."

"I think you already do."

"Why don't you spell it out for me, then?"

"I don't think I need to."

"Why? Because if you lock me up for long enough I'll make up anything just to get out of here?"

"No. I think you'll tell us the truth."

"And what truth is that? The one you want to hear?"

"To be perfectly honest, Michael, I'd prefer not to hear that you're involved in a project that could potentially threaten humanity. You seem like a decent person. Like you're trying to do something to help the world. I don't quite understand it, to be honest."

"So I suppose you think the world is alright like it is, do

you?"

"I'm not quite sure what you mean."

I am afraid that if I say too much more I am going to give something away. I have to make Don understand me, though. If I don't, he'll just keep locking me away in that cell until he finds out what he wants to know from someone else.

"I mean, look at the world. Humans are destroying it. A few years from now and it's going to be uninhabitable."

"So, what are you saying? That you think humans ought to be wiped out?" He crosses his arms and stares at me.

"No. That's not what I'm saying. I'm saying that something needs to change or we're going to wipe ourselves out."

"And how exactly do you plan on stopping that from happening?"

I want to tell him more about my cooperation research and how I imagine it will change things, but if Don follows my arguments logically – which he no doubt will – it'll lead him to the same place I and the others at Gendigm were led to: that all unmodified humans might need to be either sterilized or wiped out entirely for the plan to work. A solution we had found an alternative to. Although Don, given his current line of questioning, probably won't believe it.

"I don't," I say.

"Well, thanks for your time."

"Hang on."

"Yes?"

"Maybe you could help me with this."

"In what way?"

"Why don't you tell me what it is that you think I've done, and I'll tell you as much as I can. Have you ever considered the possibility that we're looking at the same thing from two different perspectives? That maybe I've been doing something which in my mind is perfectly fine, and which in your mind is an act of terrorism. You said I seem like a decent person. Why don't you just trust that judgement and give me the benefit of the doubt?"

"How about this?" Don slaps his hands on the table before me. "You tell us absolutely everything you've been doing for the last couple of years, piece by piece, day by day. All of your work, all of your outside contacts, pretty much everything you can remember. And if there's anything missing from that story, anything that we know about you that you've failed to tell us, then we'll keep you here. If it all checks out and makes sense, then we'll either charge you with something, if we think you've done something wrong, or we'll let you go."

"Okay," I say, thinking at the very least it will buy me some time and let me get my thoughts in order.

"I'll have a pen and paper sent to your room," Don says. "You can write it all down for us. The old-fashioned way."

CHAPTER FOUR

FOR THE NEXT few days I don't see Don. I spend each day in my room, writing down everything I can remember about my work over the past couple of years, omitting not only the most condemning information, but anything else I can leave out without looking guilty for doing so. The cell is quiet except for the occasional scream of another inmate.

When I'm not writing, I try to exercise or meditate. Anything that will help keep my mind, body and emotions healthy. I think about Annie all the time. I wonder where she is now: at home still, or safely on the New Church island we had planned to move to?

At night, instead of placing my head on the pillow, I lay the pillow alongside myself and hug it. I tuck my hands in my groin, where it is warm, and sleep fitfully. On a number of occasions I wake in the middle of the night, in total darkness, gasping for breath. Each time I remember the dream preceding my awakening: someone was trying to keep me quiet by holding their hand over my mouth.

I wonder how much I can trust Dylan. If he talks, I will go away for ever. I'll never see the outside world again: never feel the sun or the breeze, never lie down with Annie at night and feel her warm, soft body next to mine. If he keeps quiet, on the other hand, there is a chance we'll both go free. How much of a friend is he? What if he was just using the reference to Toby to keep me quiet while he tells them everything?

I think back to the time we met — sharing a room at university which he transformed into a bohemian den. Indian wall-hangings, persian carpets, bookcases filled with books, a collage of photographs of him with many different, but all extremely attractive, people, an expensive stereo, red shades over the lights and small matching lamps on our desks.

"Listen to anything you want," he told me, connecting up a laptop filled with music to the stereo.

He had more beauty products laid out in the small cabinet in our bathroom than I even knew existed for men. He swaggered around the place, doing his yoga exercises in the morning, doing push ups in the evenings after his run, admiring himself in the mirror he'd attached to the inside of his wardrobe.

At night sometimes, we'd both lie in bed with a candle burning on our shared bedside table and the window wide open while Dylan smoked either cigarettes or joints, which I took occasional puffs of, and talk.

"What do you most fear in the world?" Dylan would ask me. Or, "what is your biggest dream?"

I didn't have any other friends, so when I wasn't talking to Dylan, which I didn't do that often as he was always out,

I studied or read. I liked books where heroic characters would do extraordinary things. I myself dreamed of changing the world in some extraordinary way, saving it from the disaster course it seemed to be on. I could identify with the protagonists of those stories and got excited when I read about them. Humans were capable of such genius and I imagined myself as one of the Newtons, the Gallileos, the Einsteins of future history. Those people whose minds had somehow reached up and connected with a higher intelligence; had flown like Prometheus and joined with something greater than themselves. Inspired by the unfathomable complexity of a cloud or a flower or human biology itself, their thoughts had somehow mutated, made connections, in ways which no other human mind had ever done before, and they had created the intellectual equivalent of an eye or an ear. For a few hours, absorbed in a book, anything seemed possible.

An experiment that Dylan and I conducted at this time triggered both our fascination with the competitive versus the cooperative instinct. We were trying to determine which genes were responsible for gender expression in mice, specifically for inciting male mice to attack the young of other males. The first thing we did was to eliminate the TRPC2 gene, a pheromone receptor in the nasal passage which had been proven to make mice become bisexual by removing their ability to distinguish between males and females. This modification stopped them from wanting to kill each other, but it didn't remove their aggression towards other males' infants. Next, we knocked out the genes for encoding progesterone and testicular androgen receptors, but that didn't work either.

It was around this time that I came to a surprising but unpleasant realization: the real threat to survival and reproduction of many species, mice and humans especially, wasn't another species or even the environment at all, but other members of the same species. There must have come a time when humans had discovered it was mutually beneficial to cooperate with each other in raping and pillaging others, maybe it had even become necessary for defense – but that was as far as our altruistic nature had gone. And why should it have gone any further? There was certainly no evolutionary pressure to do so. For 150,000 years, that particular mode of thinking had worked quite well. Humans had gotten ahead in the world. But with over eight billion of us still battling it out, and the environment changing rapidly, the survival of not only one individual was at stake, but that of the entire species. Something we were biologically ill-equipped to deal with.

Then, one morning, I went into our lab to where our mice were waiting in cages. The night before, we'd put the latest batch of male mice in cages with pregnant females. Ten of the females had given birth during the night, but in nine cases not a single infant was left alive. In the last one, however, the cage of mouse RV244, something unprecedented was happening. RV244 had been born in a male body, but right from the outset he had begun to display behavioral characteristics usually only shown by females. And now, not only had he not killed the infant mice who were in the cage with him, he was sharing his food with them.

* * *

My interview with Don resumes a few days later.

"So, there are just a few other things in your statement that I'm not quite sure about," Don says.

"Yes?"

"It appears that the people at HGM Industries were introduced to Geneus through you."

"Yes, that's right." HGM industries was the dummy corporation that Gendigm had created in order to invest in Geneus.

"How did you come into contact with HGM?"

We never worked out an alibi for this one, so I tell the truth. "I was introduced to them by another scientist, Bruno Salacio, who read an article I published in Genetics Today. He apparently knew Jan from HGM, and after being impressed with my research, introduced us."

"Hmm," Don says. "Interesting."

"Why's that?"

"Bruno Salacio was found dead in his apartment three weeks ago. Just after we met."

For a moment I am stunned. Maybe I *have* been set up as a scapegoat for Gendigm. Maybe Bruno was too. Then I realize that Don is possibly lying to me again, and Bruno is not dead at all. Maybe they're just trying to frighten me, to get me to talk.

"Is that all?" I say.

"Well, some bad news I'm afraid. For you, that is."

"What's that?"

"It appears your friend Dylan is not quite as good a friend as you thought he was." Don says this as sarcastically as he possibly can. "He's agreed to testify in court, about everything you and he have been up to. About your involvement with Gendigm."

My whole body squirms as I fight for breath.

That night, I wake up in the middle of the night gasping again. In my dream, my cell was slowly filling up with water. My whole body and bed are drenched in sweat and I am freezing. I stand up in the light coming through from the passage and try to dry myself with the hand towel next to my basin. I run some warm water and splash it on my face and run it over my hands, then turn the blanket around and try to huddle underneath it again.

I can't get back to sleep. All I can think about is being trapped inside this cell for the rest of my life and dying here. I can't stop myself from shaking. I want to smash myself against the door, try to break out of here even though I know I can't. I try to breathe slowly, tell myself it is going to be alright, but I know it isn't. Even if Dylan doesn't know everything, he knows enough to put me away for a long time.

Then I think about Annie, and the first time I woke in the middle of the night to find her sweating and feverish, just as I am now.

"Annie, what is it?" I said, feeling wet sheets around her. "You're soaked."

I switched the bedside light on and put a hand on her forehead but it was pretty obvious she had a fever.

"Let me get a towel," I said, standing up and heading for the bathroom. I came back a minute later with a dry towel and a wet face cloth which I used to wipe her face down. She tried to roll over, to get out of bed, but she couldn't get up.

"We're going to have to get you to the hospital."

"No, I'll be fine," she said.

"You won't be fine. Now come on, get up and I'll take you to the Royal Melbourne."

Royal Melbourne hospital was a fifteen minute drive away. It had been privatized since the flooding, but at least it was still open.

"No, please. Let's wait until morning at least. Just bring me some aspirin."

"You don't even know what you've got."

I headed down to the kitchen. Washed out moonlight through the kitchen window was enough to see by and I took a glass from the dish rack and filled it with water. My hands shook. I thought about calling an ambulance but realized it was unnecessary. Why was it that at work I could be completely rational but when it came to Annie all reason and control left me?

"Here, take these." I propped Annie's head up under a few pillows and she managed to turn to one side. I fed the pills into her mouth and held the rim of the glass up to her lips. I put a towel down on the bed and made her roll over onto it. I checked her temperature, which was at forty degrees celsius, and I told her that if it got any higher I was going to take her to the hospital whether she liked it or not.

For the next few hours she fell in and out of consciousness and each time she came to I felt a sense of relief. The rest of the time I sat there in the dim light of the lamp, mopping sweat from her forehead and checking her temperature. I put one towel under her and another on top of her, but even those needed changing regularly.

"We need an IV drip. You're losing too much fluid," I said in one of her lucid moments, but then she blacked out again.

"I have some very bad news," the doctor said when we ran some tests on her later that day.

"What is it?" Annie said.

"You have HIV-4."

With global warming, mosquitoes had thrived, spreading to many new regions, even regulated sections of the developed world. Unlike HIV-1 and HIV-2, HIV-4 was very stable, stable enough to persist in the mosquito mouthparts and infect the next human the mosquito bit.

Annie turned to me and gripped me tightly, burrowing her nails into my skin.

I put my hand on her back. The world around me dissolved and I felt faint.

"What can we do?" I asked the doctor.

"Nothing," Annie said to me. "There's nothing we can do."

"We'll have to put her on retrovirals so you don't contract it too," the doctor said.

"I'll sell the company," I said to Annie that night, referring to the small biotech I had founded a few years earlier. "Geneus will probably buy us out. I'll sell on the condition they'll support me in doing some immune system research. We'll find a cure for this."

At that moment in our lives, despite the global catastrophe going on around us, Annie and I were at the peak of our careers. Annie was working at St Vincent's Hospital as a doctor and I had just developed an artificial chromosome that could be programmed with any number of genetic modifications and inserted into the DNA of a fertilized egg. Just a few months before, a company called Geneus had offered to buy me out.

"You can't do that," Annie said. "That company's your life."

"You're my life. Everything I do is for you. Without you none of it would mean anything to me."

"You're crazy, Michael. What do you know about the immune system?"

"I can learn. Geneus has already come up with a number of relevant genetic modifications. They were the ones who came up with a cure for diabetes by inserting insulin producing genes into the pancreas. I can insist they allow me to work with their immune system team. My artificial chromosomes could easily be adapted for that."

"And what are you going to tell them? That you want to do it because your wife is sick?"

"I won't tell them anything. I'll tell them that I think I can make a difference. Which I can."

"And if they ask you *how* you're going to make a difference?"

"I don't know. I'll come up with something," I said, and Annie gripped onto me tightly again.

* * *

The next morning, two men in suits similar to those who first arrested me come into my cell, followed by Don.

"Michael Khan," one of them says, "we are officially placing you under arrest for attempted terrorism. Anything you say or do may be used against you in a court of law. Do you have any questions?"

CHAPTER FIVE

5 years earlier...

I WOKE UP. The house was filled with dawn light.

"What time is it?" Annie, lying beside me, said.

"Nearly seven. I have to go. How are you feeling?"

"A little better."

The night before Annie had looked terrible. Ever since she'd gotten HIV-4, nearly three years ago now, her energy levels had been decreasing rapidly. It was like she was aging ten years for every year that passed.

"Would you like some breakfast? Maybe some eggs and a cup of tea would make you feel better." I had to get to work but, with Annie's illness, every second spent with her seemed precious.

"How about a double espresso?"

"How about some camomile tea?" Annie and I had an ongoing disagreement over the industrial quantities of caffeine she consumed.

"Oh please, have pity on my dying soul." She brushed dark hair away from her eyes and sat up against her pillow.

I laughed. "Camomile tea it is."

"You should get to work. It's a big day for you."

"What about you?" I leant in to kiss her gently.

"I'll be fine. I'm going in to work too. I've got a lot I need to get done." After she'd been diagnosed, Annie had left her full time job at one of the city's largest hospitals and now volunteered four days a week at a clinic in the de-reg zone.

"Are you sure?"

"Of course I'm sure. I can't lie around here all day. People need me."

"I need you."

An hour later, I walked towards the somatic therapy lab at Geneus. The corridor felt designed for more people and being alone in it, hearing my footsteps echo along the linoleum floor, made me uneasy.

Inside the lab, I swapped my suit jacket for a lab coat. I had been spending more time in my office and in meetings than actually working recently, and it was a relief to be away from the world of internal company politics and finances and to focus on my research again. I often felt like the immune system itself – protecting my project against foreign invaders.

The team – Justin, Richard, Yolanda and about thirty others – were lined up along benches absorbed in their work: prepping samples, loading the machines, and assessing the data on their coms.

"I think we're almost there," Justin said.

For the last two and half years, we had been working on a somatic therapy immune-system modification. Somatic therapy involved modifying the DNA of people who were already born. It would enable us to help people who were already sick, like Annie, and Justin's sister, who also had HIV-4.

"What have you got?" I said.

"Have a look at this." He brought up a video on my visual overlay. "This is a sample from one of our somatically modified primates."

I watched a video taken through a fluorescence microscope. Someone added live HIV-4 to one side of a multi-wall plate which contained two blood samples – one from the modified primate and the other from an unmodified one. On the modified side I watched as virally-infected T-cells died – lighting up bright red as they did so.

"Isn't that the recording from the germline modifications we did?" I said.

Aside from the somatic modifications, we were also experimenting with germline modifications – modifying fertilized eggs. We'd managed, in some cases, to improve the immune systems of new-born macaques. So far, though, we hadn't been able to do it consistently.

"No," Justin said. "That was taken this morning. In one of our somatically modified specimens."

Somatic modification, because we were working with a structure that was already built – in this case a monkey's body – was a lot harder than germline modification where we could build everything from scratch.

"What's the success rate?"

"Twenty percent," he said. "Seventeen percent have shown negative reactions and the rest have shown no signs of it affecting them at all."

Justin and I had, over the last few years, come up with a process to insert new strands of DNA into existing cells using a viral vector. It enabled much more precise targeting than any previous technology. We were getting close to perfecting it, but we still weren't quite there.

We talked on for a while, and he reported all the results to me.

Justin was a gun I had hired straight out of university. He could have gotten a job anywhere, but he stuck it out at Geneus on a lower salary than he deserved with the hope of finding a cure for his sister. I had never told him about Annie, just as I hadn't told anyone at Geneus, but on many occasions I'd wanted to. Justin's suffering was obvious and having someone to share it with probably would have made it easier.

After finishing up with Justin, I headed towards the primate lab where I was due to conduct an experiment based on some unexpected side effects of our immune system research: one that made our macaques far more cooperative. These particular monkeys were unlike any that had ever lived before. We'd inserted bonobo genes by germline transformation as part of our immune system work, and they had become matriarchal, polygamous and non-aggressive, just like bonobos.

Today we were going to perform a test to check the extent of their behavioral changes. Our macaques were going to be introduced to seven unmodified macaques. Macaques in their natural state defended their territory aggressively, whereas bonobos were more inclined to share, even with strangers.

The young macaques were restless and squawked in

their cages when I walked into the lab, but the older ones paid me little attention, sitting patiently grooming themselves.

Masanori, my colleague, was measuring cups of oats from a stainless steel drum.

"Big day," Masanori said.

"Everything ready?"

"Toby's limping. I think someone must have bitten him in the play cage yesterday."

"He probably deserved it." Toby was a cheeky little monkey who pulled the other monkeys' fur and stole their food.

"What time are the others due in?" Masanori said.

"Eleven."

I walked over to the cages, smelling the stench of urine and feces, watching the little brown and white creatures through the wire. I watched Toby make frantic loops of his cage and screech. Toby's body was almost cat-like, although he stood on hind legs. Masanori was right: he was limping.

Sika, the oldest female of the group, stared at Toby out of eyes the color of muddied water as if trying to silence him with her thoughts. Although macaques weren't matriarchal, bonobos were, and Sika was turning out to be the matriarch of this group. Milo, the alpha male, had been demoted.

The relationship between the two head monkeys had been clearly seen the day before. Masanori and I had put fruit on a tray outside the play pen, too far for the macaques to reach. We had threaded a rope through a ring in the tray and put one end into either side of the pen in such a way that they needed to pull both ends at the same time to get the fruit, something one monkey couldn't do alone. Milo and Sika had worked this trick out and between them had brought the tray within reach of the cage. It was Sika, though, who pulled the fruit inside the cage and divided it up while the others squawked and rubbed themselves against one another in excitement.

"Big day today, Sika. Let's see how they behave," I said to her. She nodded at me and grunted in a way which suggested she understood.

The monkeys were able to understand not only our tones of voice, body language and a lot of basic words, but they seemed to have a sixth sense as well. Quite often, minutes before Masanori or I arrived in the lab, they would start looking around as if expecting an arrival. They were right so often that we'd come to predict the arrival of the other by their behavior.

The monkeys started shaking their cages as Masanori took a bucket of food into the play pen. I followed him in with the remaining fruit and helped spread it out on the concrete floor.

Masanori went over to Toby's cage and tried to pull him out, but he clung on tightly to the wire and screamed.

"Okay, calm down, calm down," Masanori said. He picked up an extra-large serving of grapes from the bench and handed it to Toby. Stuffing the juicy red globules into his mouth, Toby grunted with pleasure, juice running down his chin as Masanori carried him across to the bench.

I broke off a few grapes for myself and ate them, then pushed a button which released all the other macaques into the play pen. They greeted each other excitedly, rubbing themselves against one another and grooming each other playfully – just as bonobos would – before feeding.

Masanori took Toby over to the operating table and we looked at his leg. A small amount of hair was torn away, exposing a bite mark.

"He obviously got on somebody's nerves," I said.

"Gilly probably. Gilly hates him for some reason. I don't think the behavioral changes in him are as strong as in some of the others."

We applied some antiseptic and a small bandage to Toby's wound, then released him into the cage with the others.

At 11am, I received a message on my com saying the truck carrying the seven new macaques had arrived. Masanori and I walked down to the loading bay and watched as two security guards opened up the roller door and unloaded the covered cages into the holding area. Once they'd been scanned and cleared, we stacked them onto trolleys and rolled them down the long, pale-green, disinfected corridors to the lab.

The modified macaques looked on with solemn eyes as we took the covers off the cages. The new monkeys started shrieking, shaking their doors. A couple of them had urinated.

I switched the 3D recorder on.

"Ready?" Masanori said.

I nodded.

We released the newcomers from their cages into the six-by-eight-metre pen. They ran inside, screaming like a raiding war party, immediately intimidating and chasing off some of our youngsters, like Toby who had come in for a closer look. The oldest members of the modified group, including Sika and Milo, fanned out and closed in cautiously on the intruders.

Milo started shrieking, nodding his brown head aggressively, and exposing his short fangs. Gilly and Sam followed his lead, adding to the racket. Sika tried to hush them with a low grunting, and Lady and Ginger joined in with her. The groups were caught in a standoff. The fur on the backs of their tiny necks stood proud and their bodies tensed. Sika tried a "girney" call, a gentle tranquilizer like a cat's purr that the macaques often used on their young. I recognized it as bonobo behavior translated into macaque language.

The screaming from both sides continued until Milo and the other modified macaques slowly relaxed as Sika purred to them. Seeing that they were no longer challenged, transfixed by Sika as she continued her call, the newcomers also started to quieten.

It was Lady, one of our younger females, who went forward next. She sniffed the air in front of her and scratched herself lazily as if to prove to the newcomers that there was nothing to worry about.

"You go, Lady!" Masanori whispered under his breath.

As Lady got closer, the larger monkeys from the new group started growling again, raising themselves up on their hind legs.

"We'd better get ready with the first-aid kit," I said.

Despite the aggressive display of the newcomers, Sika, Lady and Milo advanced, just as bonobos would do. As the advance continued, the newcomers' growls turned to low moans, and one of the males stepped up and sniffed Sika tentatively. Sika cooed to him and put a hand on him to groom him. The male let out a short, high-pitched scream and then slapped her before retreating. Sika held up a hand to where she'd been hit but there was no blood so I suspected the male had done it more out of surprise than a desire to hurt her.

Milo scuttled towards the one who'd hit Sika, but Sika cooed to him then turned her lips out at him and made a comical little nodding motion together with a small clucking sound. I saw the tension in Milo's body relax. One of the female newcomers, with pretty white patches around her eyes, approached Milo. He let out a low gabble and suddenly it was love at first sight and they started caressing one another tenderly.

Both groups came together then and slowly but surely they started cackling and murmuring and grooming one another.

Masanori and I turned to one another with smiles on our faces.

I walked into the board room later that afternoon. It seemed everything was coming together. The possibility we might finally be able to cure Annie made me feel as if gravity had suddenly weakened.

Klaus Hofferman, CEO of Geneus, sat at the head of the table surrounded by the other board members. He was working, his fingers moving in the air in front of him as he manipulated objects on his visual overlay. His thin gray hair was brushed back – exposing his widow's peak – and his eyes were turned down at the edges. His face was rigid except for his jaw grinding from side to side in reaction to whatever was in front of him on his overlay.

The rest of the group was also working. Usually I would join them until Klaus was ready, but today I poured myself some black coffee from the pot on the table and waited for the meeting to start.

I looked around at the board members. Beside Masanori was Rachel, the marketing director, thick brown hair over a face too slender to be the result of natural selection and more likely to be the result of cosmetic surgery. At only a couple of thousand dollars a pop, if you weren't operated-on these days you could pretty much say goodbye to your chances of ever finding a job outside tele-marketing. Next to Rachel was Zhao, the chief financial officer. Half Chinese and half Russian, he cut a striking figure in his blue pin-striped suit. Zhao worked magic on the Geneus books and it was rumored he had numerous copies of our financial files at any given time: one for investors, one for banks, and one for the government. All completely legitimate of course – it was a matter of perspective. Either way, he'd kept the company afloat through some rough weather. With economies around the world falling like dominoes, any company which managed to keep operating was doing okay for itself, especially one like ours which ate hundreds of millions in R&D.

Around from Zhao was Klaus, and on the other side of him was Anthony Simons. Anthony was chief operations manager for a number of divisions of the company and for the past year had been progressively more and more against our immune-system project. It not only threatened the other projects, he claimed, but threatened the financial viability of the entire company. Anthony and I had gotten on quite well until Klaus chose to cut Anthony's pet project – improving athletic skills – so he could redirect the funds from it towards our immune system work. These days we hardly spoke to one another. Next to Anthony was John, balding head of the legal department, and besides him sat Sue-Ling Song, Janet Greeves, and James Charlston, all major shareholders.

"Let's get started," Klaus said, letting his hands drop loudly on the table like a judge's gavel. Despite being almost eighty, Klaus looked twenty years younger, and his clear brown eyes stared around the room confidently. "I have some very bad news. Yesterday I received a call from Bill Hamilton, our man over at CryptoLabs, and they're no longer able to provide us with the investment funding they'd promised. They're going bankrupt, apparently, like everyone else in this God-forsaken world. Now, this immune-system project is taking far longer than we expected, and we've yet to see significant returns from it. At the current rate, without further investment, we're not going to last until the end of the year. We need to make a decision, and we need to make it fast."

We all stared at one another, wondering who would speak first. My heart felt like it would swell so much it would block my wind passage and I loosened the tie I'd put on for the meeting and undid the top button of my shirt.

Anthony, always eager to prove himself, took the lead. He stretched his arms forward so his muscular wrists extended out of his well-tailored sleeves. "As I've said before, I think it's time to cut our losses. This project has sapped the company dry for years and it's only going to get worse. Our custom facial-features line is turning a profit, and we could amp that up quickly if we stopped putting all our money into this immune system work."

"We can't just throw it all away now," John said. "We've spent hundreds of millions on it."

"We might have to," Janet argued.

"Can I report on this week's findings?" I said.

"Please do," Klaus said, extending a hand impatiently in my direction.

I cleared my throat. "Over the last few days we've been running tests on the latest batch of macaques. In nearly twenty percent of cases, we have managed to greatly improve their resistance to a large range of viruses, including HIV-4, AIDS, influenza and hepatitis. I've got videos here if you'd like to see them…"

"No thanks, Michael. Just give us the low down," Klaus said.

"Well, that's a forty percent improvement on last time. Forty percent, in just the last two months. I'd say another six to twelve months at the most and we'll have a viable product." With our funding on the rocks, I was desperate to convince them to keep going.

"That sounds like great news," Anthony said. "Only we've been hearing the same thing for the last eighteen months. *This is it, this is the one. The breakthrough we've been waiting for.*" And, no offense, but so far it hasn't been."

"You're right, and believe me, I'm just as frustrated by this situation as anyone. I honestly believe this will be the last stage, though."

"How can you be so sure?"

"Without getting too technical, in this batch we finally

managed to perfect the recognition of the histone modifications at each site, and it seems to have made all the difference." Trying to explain genetics to Anthony was like trying to explain relativity to a macaque.

"Is that all you've got to report?" Klaus said. "You mentioned something the other day about a new side effect?"

"Yes, there is one other thing."

I told them about the cooperation trials and how our modifications to the genome had inadvertently created more cooperative, less xenophobic monkeys.

"Nobody in their right mind is going to accept that kind of response," John said.

"Do you mean to say," Masanori said, in his quiet but firm voice, "that you wouldn't like your children to be more cooperative and friendly towards strangers?"

John's children, who had attended many company picnics and family days, were known for terrorizing the other children. Masanori suspected it was caused by a competition modification gone haywire, but I thought it was just bad parenting.

"I don't think anyone would," Anthony said, racing to John's aid. "What people want are kids who are going to compete, not kids who are going to be more cooperative."

"Cooperation has been proven to be one of the major factors in promoting not just evolutionary success but the success in daily life that leads to that," I said. "Of course people are going to accept it."

Everyone stopped for a minute to think about this.

A couple of people twisted their mouths and nodded but others just sat there. Anthony in particular was shaking his head and looking at the ceiling as if he thought I had gone completely crazy.

"Rachel, what will the market say?" Klaus said. "Do you think we could sell cooperation?"

Rachel had a confused look on her face and shook her head. "I really don't know. I don't think anyone's ever tried it before."

"Well, get onto it, then."

"There is one other small detail," I said.

"What's that?" Klaus leaned towards me.

"It seems these new modifications, because they're based on bonobo genes, also make the test subjects quite a bit friskier."

"Well, that sounds like something we probably could sell!"

The meeting went on for another few hours, and in the end Klaus asked for a survey to be done on the acceptability of increased cooperation and sex-drive.

"You'd better bloody well make something of this, Michael," he said to me as we exited the board room, putting a firm hand on my shoulder. "I've put not only my own ass but the ass of the entire company on the line for you here, and we need to see some results. Soon."

CHAPTER SIX

THAT EVENING, ANNIE called and asked me to meet her at her doctor's clinic. She said she was feeling better but wanted to get some tests run just in case.

I could have taken one of the cable cars that hung throughout the city, crossing flooded streets where traditional vehicles were unable to pass, but I decided to walk, taking the higher streets and the bridges that had been put up after the flood.

Very few people knew about Annie's disease, and we wanted to keep it that way. If someone at Geneus found out about it they would assume my zeal for the immune system project was based on more than just my conviction that I could come up with a solution. With the project already tenuous, something like this would be enough to send it plunging into the ravine of scientific obscurity and me along with it. Which company would want to hire a scientist who had cost their previous employer hundreds of millions in research funds just to try to save his wife?

I turned onto a street that had become an informal market.

"Kebabs, kebabs kebabs... Baby chickens, ten dollars each, baby chickens... A necklace sir, perfect for the lady, only twenty dollars..." The calls from the vendors were a reminder of the beginning again, of our roots, of the importance of trade to human civilization. It felt more real than the sleek shopfronts that had once glazed this particular street with their promise of perfection in luxury cars, designer clothes and diamond necklaces. A few bars and restaurants still remained, as did the banks, now heavily guarded, but there wasn't much of the old economy left. These days, almost everything was virtual.

Annie's doctor's office was in a heritage building without an elevator. I climbed up the wooden stairs. The inside of each step was worn deep from years of passing feet and the boards creaked and wobbled from lack of maintenance. Light trickled through dusty opaque windows on the landings. On the third floor I walked over to a glass door with a small name tag next to it: Dr Graham Baxter.

I went inside and was greeted by Dot, Baxter's aging secretary. Annie was there already, sitting next to a plastic plant, awaiting her test results. She stood up and we hugged, her familiar presence engulfing me.

"How are you feeling?" Doctor Baxter asked her when we went into his small consulting room a few minutes later.

Graham Baxter had been our doctor for years and his calm, quiet manner was comforting to both of us.

"I'm okay now. This morning I wasn't so great. I was running a bit of a fever." Annie glanced in my direction.

"Well, your viral load is up. Maybe that new medication

you're on isn't helping. Any side effects?"

"A bit of nausea. Headaches occasionally. Nothing I can't live with, provided I'm alive."

"That's good. There's a new trial starting up of another drug, Exymorline, and the studies look promising. Would you be interested in being part of it?"

"I don't have time for trials, Graham, you know that."

"You're not still working at that clinic are you?"

"Of course I am. I'd be bored out of my mind otherwise."

"You need to take it easy, Annie."

"That's the last thing I need – to sit around home feeling sorry for myself all day."

Baxter shook his head. "Why is it that doctors always make the worst patients?" He turned to me.

"You should try living with her," I said, smiling.

Annie and I took a cable-car back home and greeted Henry, the gatekeeper. After the flooding, the residents of our area had taken it upon themselves to block off most of the streets leading into our suburb and had installed private security at the two entrances. In the early days, before the fence was put up around the whole perimeter of the regulated zone, hungry gangs roamed the streets at night and broke into houses. As much as I understood their plight, I felt a lot safer after we'd shut the gates.

Our friends, Dylan and Sophie, were coming around that night, and when we got home I started preparing dinner. Annie, exhausted, slumped down onto the lounge.

"How did you go with your meeting today?" Annie said.

"Not very well."

"Why?"

I hadn't wanted to tell her about the results of the meeting, as I knew it would only worry her more, but she was going to find out sooner or later.

"One of our investors pulled out. We're going to have to find some more funding," I said.

"They're not going to pull the plug on your project, are they?"

"No. Not yet. They will if we don't come up with something soon, though."

"How did the cooperation experiment go?"

I told her about it.

"Did you mention that to the board?"

"Yes. Of course. They weren't that interested. Klaus asked for some research to be done but nobody seemed to care. I get the feeling I've become like the boy who cried wolf."

"Come over here," Annie said, patting the couch next to her.

I went over and she put her hand around the back of my neck and hugged me to her. We cuddled together and I tried not to think about what it would be like to lose her.

"You need to find yourself someone else, Michael."

"Don't start that again." Recently, she had been getting more and more despondent and she was convinced she was going to die. It was a topic I was unwilling to discuss, preferring instead to focus on finding a solution and trying to stay positive.

"Look at me. I'm useless. We hardly even have sex any more."

We hadn't had sex in over three months, although it had

more to do with our stressful work schedules than her illness. When I met women at work or socially I did sometimes find myself wondering what it would be like to be with them. My guilt always got the better of me, though. How could I be thinking about sex when the woman I had loved since I was sixteen, who had loved me and given me the best years of my life, was dying?

"I don't need you to have sex me. I need you to concentrate on getting better."

Later that night, I stared back at myself from the mirror as I washed the shaving foam from my face and ran gel through my hair. My hair was starting to gray, the lines around my eyes were deepening, but in general I felt my features were balancing themselves out, finding an equilibrium which in my youth had eluded me. My strong nose and chin, once ungainly, now suited me.

"Are you almost ready?" Annie called from our bedroom.

"Almost," I called back.

Half an hour later, Dylan and Sophie arrived. Dylan and I hugged one another and I admired with a tinge of envy his long thick hair. Sophie came over and kissed me, a little closer to the lips than I was used to, and I couldn't help being momentarily stunned by her beauty. She was tall and slender with a short blonde bob that framed her delicate features.

"Wow, real mangoes," Annie said, as Sophie handed a bag to her. "These must have cost a fortune."

"I've got a regular supplier and get them sent across from Argentina." Sophie came from a wealthy family and even though she was a sculptor and made very little money herself, lived a very luxurious lifestyle.

While we ate, Dylan told us about his work. A few years ago, he and Sophie had become involved with a cult called the New Church. Their leader predicted the end of the world as we knew it six-and-a-half years from now, and the group was making plans for the survival of its members by buying up taller islands in remote areas and building self-sufficient communes on them.

It was Dylan's job to coordinate construction on the islands. The group believed they could create a more harmonious society, riding out the end of the world and rekindling the old flame of humanity once everything had settled down again.

"Are you going to invite us?" Annie said. Her black eyes surveyed Dylan cooly, as if she didn't believe in his utopia any more than I did.

"Of course," Dylan said. "VIP passes to the apocalypse. Cheers, anyway." He raised his glass to us. "Here's to good friends."

I told them about the difficulties I was having keeping my own project alive.

"Maybe we should ask Rowen if he'd be interested in investing in Michael's project." Sophie turned to Dylan. Rowen Boone was the leader of the New Church, and from what I gathered, probably thanks in part to the large donations Sophie made to his organization, he was a personal friend of theirs.

"It might be worth a shot," Dylan said.

"Why would he be interested?" I said.

"He invests in all sorts of crazy schemes." Sophie smiled. "Anything which he thinks will help our members survive."

"Well, this would definitely do that."

"I'll get in touch with him."

"Thank you," I said.

"How are things going with you, Annie?" Dylan said.

"I'm fine. We got a new batch of meds in at the clinic this week, so hopefully that'll be a few less people whom we have to euthanize."

Due to the lack of specialized drugs in the de-reg zone, whenever someone was really sick, beyond help, the clinics would put them to sleep if they asked for it. There wasn't a law against euthanasia any more, and even if there had been – not many laws were adhered to in the de-reg zone. Annie often joked about putting herself down, which disturbed me but helped her to take her illness a little more lightly.

"How's the rebel situation?" Dylan asked. "Have you noticed any changes?"

In the last few months there had been reports of rebel soldiers in the de-reg zone starting to band together and train in preparation for launching an attack on the main part of the city.

"Who knows what's going on? It's all just media hype if you ask me."

"I'm not so sure about that," I said. "It makes perfect sense. It's happening in other parts of the world. And it's what humans do when they get desperate. They try to kill one another."

"I think people there are too busy just trying to survive — to plan and train for a full scale attack," Annie said. "And besides, where would they get the arms from?"

"There are always unscrupulous assholes around ready to make a buck," Dylan said.

"Yes, but they don't have the funds."

None of us said anything for a minute, a quiet tension settling over the room as we all thought about the possibility of an attack.

"What I really want to know, is when science is going to come up with a permanent cure for aging," said Sophie, breaking the silence, "I mean, all this money they spend on other things, can't they dedicate some of it to curing wrinkles?"

We all laughed, and the mood was lifted.

"There's no point stopping aging if we still die of disease," I said.

"Yes, well, I say we just enjoy life while we've got it and be happy we're even alive at all," Dylan said, pouring more wine. "In fact, you know what I think you should concentrate your research on Michael?"

"What's that?"

"Sexual jealousy." He glanced briefly at Annie, relaxing back into his chair with his hands clasped behind his head.

"Sexual jealousy?"

"That's right. Imagine if you removed sexual jealousy from the range of human experiences. We'd all be a lot better off."

"If you ask me," I said, "we'd all be a lot better off without so much sex at all. Maybe we could come into heat once a year, just for reproductive purposes, and then spend the rest of the time not thinking about it."

We all laughed again, and my heart soared with the pleasure of friendship.

As I was finishing the smoked trout on my plate I felt Sophie's calf come to rest gently on my right leg. My whole consciousness was drawn to it, and to my surprise she didn't move. I wasn't sure if she'd done it on purpose. Maybe she thought it was the table leg. Or maybe she hadn't noticed. Or maybe for her physical contact didn't mean as much as it did to me. Dylan and Sophie were poly-amorists, as was everyone in the New Church. According to Dylan it helped bond the tribe, just as it had done in many primitive societies, and as it did in bonobos. I wondered what place polyamory, or polygamy, had played in original human evolution and if it might not be a more natural form of relating than our enforced monogamy.

A week later, I hurried along the dimly lit corridor of the Geneus offices to catch up with Masanori, whom I could see up ahead. I'd been trying to contact everybody I knew who could possibly be interested in investing in our immune system research, but had gotten nowhere. I still hadn't heard back from Sophie and was starting to doubt I would.

Masanori turned to look at me as he slowed his pace.

"Michael-san." He nodded at me.

"What do you think's going to happen?" I said. Today was the report-back on our cooperation research.

"I think we're going to be told that we're idealistic fools for even imagining they might be able to find investors for something like this."

"You're probably right."

I pushed the heavy wooden door of the Geneus boardroom open and we took our places and waited patiently for Klaus to finish a call he was on.

I looked out the window at the early morning city filling with mist. Buildings rose out of it like trees in a forest, fighting for light in the ever-competitive real estate market. From here you could see over to the bay where old apartment buildings and skyscrapers stood in the water like dead trees in a lake. Some of them had been redesigned, with jetties and boats around them, enabling their residents to continue to live in them, but others had simply been abandoned or taken over by the ever-increasing population of homeless.

"Okay, let's get started," Klaus said, silencing the room with his commanding voice. "Rachel, what have you got for us?"

Rachel made a few adjustments on her com and statistics came up on everyone's overlays. I looked at the survey questions, imprinted over the world around me. I darkened the background with a short subvocal command so as to read the results more clearly. As the faces of the board members faded out the survey questions faded in.

Do you think humans should be made more cooperative?
90% yes, 7% no, 3% undecided.

Would you be interested in a genetic modification able to achieve this result?
70% yes, 21% no, 9% undecided.

If such technology were freely available, would you be interested in applying it to your own children?

15% yes, 71% no, 14% undecided.

Would you pay for such a modification?
1.5% yes, 91% no, 7.5% undecided.

Would you be prepared to accept a less selfish, more cooperative child as a side effect of a modification which substantially improved the immune system?
21% yes, 46% no, 33% undecided.

There were more questions and colored 3D graphs but the sad conclusion was obvious. I switched off the overlay and looked across the shiny expanse of polished wood to the rest of the directors in their tailored suits, with their well-trimmed hair and smoothed-out faces.

"I think the results speak for themselves," Rachel said, brushing her hair back to one side. "People want other people to be more cooperative, but they're not interested in being more cooperative themselves or having their children be more cooperative."

Masanori glanced at me with an "I told you so" look.

"Well, I guess that's not surprising," I said.

"Not surprising at all," Anthony agreed, crossing his arms. I watched as his flabby lips twisted into a snarl.

"Society has made people believe they need to compete so much – now they believe it's true." Masanori lowered his head.

"This is a ground-breaking change," I said. "Of course people are going to be skeptical of it. When the computer was invented even the CEO of IBM estimated a world demand for it of less than five. Less than five! The telephone was said to have "too many shortcomings" by Western Union. When Pasteur came up with the idea that germs caused disease, Pachet and others said it was ridiculous. These were paradigm shifts. And that's what this is. A paradigm shift."

"Paradigm shift or not," Zhao said, laying his hands gently on the table in front of him, his face almost as inexpressive as Masanori's. "I don't think we have the time or the money to go changing people's perspectives on life. And that's not our job. Our job is to make money for ourselves and our shareholders. Or at the very least stop ourselves from going bankrupt."

At the end of the meeting Klaus said that if we didn't find another investor within the next couple of weeks the immune-system project was finished.

Just as everyone was standing up to go I said, "I would like to publish a paper on the interrelationship between the genes controlling the immune systems and the socio-sexual behavior of bonobos. Maybe it'll help find an investor."

Normally Geneus didn't like its scientists producing papers, despite the fact that science was traditionally based on the sharing of research. They considered it a waste of time and a giving away of potentially valuable information. But this time everyone agreed.

After the meeting, I headed down to the somatic therapy lab. I hadn't wanted to tell Justin that our funding might be cut, but I couldn't hold off any longer.

"Justin, can I speak to you for a minute?" I said to him.

"Check this out." He motioned me over.

"What is it?"

"The stats. They're getting better." He loaded them up

on my public overlay. "Thirty nine percent success rate this time. These new bio-vectors are really working." He clenched his fists like a football player who'd just scored a goal.

"We have a problem."

"What's that?"

"They want to shut us down."

Justin stared at me. "What?"

"One of our major investors has pulled out."

"We're so close. The latest batch of macaque trials is showing some real promise. What will happen to everything we've done?"

"Nothing. That'll be it."

"Will we get to keep our jobs?"

"I hope so. Don't despair yet. Hopefully we'll find a solution. We need to find another investor, but if it doesn't work out I just wanted to give you a heads up."

Justin's eyes gaped at me and his mouth opened involuntarily. His whole body fell forward as if strings holding him up had slackened.

I took hold of his arm. "Let's just keep doing what we can."

At lunchtime, I headed down to the cafeteria: a tall, glassed-in sunroom, palms and creepers thriving between the tables. As I was sitting down to a cheese roll and a chocolate donut, a concession to my unmodified sugar-and-fat-loving taste buds, Sophie's name flashed in the top-right corner of my visual overlay with a call sign next to it.

"Sophie," I answered.

"I'm sorry I haven't been in touch. I was waiting to hear back from Rowen."

"What did he say?"

"He's overseas at the moment. They're setting up a New Church in San Francisco. He'll be back late next week and he can't consider it until then."

"That could be too late."

"That's the best I can do. Shall I set up a meeting?"

"Okay."

"He usually only takes meetings at the gatherings. Will that be alright?"

"That's fine. Why wouldn't it be?"

"No reason. I'll let you know."

CHAPTER SEVEN

MY CAR HEADLIGHTS forged a tunnel in the night, illuminating tight knit cypress on either side of the driveway. A song that Sophie had put on my stereo was playing at full volume. The whining melancholy of the music, the dark clouds passing across the full moon behind the trees, and not knowing exactly what Sophie was getting me into made my heart accelerate and my mind alert as if I had just taken a mixture of amphetamines and hallucinogens and was waiting to find out what the effect would be: heaven or hell.

I had heard a lot about Rowen Boone and about the New Church "gatherings" but I had never expected to go to one. Rowen was one of the country's wealthiest men, and his cult was one of the country's most popular spiritual organizations. As science and technology failed them, people were turning again to religion for answers. Not that the New Church appeared to have too many religious doctrines – unless polyamorous, communal living could be called a religion. Dylan liked to call it a practical religion.

At the end of the driveway we came to a white gravel turning circle leading up to a heavily illuminated Italianate mansion. We stepped out of the car while a robot attendant transferred auto-park data to the car's computer.

"Are you ready?" Sophie took my arm.

"I hope so."

Sophie and I walked across to the house together. Others were arriving at the same time, and we joined the throngs going up the stone stairs to the main entrance where a wooden door stood wide.

Inside, pillars in the foyer led up to a double-story cupola. A stone fountain contained a bowl held high by a sculpture of a naked couple.

"That's mine." Sophie pointed towards the sculpture.

"It's beautiful." I admired the ring of intertwined bodies at its base, all finely detailed.

Underwater lamps threw rippling light across the walls. Jazz music floated into the room like a flock of butterflies, notes dipping, seemingly randomly, this way then that, almost colliding, stalling, holding, continuing on again in new displays of virtuosity.

An archway on one side led to a corridor which ended in a hall full of people dancing to some throbbing electronic music. Sophie guided me around the edge of the spinning, rising, falling masses to where a terrace overlooked a lake behind the house, nodding at two security guards as we walked between them.

Upon a four-poster day bed draped in brightly colored tapestries sat a tall, thin, handsome man of about sixty, with bloodshot eyes and a well-trimmed beard. Next to him were two young women wrapped in dresses accentuating their voluptuous figures. They looked up at me out of two sets of dark-brown eyes and smiled.

Sophie slipped her shoes off and knelt on the bed and leaned across to kiss the man on the cheek.

"Rowen. Lovely to see you."

"The pleasure's all mine," Rowen replied. They embraced briefly and Sophie kissed the two women.

"Rowen, Suni and Sam. Let me introduce to you my friend, Michael."

Rowen held out his hand for me to shake and I was forced to lean forward onto the bed in order to reach him. Rowen's hand was large but I felt a weakness and fragility in his grip. "It's a pleasure," he said.

"Thank you for meeting with me."

He nodded.

The two women held out their hands for me to shake as well; their cool fingers slipping through mine.

"Please, make yourselves comfortable." Rowen signalled to the space on the bed.

I felt strange crawling onto his bed like this – even if it was a day-bed – but I slipped my shoes off on the flagstones and tried to adopt as comfortable a position as my tight suit pants and stiff back would allow.

"Would you like a pillow?" Suni noticed my awkwardness and extended one to me.

"Thank you." I took it from her.

Sophie lolled backwards, one hand drifting lazily onto Sam's knee.

"I like your suit," Rowen said.

"Thanks." The suit was part of an Armani summer

collection I'd picked up a few months ago on sale and that I was particularly fond of. I was surprised Rowen liked it, given his own attire: white linens and colored beads. "I like your house." I looked up at the floodlit sandstone walls. "Did you design it?"

"Yes. My wife and I." My gaze glanced questioningly onto Suni and Sam but Rowen chuckled and said: "No, my wife died about ten years ago. God rest her soul."

I nodded, thinking about Annie and wondering if I would ever be able to find love, or even lovers, after her death. I doubted it. Life without Annie would be intolerable. I imagined her right now, at home alone, and wanted to message her to see if she was alright.

"Would you two like something to eat or drink?" Sam asked.

"Yes, please," Sophie said, and I nodded agreement.

Suni reached in amongst the pillows. A moment later, a young Asian boy appeared behind the bed.

"May I take your order?" he said.

"Some punch and tapas for me," Sophie said. "And the same for my friend here."

"Coming right up." The boy let out a broad grin.

"Make it snappy," Suni called after him, laughing. The boy looked back and smiled at her suggestively. Rowen noticed but only smiled, his gaze drifting out towards the moonlight reflecting off the lake and the silhouettes of hills in the distance.

"So, tell me a little bit about yourself, Michael."

"What would you like to know?"

"Tell me a little about your history. I've had my people do some research on your company, Geneus. They seem like a fairly successful company. They cured diabetes by providing the insulin gene to pancreas cells, is that right?"

"Yes, that's right. They also developed a somatic treatment for Systemic Lupus Erythematosus, an auto-immune disease, and another for Hereditary Spherocytosis. That was before I started working for them. I used to own a small company, PureGen, which came up with a human artificial chromosome designed specifically for genetic modifications."

"Hmm," Rowen said, but didn't ask any more, his mind seeming to wander.

"How about you?" I said. "What were you doing before the New Church?"

"Prostitution and gambling mainly." Rowen turned back to me.

"Oh." I was not sure how to respond to this and my expression must have shown confusion as Rowen let out an unexpected laugh.

"Casinos, brothels, strip clubs, porn. You name it. My daughter runs it all now. Does a much better job than I ever did. I am here trying to make up for my sins." He smiled.

"Sounds interesting." I wasn't really sure what else to say. I was starting to wonder what kind of a crackpot this guy was and if he had any real interest in investing in my project at all. Surely Sophie wouldn't have brought me all the way out here for nothing? I glanced at her, but she was splayed out on the bed playing gently with Suni's fingers.

"Not really," Rowen said. "Just like any other business. Marketing, product and service development, human resource management, cash flow management, you know how it goes?"

"All too well."

The Asian boy returned with a tray of olives, cheese, crackers and two tall mugs of mulled wine. He placed it on the bed between Sophie and me, bowed, and left.

As we ate and drank, Rowen told me about the mission of his organization. He believed society was on the verge of total collapse and that one day the residents of his havens might have to be the ones to re-populate the planet. In the meantime, he was trying to store as much knowledge as possible on servers on his islands so that it wouldn't be lost.

It all sounded very interesting, but I couldn't help wondering if this was more of a pitch for me to join his own organization, rather than an investment meeting for him to consider investing in mine. I started to feel more and more uncomfortable. My suit and shirt seams were digging into my skin, not having been designed for cross-legged sitting, and the whole place was starting to make me anxious. All I wanted to do was get home to Annie. I considered sending Sophie a message and asking her if we could leave.

Just then, Sophie, Sam and Suni decided to go and join the party, and I watched as they walked away from us and merged with the crowd of people near the back door.

"Beautiful, aren't they? All three of them," Rowen said.

"Yes," I said, not sure of what else to say.

Rowen turned to me then and focussed his eyes on me, as if for the first time that night.

"So, tell me more about this project of yours, Michael. What is it you're trying to do exactly, and what is it you need from me?"

My heart accelerated. I took a deep breath and tried to

keep calm. I told him everything, including my research into cooperation and how I believed it could be used to improve humanity.

"Very interesting," Rowen said when I had finished, then lapsed back into silence, staring over at the lake again.

A couple of minutes passed, and Rowen still said nothing. I wanted to move around, get comfortable, but it seemed inappropriate. Then Rowen turned back to me, as if coming out of deep thought.

"Well," he said, "with medical specialists being reduced to a minimum during the turmoil that's now facing us, a modification like yours might be just what we need to help our communities survive."

"We'll probably need at least another six months to get it all working, and another hundred million in funding. I can have some exact figures sent over to you if you like."

Just then, Sophie and Sam came outside again and I watched as they joined a group on the terrace. I heard Sophie's cackling laugh.

"What is going on with you, Michael?" Rowen said. "You seem sad. Confused."

"What do you mean?"

"I mean inside. What's going on inside."

I wondered again if this was Rowen's way of recruiting members for the New Church; if he'd left prostitution for the more lucrative industry of religion.

"Nothing."

"Everyone's got something going on inside. What is it? Are you thinking how hot Sophie is? Or are you thinking about the wife you've left at home? Or are you wondering what sort of a nut I think I am?"

I let out a nervous laugh. "Something like that."

"There you go. So something is going on inside."

"Yes, I suppose it is. I'm just not that accustomed to sharing it with strangers, that's all."

"Maybe you could consider me a friend, then."

"Okay." I nodded my head, wondering where this was leading. "I guess I could do that."

"Good. So, what is it?"

I hadn't wanted to tell Rowen about Annie's illness for the same reason I hadn't told anyone at Geneus, but if I wanted his help I realized I was going to have to be honest. I got the feeling this wasn't going to be a standard business transaction anyway.

"My wife has HIV-4. She got it a few years ago."

"I can understand what that's like. Two years ago I was diagnosed with cancer."

"I'm sorry."

"I don't mind. I'm at peace with it now. It's been one of the best things that's happened to me in some ways. It's changed my perspective on everything."

"Yes, I know how that feels." I thought about how my own perspective had changed since finding out about Annie's illness. "But you're still scared, aren't you?"

"Of course I'm scared. But what else can I do? Just like you're telling yourself you can save your wife, I'm telling myself that everything's going to be alright. That's the best we can do, really, isn't it?" Rowen reached across and put his hand on my shoulder. The feeling of his hand on me, so heavy and warm, was strange, but although I was uncomfortable with it I felt bereft when he took it away. "I used to be like you, you know? Always trying to hold onto something. I think we realize, though, deep down, that nothing is ever really going to protect us."

I nodded, wondering if he was going to give me a sermon, but he stopped.

"Enough talk," he said. "Go. Go and have fun. Go and do whatever you like. Enjoy the night. Enjoy yourself. Nothing bad will happen to you. I promise. Here, before you go, give me a hug."

With any other person I would have considered this an odd request, but from this man, at this time, it seemed appropriate. I reached over and hugged him and as I felt his arms wrapping around me a peace and emptiness invaded me, a feeling of protection and warmth and lightness that I hadn't felt in a long time, and for a moment I understood why people were drawn to him.

"What about our project?" I said, climbing off the bed.

"Do you think you can find a cure for cancer?"

"How long have you got?"

"Months. Maybe a year."

"I'm sorry. I'd like to say yes, but I don't think so."

"That's okay. Let me think about it. I'll talk to my people about it. Give me some time. Now I have to rest."

"Okay. I understand. It's been a pleasure meeting you. Thank you for the opportunity." I slipped my shoes back on.

"The pleasure's all mine."

"Good luck."

"You too."

I wasn't sure why but I clasped my hands together and gave Rowen a little bow. Rowen returned the gesture then reached under a pillow and a moment later two young men appeared and helped him away.

Inside the hall the lights had been dimmed. The thumping beat of the music reverberated through the floor and up into my body. People were dancing, hundreds of swirling, dropping, lifting, flying figures, blurs of color and sound.

Suni came over to me and motioned for me to join her. She led me onto the dance floor, rocking gently with me for a minute, holding my hand as I found the rhythm.

"Just let yourself go," she whispered. "Let your body dance its own dance. Don't try to control it. Follow your feet." She span around in slow circles in front of me, then started orbiting me, as if letting her body drift into my gravitational field.

I let my feet take me where they would. They led me in an orbit of my own, small circles which gradually became larger until Suni and I were circling each other and spinning as we did so. I let myself go with the music then, let it guide me. Around me were groups of interconnected bodies, flowing into one another and writhing over one another. Suni drifted off with another man and another woman appeared before me and our bodies seemed to attract then repel like two magnets twisting and turning and bouncing off one another.

Then she too went away.

Suddenly all the stress of the last few years rose up inside me and I made my way over to the side of the hall and found a place alone on a lounge in a dark corner. I thought about Annie and all that she meant to me, about the world that I had once loved and that no longer existed. About how much destruction humans had brought upon themselves and upon everything else on this planet. I wondered if Rowen was going to give us any funding and then I thought maybe it would be better if he didn't. Making humans stronger probably wasn't such a good idea anyway. The last thing we needed was more humans in this world.

After a little while, Sophie found me. "Are you enjoying the party?" She sat down next to me and put a hand on my knee.

"It's okay."

"Would you like to come upstairs?"

"What's upstairs?"

"The rest of the party." She raised her eyebrows at me.

My pulse throbbed and my stomach clenched up on me. What was she suggesting? Annie and I had talked about the possibility of me being invited to participate in the New Church orgy, and Annie had told me that I should make the most of it. I had told her I wasn't interested, but Annie had laughed and told me to give it a try: she was much more practical about these things than I was. I couldn't deny that I was attracted to Sophie – any man would have been – but the idea of betraying my wife was painful just to think about.

Another part of me, though, knew that at some point I would have to let her go. She was dying and, without a cure, probably only had another two years at the most. And the chances of us finding a cure, especially now, were not good. If I was honest with myself they never had been. Even if we could get our modifications working, the possibility they'd cure HIV-4 was less than fifty percent. The world was falling away from me and everything that had previously kept me supported was fading.

"Well?" Sophie said. "It's not polite to keep a lady waiting." She took my hand.

Was Dylan okay with this? Would Annie really be? If there was one thing I'd learnt about women over the years it was that they didn't always say what they meant.

I felt as if I were standing at the open door of a plane, three thousand meters above the ground, about to skydive for the first time in my life.

"Okay," I said to Sophie, deciding to follow her upstairs but do nothing more. At the very least it would make an interesting subject of scientific study – something to report back to Annie about. She'd joked about wanting a full rundown.

"Should we invite someone?" Sophie said.

"What do you mean?"

"How about that woman over there?" Sophie pointed towards a very attractive woman just slightly younger than I was.

I hesitated. How could I tell Sophie that I wasn't going to do anything? Or was I just kidding myself? Did I really want this to happen but just hadn't admitted it to myself?

Either way, I couldn't stay where I was. I looked and felt like a fool.

"Come on, coward." Sophie nudged me with her elbow. Before I knew it she had stood up and was walking across to the woman. The woman didn't speak but put her hand gently into Sophie's. They headed for the foyer. Sophie glanced back at me and I followed.

We wound our way up the stairs and onto the interior balcony, looking down upon Sophie's fountain. Dimmed chandeliers spread a faint red glow against the walls. People, entirely naked or almost, lounged against walls or in arm chairs.

Sophie was ahead of us. She strode past a number of closed doors until we reached one which was open. Inside were mostly naked figures on an enormous four-poster bed, a diaphanous screen around them. We stood and watched for a minute, then went to the next open door, a similar room with a similar bed, but empty.

Sophie and the woman disappeared inside and I stood at the threshold, wondering what to do next.

CHAPTER EIGHT

MY BODY SLUMPED down into the chair in my office. It had been a week since the party at Rowen's and there was still no word on whether or not he was going to invest in our project. I was starting to think the whole thing had been a waste of time, and I was angry with myself for getting both my own and Annie's hopes up.

I checked through my mail messages. There were a few internal messages, a few from other geneticists around the world, and then there was one from a man named Bruno Salacio. I had met Bruno once at a neuroscience conference. He was a well-regarded evolutionary biologist.

Hi Michael,

I'm contacting you because I've just read a paper of yours that I've been asked to referee concerning your studies with bonobo genes in macaques and I think you might be interested in a new line of research that we are about to undertake. I was wondering if we could arrange a

meeting?
  Bruno.

The message was strangely unforthcoming. Bruno's signature had a number so I connected to it, but it went to voicemail and I left a message. I asked the net for more information about him, but all I could gather was that he worked for a company called FutureGen, a biotech similar to Geneus.

As I was eating lunch that day, Bruno's name appeared on my overlay. I answered the call and Bruno asked me if we could meet but wouldn't tell me why. We agreed on a time and a place: at Melbourne University that afternoon.

I sat staring out the glass windows of the Geneus cafeteria onto the small paved courtyard, wondering what he could possibly want with me. Maybe FutureGen wanted to invest. Or maybe they were going to try to poach me. If they had the money I might consider it. I could take Justin, Masanori, Yolanda and Richard with me and make a fresh start. Except Geneus had a non-competition clause in my employment contract and time was running out to find a cure for Annie.

Later that afternoon, I took a cable car from near my office building to the other end of town, floating between plane trees and above power lines. I looked down at the masses of people crowding the streets: a mix of cultures and sub-cultures from all over the world.

I got off at the station closest to Melbourne University and walked across. Armed guards stood at the entrance with machine guns and I had to show them my identification and have my body scanned. Two years before a bomb had been set off there, apparently by an eco-terrorist group angry that the university had accepted funding from fossil fuel companies. It had killed thirty-seven people.

I walked between a line of elms and the modern, concrete, buildings to where the old, sandstone, buildings started with their tiled roofs and ivy-covered walls. Clusters of students talked and laughed in the spring sunshine. I remembered my own time there, that innocent abstract world where everything was theoretical, where anything seemed possible. I remembered my life with Dylan, sharing a room in one of the on-campus colleges, and how during our third year, Dylan had decided to do his thesis on bonobos.

Dylan was especially interested in the bonobo mating habits, which seemed to closely parallel his own. In typical Dylan style he organized an expedition to the Congo in a matter of weeks and asked me if I wanted to join him. At the time a civil war had just ended in the Congo and all the travel advice warned us not to go. It wasn't so much that I wanted to go to the Congo, but that I wanted to try to keep my only friend out of trouble.

After a twenty-four hour flight, a nine hour bus trip, a two hour jeep ride and a two day boat ride up a river surrounded by jungle – where the only signs of human life were tiny villages of thatched huts and the fishermen and traders on log canoes who serviced them – we finally arrived at a village. Our guide, James, a very black man with a very white smile, told us we would be able to find the bonobos there.

We spent the next few weeks observing these peace-loving creatures. Almost every circumstance in life –

whether it be finding new food or meeting another troop – seemed to demand a round of almost indiscriminate sex. Aggression between members was almost non-existent, and even when they came across other groups they welcomed rather than rejected them.

On our way home from the Congo we stopped off in Tanzania to spend a few days at the chimpanzee research center in Gombe. Here we saw something totally different. Male chimps, especially those competing for alpha male status, spent a good deal of time and energy displaying aggressively for one another, something bonobos never did. Females were bullied and often attacked by the males and even other females, and while they were cooperative in family units or among cliques, as a rule they didn't help each other. The one time we saw them come into contact with another troop there was an aggressive standoff before both groups went their separate ways.

It was in Africa that I decided to analyze the bonobo genome and see where it differed from both chimpanzees and humans, and where Dylan decided to live in a way more similar to his bonobo cousins.

"Michael, nice to see you again. Thanks for coming." Bruno, a heavy-set man, bald on top but with a beard to make up for it, offered me his hand.

"Bruno, likewise."

Bruno led me across a grassy clearing. We went under a stone arch to a courtyard where a single tree was growing, its bare branches twisted into ever-smaller spirals, leaves just starting to bud.

"So, you're interested in my work?" I said.

"It was actually a mutual acquaintance, Rowen Boone,

who asked me to meet with you."

"Rowen?" My heart did a double-take.

"Yes. He mentioned that you were involved in a project that our organization might be interested in investing in."

"FutureGen?"

"No. That's just my day job." Bruno smiled.

"You're part of the New Church?"

"No, no, we're something else entirely. Here, come through."

Bruno led me through some large double doors into a cool hallway and then to a small office with stained glass windows that looked out onto a native garden. He shut the heavy door behind us.

"Have a seat," Bruno said, motioning to a club lounge.

I sat down and Bruno lowered himself into a chair across from me.

"The possibility of genetic modification changing the human race in a favorable way is something that I have been interested in for a very long time," Bruno lowered his voice and leaned in towards me. "Being an evolutionary biologist, I'm always interested in the way certain species have evolved, particularly *Homo sapiens*, and I, like you, presumably, can't help thinking that we've evolved to a very dangerous point and haven't gone any further."

"Just smart enough to kill ourselves and everything else along with us," I said, still wondering how Bruno knew Rowen and how much Rowen had told him.

"Exactly. Now, Rowen mentioned Geneus's lack of funding."

"Yes. We've been looking for investors."

"He said that. He also mentioned that part of the reason

you're so desperate to find an investor is because your wife is sick with HIV-4. Something Geneus doesn't know about."

I looked at him and felt my intestines start to stir. How could I have been so stupid as to confide that to Rowen? I put my hands on my knees, wanting to stand up, but I stayed where I was.

"Don't worry. Your secret's safe with me."

"What is it you want, then?" I was angry, more at myself than anyone else, but I tried to contain it. I couldn't afford to get Bruno off-side.

"We want to invest in the project," Bruno said.

"Who?"

"I can't disclose our organization."

"Why are you meeting with me, then? Anthony Simons is the man to talk to for new investment."

"Because we want you to provide us with information. Information about the state of the project. The processes. Everything you do."

"You'd have access to much of that as investors, anyway." I was afraid that if I didn't do what he wanted he would tell someone at Geneus about Annie and I would lose my job and be made a pariah.

"Yes. You're right. But it's access to what we wouldn't get as investors that we're interested in."

I suddenly realized what he was talking about: industrial espionage.

"I'm sorry. I'm not your man," I said, starting to stand up but hesitating.

"Hold on, sit down a moment." Bruno waved me down. "Just hear me out."

I had little choice.

"The reason I mentioned your wife was not to extort you, but because I need to be able to trust you."

"It's hardly the best way of going about it." I took a deep breath.

"I gather from your papers and your research that you are no happier with the current evolution of *Homo sapiens* than I am. My question is, how unhappy are you? What do you think's going to happen to us over the next fifty to a hundred years, and what would you be prepared to do to change that?" Bruno stared at me unblinkingly. His voice was deep and sure of itself, and I suddenly felt even more afraid than I had a moment ago.

"Why?"

"Just tell me."

"Okay," I replied, my heart still pounding. I thought about the de-regulated zones, the civil wars breaking out around the world. "I believe society is returning to a more primitive state. The most cunning and aggressive members of the species are rising up and leading the poor and the hungry, protecting them in return for their loyalty, their money, and their lives. They're fighting it out, both here and overseas, for resources and territory. I'm not sure we'll ever be able to return to civilization as we know it, as all of the easily obtainable resources that allowed us to develop this far have been exhausted. I think for the next couple of hundred years at least, if not for thousands of years, we'll enter into a period similar to the dark ages, where war and aggression will win out over reason and justice. As to what I'm prepared to do about that, I'm already doing it. I believe an improved immune system will stop much of the suffering that's been caused by disease throughout history. Even if people are poor, at the very least we can keep them healthy."

"What about your research on cooperation?" Bruno said.

"What about it?" I shrugged.

"Wouldn't you like to continue with that?"

"Of course I would. But I don't think that's going to be possible."

"How about if I told you it was?"

"Even if I had the funding, I'm not sure I've got the time."

"What if I told you that we could provide all the funding you needed, both for your immune-system research and your cooperation research?"

"I'd want to know what the price would be." It seemed Bruno was here to make me a genuine offer and not just to blackmail me. Maybe this was Rowen's way of investing in our research without being directly involved.

"Total secrecy. And total commitment to the organization." Bruno's eyes behind his glasses were out of proportion with the rest of his face.

I looked down, but didn't answer him.

"So?" Bruno said. "Are you interested?"

"Of course I'm interested."

"Are you interested enough to agree to die if you ever tell anyone about this conversation?"

My heart started up again, so strongly I could feel my neck and chest constricting.

"Yes," I said, softly. "I suppose I am."

"I'm not doing this to threaten you, Michael. I have to

know that if I give you any more information you will be willing to keep it to yourself. You don't have to agree to accept my help, but you do have to agree to never mention a word of this to anyone."

"Okay," I said, hardly breathing at all now.

CHAPTER NINE

"WHAT'S WRONG?" ANNIE said, as I walked into the house that evening.

I wondered if Gendigm, the organization that Bruno worked for, was monitoring me already. Maybe they had been for a while now: ever since my meeting with Rowen. Even before then. Suddenly everything looked threatening and suspicious: a loose light fitting, the slightly skewed painting of a garden scene in our living room, a hollow elephant sculpture we'd picked up in Kenya.

At the same time as being deeply afraid, I felt the stirrings of hope. If Gendigm had unlimited funding and was willing to fund both my immune system research and my cooperation research, anything was possible. We could find a cure for Annie's disease and cure not only her and Justin's sister but tens of thousands of others around the world. We could create a germline modification of the immune system that would protect future generations from disease. We could even create a nicer, more empathetic version of humans, although whether anyone would ever want that or not I didn't know.

"Michael?" Annie prompted, and I realized I hadn't answered her.

"Sorry. Nothing. Just a hard day at work, that's all." I stared at the elephant again. I had to tell her what had happened with Bruno, but I had to find a way to do it that couldn't be detected. Bruno had insisted on complete secrecy, even from Annie.

The next day, I received a message on my com from Bruno saying that he had set up a meeting with Gendigm that evening and that he would send through the encrypted access information.

That night, I told Annie I had a meeting with a potential investor and went into my office and locked the door. I connected into v-space and went to the IP address that Bruno had sent me and entered in the access details.

I found myself in a virtual boardroom very similar to any normal boardroom, except that outside the windows, which completely surrounded us, were stars and galaxies in a totally black night.

"Michael, welcome." Bruno's 3D avatar came over to meet me.

A number of other people were sitting around the table already. I walked clumsily towards a chair. I didn't spend much time in v-space, and my motor skills there were not very well developed. After some trouble I managed to sit my avatar down and I greeted everyone. Their voices all had the slightly electronic twang of a scrambling device – presumably so that they could never be recorded and recognized.

"Take a moment to get acquainted," Bruno said.

From each of the avatars I pulled up a short biography. No real names were mentioned, but there seemed to be an impressive list of people in the room: CEOs, scientists, an ex-politician, an army colonel, and a number of NGO executives.

"This isn't all of us, by any means," Bruno said. "But we're part of the core group."

"Thanks for taking the time to meet with me."

I was glad I was in v-space or the fact that I was clutching the arms of my seat and sweating profusely from my underarms would have been noticeable.

"Well, first you'd probably like to know a little more about who we are and what we want?" Bruno said.

"Yes, please."

"Gendigm was created nearly fifteen years ago. We're a slow growing organization but now have over two hundred members in thirty-five countries around the world. Our main goal is to transform the human race through genetic modification. We believe we're approaching a bottle-neck, a time when the numbers of our species will be so diminished that an evolutionary leap may be possible. I'll send a list of our current projects to your com — have a look over them when you get the time."

"Meanwhile, we're here today to discuss your own research. We believe it could well become one of our most important projects." Bruno turned to the rest of the group. "As all those who have read the brief know, Michael is involved in a project targeting the human immune system, with potential also for making humans more cooperative and empathetic. We're here to discuss whether or not we should invest in his company, Geneus. It's estimated they'll need another hundred million at least before they've got a workable solution."

"How long will it take, Michael?" Frank, labelled as the treasurer, asked. I admired the detail in the rendering of Frank's jaw — almost lifelike. He must have had some pretty high-powered tech at home, or wherever he was located. Probably in a bunker in Sweden; one of those new underground hotels with high-res windows and hydroponic farms.

"At least six months. The benefit of this technology, though, is that we can apply it to other things. Our new delivery method, using histone code recognition, has almost been perfected. We might even be able to augment the entire immune system of those already born — somatically."

"Can you tell us a bit more about your cooperation research?" Zoe, another geneticist, said. "I don't quite understand how those who have been modified would differ from normal humans. We're already a very cooperative species."

"We're also xenophobic. We're good at cooperating in groups, but two groups won't cooperate together unless they're able to identify with one another. And even then we often require a third group who we label as "the enemy". Our modified macaques no longer have such a strong "us and them" paradigm. And even within the group itself, everything is shared equally, usually under the control of a matriarch, rather than dominant males taking more. Bonobos, unlike chimps and humans, evolved in an environment where there were plentiful supplies of food and few competitors. Females formed strong coalitions which thwarted male aggression, leading to it being selected against, and higher levels of cooperation selected for. We're still not exactly sure what the mechanisms are, and how they'd play out in humans — although we suspect bonobos' greater empathy and polygamous sexual natures play a role. "

"Well, from everything I've read, I think this modification could mean the difference between our modified humans surviving or not," Zoe said.

"How are we financially, Frank?" Bruno said.

"We could do it, but it's money that could easily be put into other things. If it doesn't work, it's a lot to waste."

"What about the bio-dome project?" Robert, an eco-engineer, interjected. "Without somewhere to live, it doesn't matter how well we modify people."

According to Robert's biography he was the leader of a project creating self-sufficient pods which could be completely shut off from the environment around them. I'd read about similar projects before, but they all had the same problem: getting the eco-systems to balance. Chemical levels in the air were difficult to stabilize and weeds and insects were a constant problem. Nature wasn't so easy to imitate.

"Hopefully we'll never get to the point where we even need bio-domes," Zoe replied.

"Current models show unsustainable levels of groundwater nutrient overloading for at least a hundred years," Robert said. "If things get too bad, we're going to need some way of controlling our environments."

The group talked on for another couple of hours and it

was decided that the only way Gendigm should become a part of Geneus was if they could take a controlling share. Without that they would have very little control over the direction of the project. If we were ever successful in doing what we wanted to do, they wanted to control how the technology was applied. Klaus, they presumed, would want to sell it for as much as possible, whereas the members of Gendigm were more interested in making sure it was distributed as widely as possible. They even mentioned making it open source — something they would definitely need total control for, as there was no way Klaus would ever allow that. An open source genetic modification would be freely available for anyone in the world to apply. If the technology was perfected, a bio-vector containing the modification could even be put into pill form.

"The problem is going to be convincing Klaus to let go of Geneus," I said. Klaus held a fifty-one percent share in the company.

"Maybe we should get Jan Peters in there," Frank said. "Jan is the best negotiator I've ever seen. If anyone can convince Klaus, it's Jan."

"Whose opinion does Klaus respect most, Michael?" Roland, one of the CEOs, asked. "If we can convince that person, we might be able to get them to convince Klaus."

"Anthony Simons. Unfortunately, Anthony is against our project. He thinks it's never going to make money."

"Who else is there?"

"Zhao, the treasurer. If we could convince Zhao then he might put pressure on Klaus. Zhao's a numbers man."

"Well, let's talk dollars and cents to him then," Frank said.

After the meeting was over, I came out of my office and into the living room.

Annie was sitting watching something on her visual overlay, and she didn't look up at me. For the last few days she had been acting strangely, and I wanted to ask her what was wrong but knew that when she got into one of her moods it was usually best to wait until it had passed.

"Well, things are looking promising," I said.

Annie looked up at me. "In what way?" she said, although there was a lack of interest in her voice.

"They're interested in investing. Although they want to take a controlling share."

"That's great," Annie said, and went back to her reading.

I was almost going to say something, but the last thing we needed was an argument, so I went into the kitchen and made myself a cup of tea.

"Would you like a drink?" I called to Annie.

"No thanks," she called back, her tone still flat.

Over the next several months there were many meetings behind closed doors. Jan Peters, Gendigm's representative, working for a dummy corporation called HGM industries, met first with Zhao, then with Klaus, then with a few other key figures on the Geneus board. More than a financial decision, or even a power struggle, it was a psychological and emotional attachment to the company that was making Klaus's decision to let go difficult.

Letting go of Geneus would essentially mean the end of his life's work and the beginning of the end of his life itself. Klaus was still strong and fit for nearly eighty, and the idea of letting go of the one thing he'd spent his life working on, that had given him meaning, purpose and drive all these years, was, understandably, a step he was finding it difficult to take. He was also a control freak, as most people in positions of power were, and he felt he had been manipulated into this decision, rather than coming to it by himself, which he wasn't happy about either.

Anthony was still completely against the takeover, suspecting, rightfully, that if it happened he would never become CEO of the company and that he might even find himself without a job. The other board members were split, but in the end it would come down to Klaus's decision anyway.

One day a meeting was called and I hoped the decision was all but made.

Jan came into the room and shook hands with everyone.

"Okay everyone," Klaus said, "Jan's here to present the details of HGM's final offer."

Jan took his position at the front of the room. He wiped his lips and stared at us all for a moment, as if considering. "Thanks Klaus, and thank you everybody for your time here today. As you know, HGM industries is interested in purchasing a fifty-one percent controlling share in Geneus. We believe, as do a number of you, that Geneus is indeed on the verge of genius and that with some good investment we can bring to fruition all that you here, especially Klaus, Michael, and Masanori, have been working on for the last three years.

"You already know the technical details of the project, so I won't go into those again, but I would like to share with you our vision for the future of Geneus and give you some projected figures. I would also like to inform you of the changes that we would make to the company structure and the positions, salaries, and bonuses that you and the rest of the Geneus employees would be provided with were this takeover to go ahead."

Jan spent the next two hours covering all the details of the proposed takeover. Thankfully he didn't mention anything about getting rid of Anthony and, by the end of the meeting, even he was looking happy about the possibility.

"So, what do you think?" I said to Klaus as we filed out of the meeting room.

"It's looking promising, Michael. Very promising," Klaus said, putting his hand on my back.

CHAPTER TEN

"YOU KNOW WHAT we should do?" I said to Annie that night when I got home, buoyed by the idea that we might finally have an investor in our project.

"What's that?"

"Take the weekend off."

It had been years since we had taken a vacation, and although we were still together, in the last few months our relationship had become uncomfortable, like ill-fitting clothes, and we often snapped at one another for irrelevant details. The scale — with our compatibilities on one side and our incompatibilities on the other — seemed to be tipping into the negative. I wondered what had changed, but all I could think of was Annie's illness. In the last few months she'd seemed more lethargic than ever.

"I don't know. We're both so busy. I'm supposed to be doing vaccinations this weekend. Where would we go, anyway?"

"I read the other day about a converted cruise ship.

Apparently it's in the waters off the east coast and can be accessed by helicopter."

"Not exactly my idea of a holiday destination."

"No, but there aren't many other options left. And we need a break, Annie. If this deal goes through I'm going to be flat out for months, and before that happens I'd like to spend a little more time with you." I moved closer to her but she backed away.

"We spend plenty of time together," she said, annoyed.

"Not doing anything nice, though."

"How much does it cost?"

"Let me check." I did a search on the net and found the company's site. "Here, check this out, they have a v-space tour."

I sent the link across to Annie's com and together we were taken on a virtual tour of a cruise ship that was the size of a small town. It had swimming pools, tennis courts, a shopping mall, restaurants, concert and theatre halls, and a floating reef off the side where you could scuba dive amongst tropical fish.

"It does look very nice," Annie said.

I talked to the virtual booking assistant and within a couple of minutes I'd booked us a suite.

The next day we took a taxi out to the airport, which was right on the edge of the regulated zone. From there we boarded a helicopter with six other couples, a group of three elderly ladies, and two businessmen, and began our ascent across the Dandenong ranges.

The Dandenongs, just outside of Melbourne, had once been covered with a spectacular forest, but now housed a cancerous growth of concrete and shipping container houses. It was here that Annie's clinic was located and that the rebel forces threatening the city were apparently grouping.

Two hours later our helicopter swept out over the ocean and on the horizon I could see the huge floating fortress of the cruise ship.

We were soon aboard and checking in at the reception desk. We were only staying three days so hadn't brought much luggage, but the porter insisted on carrying our small case anyway. Annie and I looked at one another as we were led along an interior walkway. Two stories down to our left was an indoor garden with palm trees and park benches and about six stories above us was a huge glass roof. On our right were the doors to the rooms, and about half way along the porter slipped a card in one of them and motioned us inside.

The room was just like a hotel room, with a king size bed, a small writing desk, some armchairs and a bathroom separated off by a glass screen. From the two round windows in the far wall you could see right out across to the horizon.

"Here you are, sir and madam." The porter lifted our bag onto a low shelf and bowed before leaving.

The door closed behind him with a click and we were left in silence.

I leant down to try to kiss Annie, but she pulled away from me and walked across to the window.

"A drink?" I asked, picking up a drinks menu from the counter top.

"You have one. You know alcohol makes me sleepy during the day."

"It's not like you have to do anything."

She didn't answer.

I had hoped this break would bring us back together, give us some time to talk things over – everything that had gone unsaid between us as we focussed on work – but if Annie was going to act like this all weekend then being stuck in this room together would be difficult.

We'd promised each other we weren't going to do any work while we were away, but already I was looking forward to getting back to the lab. With the new funding we were getting from Gendigm, the possibilities would be endless.

Then, for the first time, I wondered if helping Gendigm take over Geneus was really the right thing to do. I had been so focussed on the possibilities that the threats had hardly crossed my mind. What if they were simply trying to take over the company for their own purposes? How did I know who they really were and what they really wanted?

Annie walked over to the window, and I watched the light shining off her thick, dark hair. I longed for the way things used to be between us, when we could talk together for hours, sparking one another's imaginations, feeding one another with ideas. I realized how totally absorbed in work I was and how my obsession with keeping Annie alive didn't allow me to enjoy the precious time I *did* have with her.

All this time I'd wanted to share with her what was happening with Gendigm, but Bruno's warning on that first day stopped me. I had no idea how much surveillance they had on me. I knew it was possible to hack into people's coms, and although I had some heavy duty firewalls protecting mine, installed by Geneus to prevent industrial espionage, I wasn't sure what they were capable of. Presumably if they had the money to take over Geneus they had the money for almost anything.

"Let's go and explore," I said to Annie, wanting to escape from this claustrophobic room.

"No. I think I'll stay here and rest."

"I'll see you later then."

I pushed the door a little harder than necessary and it closed with a bang behind me. I headed for the upper deck; I needed some space, some thinking room. Maybe I'd forced Annie into this trip. Maybe that was why she was angry with me. But it went deeper than that. She'd been like this for months. There was something else.

I walked up a steel staircase to the roof of the ship and stood against a metal railing and stared at the horizon. The sun was low and glittered off the surface of the ocean to the west. Other people were up there too: young couples in pastel colors hugging one another in the breeze, a few older people clasping the rails and staring out at the ocean, that immensity which must have reminded them of that to which they would soon return.

I wished that Annie was up there with me and that she was healthy again and that we could go back to our room together and make love together for days on end like we used to. I remembered the last real vacation we'd taken, before the flooding. We'd gone to Mexico and spent two weeks in a colonial hotel staring out from our balcony to palm trees swaying in the beach breeze. Every day we'd gone swimming and eaten seafood at the restaurants with their tables and chairs spread out on the sand.

Half an hour later, when I went back down stairs and made my way to our room, Annie was half asleep on the bed and I sat down next to her.

"Are you hungry? We should go and get something to eat?" I said.

"Okay." She sat up.

I wanted to ask her what was wrong, but I was afraid that if we got into a fight then it could turn nasty. There was so much stored up frustration between us and I was so exhausted from everything that was happening with my project and Annie's illness that if Annie got nasty, which she sometimes did, I might not be able to control myself. We were better off trying to be nice to one another and restoring some goodwill first, rather than dredging up all our anger and frustration. There was little we could do about our situation anyway.

"Let's go then," I said.

"Give me a minute."

I waited for her to change, and then we went down to one of the restaurants and sat through a tense meal.

As we pushed back into our room, Annie said she was going to take a shower and disappeared into the bathroom. She pulled the blinds down across the windows and I heard the water going on. I hoped she would invite me in, but after a few minutes, when she hadn't, I decided to leave her alone for a while. I needed some space, and by the looks of it she did too.

I went back to a bar I'd seen near the restaurant and ordered a G and T. Before I knew it I'd had three and was onto my fourth.

Just as I was ordering my fifth an attractive woman

about my age sat down next to me. She smiled at me and I smiled back.

"Are you here alone?" she said.

"Yes," I said, meaning that I was in the bar alone but realizing that might not have been what she meant.

We started talking. She had just divorced from her husband, she told me, and was finally enjoying her freedom. They hadn't loved one another for years, apparently, but they'd stayed together out of habit. It wasn't until she'd caught herself one day with a handful of sleeping tablets and a bottle of whisky that she finally found the courage to make the change.

"And how do you feel now?" I said, the room wobbling in a way I was sure wasn't due to the ocean.

"Better than I have in twenty years!" Her enthusiasm was infectious.

Annie sent me a message then, asking me where I was.

"Just let me go to the bathroom," I said to the woman, Gloria.

I messaged Annie that I was down in the bar, but she didn't message back. I presumed she was still angry with me but that her worry for me had reached an intolerable peak. I wondered whether I should go back to her, but decided against it. I was feeling good for the first time in years.

At 2am, I finally staggered back to our room. Annie was asleep, or at least appeared to be asleep, so I went into the bathroom and took a shower. When I lay down I put my hand slowly across onto Annie's warm body and was relieved when I felt her shuffling towards me and pressing her back up against me.

"Where were you last night?" Annie asked when I awoke.

Harsh light was coming in the window and I wanted to keep my eyes closed, but forced myself to look at her.

"I told you. I was in the bar."

"Who with?"

"A woman I met there."

"So, you just pick up random women now, do you?" She had her hands on her hips.

"No. We got talking. That's all. Am I not allowed to talk to other people now?" I sat up and stared at her.

"Not when you invite me away for the weekend and then disappear you're not."

"I thought you wanted some space. We haven't exactly been getting along very well recently, have we?" I shook my head and looked down.

"And whose fault is that?"

"I don't know. Whose fault is it?"

I'd learned over the years that as often as not I was just as much to blame for situations which I initially held Annie solely responsible for, so I tried to stay open to that possibility now. Blaming her for her illness, which I often wanted to do, was not going to help either of us.

"Yours, Michael. It's your fault. If you weren't having an affair then none of this would be happening."

I turned up to face her. We locked eyes and I shook my head. "What are you talking about?"

"I'm talking about the affair you've been having. With Sophie I presume. Ever since that stupid gathering you went to you've been creeping around like a guilty teenager."

"What do you mean creeping around like a guilty teenager? I'm not having an affair with Sophie or anyone else. I told you about the gathering, and nothing happened."

After watching Sophie and the other woman go into the bedroom that night, I'd turned around and walked downstairs. When I got home, I'd recounted to Annie the whole situation and she'd laughed and called me a coward, but now it seemed that she didn't believe me.

"Well what the hell have you been doing then?"

I suddenly realized what was happening and I burst out laughing.

"What the hell's so funny?" Annie stood there in her bathrobe, arms crossed.

"Oh Annie. Come here. Sit down. Please." I patted the space on the bed next to me but she wouldn't budge.

"What is it, Michael? Tell me?" She was trying to remain firm but her voice had softened.

"You're right. I'm sorry. There is something I haven't told you. But it's got nothing to do with Sophie or any other woman."

"What is it then?"

I realized that I was going to have to tell her everything. I hoped that Gendigm wasn't listening and, if they were, that they would forgive me this one betrayal of their secret or at the very least consider me too useful to dispose of.

I told Annie everything that had happened with Bruno and Gendigm, and she stood there in disbelief and then sat down on the bed beside me, facing me.

"This sounds way too dangerous, Michael. I don't think you should be working with these people. You don't even know who they are."

"I know. But we need the funding. Without it Klaus will shut the project down."

"So let him."

"I can't. I don't want to lose you." I took her hands. I could see the relief but also the new fear in her eyes.

"And I don't want to lose *you!* I don't want you risking your life for some shady organization. Who knows what they'll make you do?"

"What do you mean?"

"I mean – once they've got you working for them they could ask you for anything. Why so much secrecy? Something's not right."

"Maybe. Maybe not. What choice do I have?"

"We can go away together. Leave the country."

"What about your disease?"

"Let me go, Michael."

"I have to give it a try. I can't just let you die." I squeezed her hands tightly. "And it's not just for you, Annie. It's for everybody with your disease. With any disease." I knew that Annie would never agree to let me do it for her alone, but maybe this would convince her. She put her face in her hands and I put a hand on her back. "It's our only choice."

"I'm so sorry," she said. "I'm so sorry I've been acting like I have. I really did think you were having an affair." She shook her head and laughed and looked at me straight in the eyes, begging me to forgive her.

"It's okay," I said. "I love you."

"I love you too."

CHAPTER ELEVEN

TWO DAYS LATER, I walked into my lab, whistling. I used to whistle all the time, but over the last few years my desire to whistle had waned. Catching myself at it again made me smile and I pumped out a bad rendition of "Greensleeves" that I'd picked up from my grandfather.

I stood at my office window and looked out over the city, seeing my own face in the window and seeing my father's face in it. It was cloudy and a strong breeze was blowing the leaves off trees. I liked autumn. Even in this concreted-over and virtualized world there was still something ominous about it which stirred deep emotions in me: the desire to prepare for the oncoming winter.

My overlay showed a message waiting and I brought it up. Klaus had called a meeting. This was it. He was finally going to tell everyone he'd accepted HGM's offer. If all went well, we'd have the funding for the rest of the project by the end of the month, and within six months we'd have our modifications to the immune system ready.

Half an hour later, I was seated with the directors of Geneus. I was surprised to see that Jan wasn't there but realized this acceptance of defeat was probably going to be difficult for Klaus, and he no doubt want to keep it in-house.

Klaus stood up before us, his barrel chest strong in his tailored gray suit.

"Thank you for coming in," he said. "Today we have some very important news for you. It's something which is going to affect the entire future of our company and that many of you may not be very happy about. I myself am not so sure it's the right decision but I seem to be left with little choice. If any of you decide that this company is no longer the place you want to work once the decision has been finalized I will completely understand."

Why would anyone want to leave? The terms that HGM had proposed were beneficial to everyone.

"Before I say any more, though, I'd like you to hear from Anthony. He has been the one instrumental in securing this deal."

Anthony? What the hell did he have to do with this? I saw the smug look on Anthony's face and suddenly my pulse quickened.

"Thank you, everybody." Anthony stood up and looked around the room before going on. "As you all know, Geneus has had financial problems for quite some time now. Up until a few weeks ago we only had one option – and that was to allow HGM Industries to take over the company. Although this would have helped the current project and those involved in it, it was not going to be the best course of action for Klaus, who was going to lose his place as majority shareholder. I myself have been working hard to secure other lines of funding and just recently have managed to gain a meeting with the Defense Department who have come to see the great possibilities that our technology could provide—"

"Hold on a minute," I interrupted, but Anthony put his hand up to silence me.

"Questions afterwards, please, Michael," Klaus said.

"As you know," Anthony continued, "Australia is in an incredibly vulnerable position at the moment, with a possible civil war on our hands, and Indonesia, who desperately needs land and resources, very close to our doorstep. The Defense Department believes that biological warfare could be a real possibility if a new world war were to start, and that we are better off preparing for that likelihood rather than relying on old conventions that outlaw it. The world is changing and if a war takes place it's going to change beyond all recognition. Anyway, the long and the short of it is that the Defense Department has asked us for a meeting. Klaus and I will be going to see them on Thursday. Michael will also be coming, if he agrees."

I sat there in silence. I could not believe what I had just heard. Was Klaus really so desperate that he was considering this? Everything I thought I had achieved over the last few months had just collapsed from under me.

"Are you really in agreement with this?" I said to Klaus.

"What option do I have, Michael?" He held his hands out.

"We had an option."

"To lose my company? That's not an option. The Defense Department will provide us funding for our research rather than requiring a share of the company."

"I haven't worked on this project for years just so we can use it to kill people. And you know as well as I do that once we start working for the government they'll put a stranglehold on this company so tight you might as well not own any of it."

"We're not going to kill people, Michael, we're going to save them," Anthony said. "If the Indonesians decide to use bio-weapons on us how many of us do you think are going to die? Do you think they're really going to care if they wipe out half our population?"

I shook my head and took deep breaths.

"I think it's a very reasonable idea," Zhao said. "The Defense Department has the largest budget of any governmental department. Working with them will provide almost unlimited funding to our projects. Many great technologies have developed from military experiments. It's a win-win situation for everybody."

"What is it exactly they want us to work on?" Masanori said.

I had hoped that Masanori at least would back me up in this, but maybe he didn't really care.

"Well, we're not quite sure," Anthony said. "I suppose we'll find out at the meeting."

Speculation swirled around the room as to what they would want us to work on and how our technology would be deployed.

"Are they interested in our cooperation research?" I said. "Surely that would be beneficial to the military."

"I did mention it to General Savage, my contact there, but he didn't seem to pay it much thought," Anthony said. "It's the somatic modification of the immune system that they're really interested in."

"How much funding will we get?" John said.

"Hopefully, whatever we need," Anthony said, clasping his hands together.

I had to do a mental and emotional about-face as quickly as possible and start showing as much enthusiasm for this project as everybody else seemed to be. Masanori knew as much about our processes as I did and I was certain that Klaus would put him in charge of our department and get rid of me in a heartbeat if it came to it. Klaus and I had a good relationship, but business was business. With a Defense Department contract in his hands, his company would be safe and well-funded, for a little while at least. Not only that, but he was patriotic enough to believe that working for the military was the right thing to do.

All I knew was — as soon as we started working for the military we were never, ever going to come up with a cure for HIV-4. There was a vaccine available for it now. Why would they bother?

That night, I went home to Annie. I didn't want to tell her until the decision was final, but I knew that the deal was as good as done. Our technology would help the military in so many ways, especially if bio-warfare was a risk.

Annie was cooking dinner, drinking white wine and listening to classical music when I arrived. She was smiling when I came in, but as soon as she saw my face she put her glass down and switched off the music.

"Are you okay?"

"Not really." I went over to her and hugged her as hard as I could.

"What's wrong?" She stroked my hair.

"It's all over."

"What's all over?"

"They've gone to the military. Klaus has sold out to the fucking military. We're going to be working for them from now on."

"What do you mean? I thought it was a done deal with HGM Industries?"

"They've been working away on this behind my back. Anthony somehow got a meeting with the Defense Department, and I've got to go up there later this week."

I was shaking with anger and Annie led me over to the sofa.

"Sit down. It's alright. It's going to be alright. Something else will come up. You can take your research somewhere else."

"I'm going to have to. We are so close. I can't believe it. After everything we've done, to come this far and have it all go to shit."

"You'll find a way. Something will work out. And if not, sometimes we have to accept things as they are."

"Not this, though."

"Even this."

I stood up and took the bottle of wine from the bench and finished it off.

"There you go. See? All better," Annie said.

"It's not all better at all."

We ate dinner and discussed possibilities. We could try to convince Gendigm to invest without requiring a controlling share, or we could steal all the research and start working for Gendigm in a secret lab somewhere, coming up with our own version of the process that wouldn't conflict with Geneus's. Maybe we could even get Geneus to sell their data to Gendigm, seeing as they probably wouldn't have a use for a lot of it now. We drank three bottles of wine and our plans became more and more hair-brained, leading right up to me being a double agent for the Indonesians in return for the money to go on with our immune system research.

I went to sleep early but woke up at 4am in a whirl of anxious thought that I wasn't able to control. Annie was still asleep, so I crept out of bed and went down the corridor into my office. I hardly needed an office these days, as everything I needed was on my com, but I still had a bookshelf in there with some old books on it and my favorite leather armchair which Annie wanted me to get rid of.

I had been so stunned the day before that I hadn't let Gendigm know what was happening, so I sent a message to Bruno. Then, with nothing else to do, I started playing an old video game that I used to play back in university. It was a jet fighter simulation, where you had to shoot as many of the enemy planes as you could before they shot you. It was absorbing and for a while it helped me take my mind off things.

Then my com beeped and I logged out of the game and checked my messages. Bruno had sent me a reply. There was nothing that Gendigm could do for the moment, but he told me that having access to military facilities and equipment might not be the worst thing in the world. There might still be hope yet, he said, which I didn't really believe but found comforting nonetheless.

CHAPTER TWELVE

THAT THURSDAY, I boarded the company jet with Klaus and Anthony. Trying to appear enthusiastic about this project was even harder than trying to remain positive with Annie about her chances of survival. The only good thing I could see coming out of this was that we would finally have the technology to bring about the somatic modifications that we'd been trying to achieve – although I knew the purposes this would be put to were totally the opposite of what I wanted.

I wondered if the military was going to perform a background check on all of us and potentially turn up evidence of Annie's disease. One of the things that had attracted us to Dr Baxter in the first place was his insistence on doing everything manually, so unless they'd had me physically tracked, they probably wouldn't find anything.

The plane took off and Anthony and Klaus chatted excitedly about the possibilities of working for the military. I stared out the window at the large curve that marked the edge of the de-reg zone. On the regulated side, things were green and ordered. Then came a jumbled mess of gray and brown shanty towns. Beyond that, it was mostly desert.

An hour later, we arrived at a military airport about a hundred kilometers west of Canberra. We were met by two young bureaucrats in suits and transported to the huge, gray, flying fortress of a military helicopter. We followed our guides up a short ramp into the back, and the door lifted up and closed behind us. There was a bench along each wall, made for ten men each. We strapped ourselves in and in less than a minute we were being hauled skyward again.

The trip took longer than I expected and by the time we landed I had absolutely no idea where we were. When we stepped out, all I could see was a clearing in a pine plantation just large enough for the heli-pad. The straight rows of nearly identical trees seemed to go on forever, and the scent of pine needles hit me.

Four officers were waiting for us in full uniform. A bulky, blue-suited man of about sixty, blonde hair and blue eyes, came towards us and greeted us.

"I'm General Savage," he shouted to us over the whir of the winding down blades. "Pleased to meet you."

We introduced ourselves and General Savage led us towards a concrete shelter on the side of the clearing. The uniformed officers fell into line behind us. We climbed aboard a lift and slid deep into the belly of the earth.

Doors opened onto a wide reception area where two young women were working. A glass wall separated us from an open plan office with dozens of busy workstations.

"Just this way," General Savage said.

We followed him through a side door, past a security

checkpoint where we were scanned, and along a glass corridor into a meeting room. Here, our entourage waited outside.

A table for eight sat in the middle of the room and we all took seats. Opaque windows filtered soft light, no doubt artificial yet producing the effect of sunlight.

"Coffee, tea?" Savage said. "We're just waiting for the Prime Minister, and a couple of my colleagues."

"The Prime Minister is coming?" Klaus said, obviously impressed.

"Yes. She wanted to weigh in on this. This is an incredibly important step for us, as I'm sure you'll understand. Bio-warfare goes against all the conventions of war established in the last hundred years. Any thought of even preparing for it must be taken very seriously."

"Of course," Klaus said.

A few minutes later, a face I'd seen hundreds of times on the net but never in reality came into the room, surrounded by three other aging military officers similar in appearance to General Savage. Introductions were made and we all sat around the table.

Susan Green, prime minister of the regulated zone of Australia, was nearly sixty and looked it. Most older women these days opted for stem-cell skin reconstruction, but Susan probably thought her lined face leant her an air of authority. She scanned us all with quick, intelligent eyes and said, "Thank you for coming,"

"It's our pleasure," Klaus said.

"We're here today to talk about your research into the genetic modification of the immune system," Susan said. "I'm led to believe that you have come up with a way not only to improve the immune system of the new-born but of those already born. Somatic modification, is that right?"

Klaus and Anthony looked at me.

"That's right, Mrs. Green," I said.

"Please, call me Susan," she said.

"Thanks. We still haven't fully completed our research but we do believe we have developed a technique which, combined with the right gene insertion technology, will be viable." I explained how our current modifications had proven to make monkeys far more resistant to disease and how all we needed was to improve the mechanism to accurately perform those modifications.

"It does sound extremely promising," Susan said.

"What is it you would like to use the technology for?" I asked.

The four military officers looked at me as if I were being impertinent.

"I think that's a matter of national security," General Savage said.

"It's okay, George," Susan said. "They're going to need to know anyway." She turned back to me. "It's come to the attention of our intelligence agents that the Indonesians have developed a similar technology to the one you're working on. It's our belief that they are going to release a virus that will quickly decimate groups of people — whole platoons for example — yet which their own soldiers will be immune to."

The threat of bio-weapons had been looming for years, but, as with nuclear attacks, they hadn't happened: presumably due to the fear of worldwide contagion affecting even the users of such weapons. If the

123

Indonesians were working on immune system modifications like ours, though, that might no longer be an issue for them.

"Well, do you think it's possible?" Savage said. "Could you modify the immune system to counteract such an attack?"

"Without knowing what the disease is, it will be hard to say," I said.

The military officers and the Prime Minister all looked at one another. "Well, we do have some initial samples that our intelligence agents were able to recover," Susan said.

Klaus, Anthony and I all looked at one another. For the first time in months I felt solidarity with Anthony. This was something that could potentially affect our entire country. A country which, despite the massive changes it had been through in the last ten years, I still loved.

Then I wondered how true this was. How had they gotten samples of this virus? Maybe this was a virus they themselves were working on and now wanted to protect our own soldiers against.

My mind swirled with possibilities.

"Let's go down to the labs," Savage said.

Two floors down from the offices were five floors of laboratories. On the first of these we were introduced to Dr Kate Darlinghurst, head scientist on the project. Kate was a tall, shapely woman in her early forties, with thick, brown hair that was clipped at the sides but fell almost halfway down her back. Her nose was straight, her chin firm, and her eyes deep with intelligence.

"It's a pleasure to meet you, Michael." She shook my hand much more warmly than those of Anthony or Klaus.

She even seemed to be more impressed by my presence than by that of the Prime Minister, and we rapidly fell into conversation together. Apparently she had been following the articles I had written for various genetics journals with interest, including the most recent one on the link between bonobo immune system genes and their social behavior.

General Savage led us along the corridor, and we went into another meeting room and sat down.

"What we're dealing with is a modified strain of the Ebola virus," Kate said. "It's airborne, has an incubation period of less than twenty-four hours, and a ninety-five percent mortality rate."

My whole body cramped up on me. I had read about the possibility of Ebola becoming airborne, but doubted anyone would ever risk it. A virus like that would wipe out most of the world's population in a matter of weeks.

"If you'll just switch your public overlays on, I'll show you some footage," Kate said.

With a subvocal command I switched to my public overlay and a grainy video of four people in a glass room appeared appeared before my eyes. I darkened the background.

"This video footage was captured at the same time we managed to get hold of a sample of the virus. Here we have four subjects, who all appear to be in perfect physical condition. In just a moment we're about to see another subject introduced into the room, one who has been infected with what we've decided to call Rebola."

A door opened at the back of the glass room and another person, a small, emaciated man, was brought in by two people in haz-mat suits. They kept him there for a short while and then led him out again.

"Within less than five minutes of sharing a confined space with an infected individual all other individuals will be infected," Kate said.

I jolted backwards in an instinctual reaction of fear, even though what I was seeing was only a video.

"This is a day later," Kate continued.

The video timestamp changed and we saw the same group of people experiencing extreme respiratory distress and hemorrhaging from their mouths and noses.

I imagined the horror of dying like that. I was almost thankful that Annie had HIV-4, which was benign compared to this. At least it had given her time.

"And someone came up with this?" I said.

"Sick fucks, aren't they?" General Savage swore, then turned to Kate and the Prime Minister. "My apologies."

"No apology needed, General," the Prime Minister said. "Well, what do you think, Michael? Do you think your modified immune system would be able to handle this?"

"It all depends on the mechanism." I turned to Kate. "What kind of antigens does it produce? How does it escape the antibodies at the moment."

"Similar to the Ebola virus — it's the speed at which it works. But there are also a few notable differences," Kate said, and ran me through a fairly lengthy explanation.

When she'd finished I turned to the Prime Minister. "In answer to your question, Susan, we're really not going to know until we try. And we can't try until we've developed a reliable method of somatically modifying the immune system."

"Okay, let's get to work then."

After a tour of the labs we went back to the meeting room above, and two men in suits came in. Klaus and Anthony started some preliminary negotiations.

"Are we going to be able to continue working from our current labs?" I asked. "I doubt anybody will be that happy about moving out here to the middle of nowhere."

"You'd be surprised how comfortable our facilities here are," General Savage replied. "I don't know, Bill, what do you think?" He turned to one of the men in suits.

"It seems some of the initial work could be performed in the current Geneus facilities; the work involving bringing the modifications to fruition. Once that's been done, the actual viral testing itself will have to be done here on-site. Of course, security in your lab is going to need to be completely overhauled. No doubt you have reasonable security already, but this is the military, gentlemen."

"Of course," Klaus agreed. "Whatever's necessary."

CHAPTER THIRTEEN

THAT NIGHT, I returned home to Annie.

"How'd it go?" she said.

I shook my head and told her about the virus I'd witnessed, and how the military claimed the Indonesians were planning on using it.

"Do you think it's true?" Annie said.

"I have no idea. If governments are going to resort to bio-warfare then that's the end of all of us. Even if we come up with a somatic modification for this virus there are always going to be more."

"At least the rest of the eco-system might have a chance to recover." Annie smiled cynically and took hold of my hand.

"You're right. It might not be the worst thing in the world."

"Maybe we should just go away."

We'd talked about this possibility before. I'd done some research over the past few months and it seemed there were a number of companies who specialized in anonymous transfers to completely self-sufficient floating sovereignties like the cruise ship we'd just spent some time on. For the right price, you could disappear forever.

I tried to imagine the type of people you'd meet in a place like that: a combination of CEOs and entrepreneurs fleeing taxation and criminals fleeing the authorities. What would it be like to drink vodka with some tattooed Russian mafioso for the rest of my life? Probably alright, if the facilities were anything like the ones on that cruise ship. And with Annie by my side, at least for a few more years, it might not be the worst way to end things.

"If we go away then there's no chance we'll ever find a cure for your disease," I said.

"I don't know if you're going to find one now, anyway. At least we'd get to spend some time together. If you take this contract I'm never going to see you."

She was right. The contract would require me to spend months if not years at the military lab.

"Come with me," I said.

"What about my work here?"

"You could give up your work. You should be taking it easy anyway."

"I don't want to give up my work. If I'm going to stay here, and I'm going to die, I want to make sure my life means something to someone other than myself."

"Maybe I could find some work for you with the military."

"Maybe," she said, but I could see she didn't want to. And to be honest, even if she was there, I'd still hardly see her. This project was going to require the undivided attention of all my waking hours.

"Let's think about it, then. We've still got time."

The next day, Annie came home from her clinic very distressed.

"What's wrong?" I said.

"Sam's sick. Rabies. And we don't have any vaccines. I don't know what to do. Although it's probably too late to do anything now anyway."

Sam was the son of a man called William, who had once lived in the de-reg zone and saved Annie's life, but lost his own in doing so. Annie had been leaving the clinic just behind William, who was there with his elderly mother. A car had pulled up out the front and two men with machine guns had gotten out. There was another man, ahead of Annie, who had just been sewn up for gunshot wounds, and the men in the car had obviously wanted to finish him off. William had turned around and pushed both his mother and Annie back inside the clinic. Four machine gun pellets had caught him in the back, though, and he'd died within minutes.

"I can synthesize the antibodies in the lab if you like, and see if we can help him," I said.

"Anything," Annie said. "I owe my life to these people."

At William's funeral we'd met Gilda, his widow, and had been supporting her and Sam financially ever since, but I knew Annie still felt a great debt to them.

The next day, I explained the situation to Klaus and asked him if I could use the labs. Klaus was so happy about the military contract that he said yes right away.

That evening, Annie and I sat side by side in our car as it transported us to the de-reg zone.

I had only been to the clinic there once before and had forgotten how depressing it was. There was almost no money for a clinic like this except for occasional donations from aid organizations, and when we arrived the small, crowded waiting room was full of patients who really should have been in a proper hospital.

The boy, Sam, was led into Annie's tiny consultation room by his mother, Gilda, who looked desperate. She helped him up onto the bed, and Annie explained to her what we were going to do.

"What will happen if it doesn't work?" Gilda begged. "Will he die?"

"Yes, he probably will," Annie said.

Gilda put her hands up to her mouth. "What are the chances of it working?"

"We really don't know. It's been a while since he was bitten. Maybe if we'd gotten to him earlier, but now it's hard to tell."

"It's the best chance he's got, though, isn't it?"

"Yes, it is."

"Okay then, please, go ahead." Gilda put her hands together and closed her eyes, and I could hear her praying.

That's not going to save him, I wanted to tell her, but I realized the person being saved by her prayer was not her son but herself: giving her the strength and courage to continue.

Annie quickly injected Sam with the antibodies. He needed to be kept in a bed and monitored, but there were no such facilities at the clinic.

131

"What if we stay with him?" I whispered to Annie as Gilda continued to pray. "We could go to their house and do what we can for him there."

It was almost impossible for non-reg citizens, as they were known, to get inside the regulated zone, but there was nothing stopping us from staying outside.

Annie looked at me and took my hand. "Are you sure?"

"Yes."

"Don't get too close," she warned. "It's a lot worse out there than you can imagine."

We sent Gilda home and told her that we would come and visit her that night.

"It'll be dangerous. I'll have to get permission," Gilda told us.

"Okay," Annie replied. "Call me here at the clinic."

Gilda hugged us both and then, despite her small size, picked her son up and carried him out the door.

That evening, we drove slowly through a street dotted with potholes. On either side of the road concrete shacks had been built between shipping containers and tin tents.

"What do people here eat?" I asked.

"Chickens and eggs, mainly," Annie said. We had passed more than one free-roaming hen on the way in, although I presumed most people had theirs well-protected. "Micronutrient and vitamin supplements sometimes, when aid organizations hand them out. And any animals they can get their hands on, which are usually dogs and rats, I think."

"Let's not stay for dinner, then."

Annie turned to me and smiled.

Our car passed a feral looking gang of teenagers, all with torn clothes and matted hair. They looked in at us like we were aliens, and I imagined they didn't see too many "normal" people out here any more. Some of the younger children probably wouldn't even remember what the world used to be like.

A kind of local law and order had been established in these shanty towns, and locals tended to look out for one another. They were mainly run by local cartels, though, and before we'd come in here calls had been made by Gilda to the leaders of her local "council" to get permission. Most of the cartels liked what the clinic was doing, as Annie and her team had sewn them up on enough occasions, so we had been allowed to pass.

Eventually our vehicle pulled up outside a shipping container, and Annie told me this was it. We went inside and found Gilda stroking Sam's head as he lay in the corner on a mattress. The stench inside was awful — of unwashed bodies — but I soon got used to it. Gilda's mother was out the back, which we got to via a hole covered with a blanket. She was stirring some stew over a forty gallon drum. I wondered how they got enough fuel for cooking. A couple of the neighbors were sitting around on the wreckage of old camping chairs and upturned tires, waiting for the meal. If they all cooked together, it was presumably easier.

I needed to use the toilet and wished I'd gone before we left the clinic. Gilda told me where it was and sent one of the neighbor's boys to accompany me.

"Jut down 'ere," he said, speaking with a twang so strong that I had trouble understanding him.

He led me to a series of small sheds that had large

plastic wheely bins underneath them to collect the waste. I was surprised to find it so well organized. Although it stunk, at least it was hygienic.

After I'd finished I asked the boy where the contents of the bins went when they were full.

"Down the creek," he told me, pointing.

Back at the house, Annie was checking Sam's temperature. It seemed to have gone down, and she patted his head with a clean cloth she'd brought that she was dipping in a bucket of water.

"How is he?" I asked.

"He seems okay so far."

That night, someone produced a guitar and someone else a bottle of home-brewed spirits and they all sung songs around the fire. I leant back in my dilapidated camp chair and stared up at the stars, brighter than they ever were in the city. Despite their poverty, there seemed to be a bond between these people that I rarely experienced in the regulated zone.

When we went to sleep in our car, after checking one last time on Sam and receiving hugs from both Gilda and her mother and pats on the back from some of the other neighbors, I felt a deep solace.

The next morning, we took Sam in to the clinic and ran his blood tests. His viral load had dropped. Gilda was overjoyed despite Annie's warnings that it was still too early to predict the outcome.

That night, we drove home exhausted.

"I guess we probably shouldn't run away, should we?" Annie said to me as we neared our house, reaching across and taking my hand.

I turned to look at her silhouette in the dark car, lit up by street lights. Her eyes and skin glistened.

"No. Probably not," I said.

CHAPTER FOURTEEN

THREE MONTHS LATER, Masanori, Justin, Yolanda, Richard, and a number of other members of our team and I were all transported to the military base. Annie had decided to stay home and continue her work at the clinic, but I hoped she would follow me soon.

The afternoon we arrived, Kate and her assistant, Silvia, took us all on another tour of their laboratories. There were five floors altogether, over two-thousand square meters in total, filled with every piece of equipment available and the staff to operate it.

"And in here is where we will be conducting the research using the new equipment." Kate opened the door to a large section of the lab. Over the last three months they'd built a machine, based mostly on our plans, that created viruses capable of inserting genes precisely at any given location.

"Would you like me to show them the software?" said Shung, one of the technicians: a short, cute Asian woman with a fringe that kept falling in her eyes that she kept brushing away again.

Justin, who was standing next to me, pushed to the front. He was eager to see his creation made reality. He still believed that, as soon as we had done what the military wanted us to do, we were going to be able to use the technology to apply to our immune system modifications. I still hadn't had the courage to tell him that probably wasn't going to happen. The military had insisted our process was not to be used in any other application. Klaus had told me to keep the information to myself, but I felt Justin deserved a warning. I just hadn't found a way to tell him yet.

"Sure," Kate said. "Just a brief demonstration."

Shung activated a screen on our public overlays. With a few movements of her hands in the air she brought up a sequence of nucleotides. "This sequence comes from chromosome twelve. Av457 to be precise, responsible for hair color. Now, if we open up this folder over here, we can see that we have the strings for any hair color we choose." She brought up an array of 3D heads with different colored hair. "All we have to do is select the string we want replaced, like so, delete it, which will be done using restriction sites coded into the bio-vectors, select the exact insertion points, like this, and then drag and drop the new string into place." She dragged one of the files across and dropped it onto the double-helix icon, which incorporated the change. "And on voice command, the robotics make what you've just designed."

"Tell me about the workflow," Justin said.

"Very efficient. You can save this operation and then move straight on to the next task. You can switch between genes, between chromosomes, all very easily."

Justin asked her a few more questions and by the way she kept flicking at her hair even when it wasn't in front of her eyes, I wondered if we might have a laboratory romance on our hands.

We spent the next few weeks analyzing the Rebola virus. Kate and her team had already sequenced the genome and worked out its infection and replication strategies. I checked through every inch of its genetic code to find some trace of its engineer. Like computer programmers, genetic engineers often left signatures of code which marked a design as their own, or left commented sections to serve as place-markers for themselves or future engineers. Many had specific ways of ordering things, and I had seen enough code in my life that I could often recognize which university an engineer came from if not the specific engineer themselves. This one was completely clean, though. Which was no surprise. The engineer, or engineers, had obviously gone to a lot of trouble to keep it that way.

Kate and I became friends, but for some reason I didn't completely trust her. It might have been because I didn't trust anybody working for the military. The military had an agenda that went far beyond keeping the everyday citizens safe. It was controlled by corporate interests, and whether or not the people working inside believed the bullshit or not didn't make them any less guilty.

A group of us sat down together for dinner one night and Justin, who was sitting next to me, started telling me excitedly about how cool the new software was; a machine he'd affectionately named HAL.

"I can take out a single gene at a thousand paces." He laughed, mimicking shooting with a sniper rifle.

"He's very good," Shung said, who was sitting next to him. "I've never seen someone work so quickly."

"He's one of our best," I said.

"Almost as good as I am." Shung pouted at Justin, and they went into a little giggle of cutesie-talk.

Once they'd finished, Justin turned back to me. "So, when do you think we're going to be able to start applying it to our immune system mods? So far all we've been doing is focusing on this one virus."

"I'm really not sure," I said.

After dinner, I asked him to meet me in the garden foyer of the accommodation wing.

"What's up?" He came over to me later that night. His hair was scruffy, and I wondered if he'd been playing around with Shung. At least it might help him to take the news a little more lightly.

"Sit down," I said.

He sat down, looking at me. His gaunt face and large, watery eyes twisted. I looked around to make sure nobody else was listening. There was a cleaner over by a small fountain, but apart from her the place was empty.

"I'm afraid Geneus is not going to let us go on with our somatic immune system trials."

"W-what? Isn't that what HAL is for?" When Justin got nervous he stuttered.

"No. The military is insisting that we concentrate on producing a resistance to Rebola."

"But that's crazy. All we have to do is p-program HAL to make the modifications we've already come up with. It's a-all ready to go. A final macaque trial and we could start on the human trials."

I shook my head. "They say they don't have the resources and that's not what they're interested in."

"But, what about Penny?" Penny was Justin's sister.

"I know. I understand." I clasped my hand around his arm and held him firmly. "I know exactly how you feel."

"How long have you known this for?" He stared at me, pulling away.

"Just a few weeks. Since just before we left. Klaus told me not to tell anyone."

"But you know how much this means to me?" Justin put his hands on either side of the chair as if he were about to stand up and walk away.

"Which is why I'm telling you now."

"You should have told me then." He slumped down and put his face in his hands. I wondered if he was going to cry. He'd been so happy these last few weeks, despite the pending threat of a virus that could potentially wipe the human population out within days.

"There's something else I need to tell you," I said.

"What's that?" He said without looking up at me.

I stared around the large atrium-like room, a soft glow coming from the opaque white roof. Climbers and ferns grew down here even better than they did in a rainforest. The air was slightly humid and had a damp, musty tinge to it. "My wife has HIV-4, too."

"Annie?" He raised his head.

"Yes. She's had it for years. Apart from our families and some close friends, you're the only one who knows."

He started shaking, moving his head from side to side

as if he didn't know what to do any more. "Is that why you've been working on this project all along?"

"It's part of it. Not the only reason."

"I'm sorry." Tears welled up in his eyes which he didn't wipe away.

We both sat there for a few minutes, lost in our own private thoughts.

"What can we do?" Justin broke the silence.

"I don't know. I had thought of going ahead with the trials anyway, but everything is so regulated here, I don't know if we'd get away with it."

"Shung keeps an eye on that machine like a hawk. The logs are checked constantly and not just by her."

"I don't know, then. The other thing I'm worried about is exactly what they've got us working on."

"You mean apart from Rebola?"

"Yes. Don't you think it's strange, working on just one virus."

"What do you mean?" He finally wiped away his tears and stared at me out of red eyes.

"I don't know. Maybe they're going to come up with a virus of their own."

"Bio-warfare is completely against the Geneva convention."

"Do you really think they still care about that? The whole world is going to hell, Justin."

Justin put his face in his hands again and more than thinking about the world going to hell or the evils of bio-warfare I could tell he was thinking about his sister.

"She'll be okay," I said gently, putting a hand on his shoulder.

"Do you really think so?" He shook his head and looked up at me.

"Yes. She will be. We're going to find a solution to this."

I went back to my room feeling a huge sadness but also relief. I had wanted to tell Justin about Annie's illness for so long, and finally coming clean with him and having him not hate me was as much as I could ask for.

I lay down on my bed and called Annie. She answered and her image appeared in front of me on my visual overlay; she was in her office working.

"I finally told Justin," I told her.

"Was he upset?"

"Of course. I told him about you as well."

"Did that make him feel better?"

"It seemed to. It made me feel better. At least I've got someone on my side now. And hiding it from him was awful."

"Do you think he'll be able to find a way to help you?"

"If anyone can it's him."

"You two designed that thing — surely you can find a way to use it without anyone finding out."

"Even if we could, the modifications we came up with were never tested on humans."

"If someone's about to die, what does it matter?"

"Yes, you're right."

"So, test it on me."

"Or on someone else who's going to die sooner." Annie still had at least two years left and I didn't want to risk her health any more than necessary.

"If you build in a chemical safety trigger to shut the

modifications off, it won't matter."

"Provided we get to it in time. And the shock isn't too much for your system."

"I'm going to die anyway. We might as well try."

I stared up at the white plaster ceiling, and was suddenly uncomfortably aware of the half a kilometer of rock and soil that was above me. I imagined it collapsing in on me, crushing me. I wanted to get out of there, get up to the surface. I took deep breaths.

"I'll talk to Justin," I said. "There is a training mode built in to the system — if we can somehow bypass the GUI and code the changes in directly via the command line then nobody need find out about it. We didn't write the software, though, so I'm not sure how easy that's going to be. Justin might be able to find a way."

The next night, I waited for Justin in the same place we'd met the night before — the garden. Out of all the rooms in the underground complex this place made me feel the most relaxed. Just the presence of plants, the thriving greenery, the warm but soft light, made my mind stop its mad rush for a second and contemplate my surroundings. Behind me grew tall strands of bamboo, and I admired their smooth slender trunks. In front of me were camelias, in full, blood-red bloom.

Justin and I used to play chess together, and while I waited I called up a chess app on my com.

"Black or white?" I said to Justin when he arrived, sending him a link to the game.

"White."

The board spun around slowly in front of me, at thirty

percent opacity so I could still see Justin behind it. I shrunk it a little and moved it down. "Your turn then."

He moved his pawn and I moved mine.

"What is it you wanted to tell me?" he said.

"I think I might have thought of a way to program some bio-vectors without getting caught."

"How?"

"Well, you know how the machine has a training mode for students?"

"Yes."

"The module was built with an instant delete function, as soon as you log out. The code for vector design is unencrypted. If you could find a way to hack in and do the coding by hand, bypassing the GUI, nobody would ever find out about it. Do you think you can do that?"

He looked up at me with a large, cheeky smile on his face and I imagined him as a fifteen year old boy hacking into corporate servers just to mess with them. "I can try. Aren't there limitations on the training mode, though?"

"Yes. There are. There's usually a limit to the amount of instructions that can be programmed into the vectors, but not if we're doing it by hand."

"I'll look into it," he promised. "But how are we going to test them once we've created them?"

"Annie said she'd do it," I said and took my next turn.

CHAPTER FIFTEEN

OVER THE NEXT few months, we worked hard at adapting our immune system modifications to interrupt the effects of Rebola, and finally we came up with what all our testing promised to be a solution.

Up until now we'd been using SCID-hu mice: mice whose entire immune systems had been deleted and replaced with human tissue from aborted fetuses. Their immune responses were as close to human as we could get. By somatically modifying them, we'd given them an immune system that was capable of recognizing and eradicating the Rebola virus within hours, before any serious damage was done.

To prevent any complications when we started applying the modifications to humans, we coded in a chemical failsafe inducer which would reverse the changes to any modified cells if necessary.

Even still, the night before we were supposed to test our first group of human subjects, I felt worried. Kate had assured me there was no way we would actually have to infect the subjects with the Rebola virus itself, but this was the first time in history that such a large-scale modification to the human genome had been attempted.

Memories of everything I'd ever read about the Nazis' Action T4 and their eugenics programs came back to me, and I wondered if I wasn't somehow caught up in something similar. I had wanted to use my knowledge and skills to help people, to improve the human race — how had I ended up working for the military?

On a number of occasions I'd wanted to leave but had decided that staying was probably the best thing I could do. If Rebola really was going to be unleashed against our citizens then I needed to help. Without protection, we'd be wiped out faster than our aboriginal population had been by smallpox. And in case the military was lying, and they were creating this modification for their own purposes, then being on the inside would be better than being a lonely voice of opposition on the outside.

The morning of the first tests I woke up at 5am, sweating. I wondered if I'd contracted a virus, but the labs and staff were so ruthlessly clean it was unlikely.

I went down to the lab at seven. Kate and Masanori were already there, along with a number of younger members of the team, and soon after, Justin, Yolanda and Richard all arrived.

"Does anyone know yet who we are going to be working with?" Yolanda asked.

"No idea." Kate shook her head in a way that made me think she didn't really care.

"I just hope there are no adverse effects," Justin said.

"And that if there are then our failsafe inducer works fast enough to stop them."

At 9am, Savage came into the lab and told us we were going to be working with maximum security prisoners who had been convicted of terrorism. Half an hour later, the first of these was led into a small consulting room just off the laboratory by two soldiers. His skin was pale but his eyes and hair were dark, just like mine, and I immediately recognized him as having middle-eastern origins.

The man looked at me, fixating on my eyes for a moment, no doubt recognizing in me a blood relation. His gaze was intense, but I realized it was more pleading than threatening. I couldn't hold his stare and turned away to the bench where the syringes containing the bio-vectors were lined up. Not too soon, I hoped. I didn't want to frighten him in a way that I knew would make him crazy. I'd seen it in the chimps before — screaming and struggling, needing to be held down and sedated. It made everyone's lives worse, including their own.

"What are you going to do to me?" the man asked in an English so thick I could only just understand.

"It's a trial, a medical trial," Savage said slowly to the man. "Nothing to worry about."

The man was lowered down into the chair in the middle of the room, six of us surrounding him. He said something in Arabic that I caught only a snippet of: a prayer. Kate came over to the bench, took the first syringe, then pulled the man's shirt sleeves up and quickly injected him with the viral vector that would hopefully modify his immune system enough to make him resistant to Rebola.

"There you go, all done." Kate smiled and patted him

147

on the back.

The man was helped up from the chair and glanced one last time in my direction before he was taken from the room.

Another ten prisoners were brought in, and we repeated the process with all of them.

It would be two weeks before we could see the full effects of our modifications, and during that time we kept a careful watch on our test subjects, taking blood samples and testing them for genomic DNA modifications and hematopoietic stem cell potential.

We had to spend a bit of time with the men, and I got to know them individually. Ghanim was the man we'd injected first, the arab who had looked at me strangely, and once, when we were alone together, I asked him about his life.

He was a soldier in the army, he told me, and he had volunteered for the duty of self-sacrifice. He had come to Australia to take part in an attack on Sydney, a series of suicide bombs that would have taken out Government house.

"What are they doing to me?" he asked, hoarsely, as if he didn't really want to know the answer.

I shook my head. "It's a trial. On your immune system."

"Will it make me sick?"

"No. Hopefully it will make you stronger. Do you have family?"

"Yes."

"What is your family name?"

"Al-Saadi. And yours? Are you Arab?"

"My father was. Khan is my name. Where are you from?"

"Iraq. A town called Karam Kadal. Very small." He smiled, obviously remembering his home town.

"Wife? Children?"

He shook his head. "Just two brothers. My parents died. I have to look after them."

I wanted to reach out and touch him, put a hand on his shoulder and give him a display of human affection, but I couldn't bring myself to.

"As-salam alaykum," I said to him as I left, the only Arabic I could remember, which meant something along the lines of: "peace be upon you."

By the third week, we started to notice some fairly significant changes in the hematopoietic stem cells being produced in the bone marrow of our test subjects. At around the same time, a couple of them got sick with something similar to an auto-immune disease. We immediately activated the failsafe inducer, and within twelve hours the negative effects had abated.

That night, I went to Justin's room after receiving a message from him. I sat down in the armchair while he sat on the edge of the bed.

"I've found a way to hack into HAL," he said.

"So can we make the modifications?"

"Yes. But I think we should test it first. You saw what happened to those men this week." He was referring to the auto-immune reaction our prisoners had had.

"We're so much further along with this, though. We've

been working on it for years."

"Not on humans, we haven't."

"How long has Penny got?"

"Probably a month or two, at the most."

"Then we have to try it. We can use the same chemical trigger we've just used to switch it off in case it doesn't work."

"How do we get it out of here?"

"I've got a break coming up in a fortnight. I'll take it out then. We can mix the powdered form of the virus with some self-sealing polymers they've got over in lab five. I saw Yolanda using them the other day."

Just before my trip back home, I got a message from Justin.

"All ready?" I said as I entered his room.

"Yes, all here." He held up a pill-sized bubble — the virus in its protective coating. If we'd had the right equipment we could have created a pill whose coating would dissolve upon contact with stomach acid, releasing the bio-vector, but as it was I would have to dissolve and inject Annie with it.

"Are you sure about this?" Justin said.

"Not really. Are you?"

"Not really."

"I won't blame you if it doesn't work, and I don't want you to blame yourself, either."

"I won't be able to help it. Of course I'll feel responsible."

"It's the only way and you know it. Think about not only Annie and Penny but all the other people out there living with this disease as well."

I wasn't any more confident about this than Justin was, but I was his boss and I had to keep up a show of strength for him. Penny was much closer to the end than Annie was.

Chapter Sixteen

I ARRIVED BACK in Melbourne at 9:15am on a Thursday morning. It was August, but it was already hot. I walked out of the terminal after collecting my bags and the sun bore into my skin. A car was waiting for me. Despite the heat, all I could think about was how much I wanted to see Annie and how much I hoped our somatic therapy modification was going to cure her.

Sitting in the back of the car on the way into the city, I thought back to our honeymoon, twenty years ago, in Italy and France, before the flooding, traveling around the countryside in a rental car, stopping in villages where we would make love in the afternoons before going out ravenous for drinks and meals in the evenings.

I remembered when we'd gone to look at the first house we owned together. It had seemed very expensive at the time, but we'd both fallen in love with it. We borrowed money from Annie's mother for the deposit and on the day of settlement we ate Chinese take-away on the floor and slept on a camp mattress in the main bedroom. It was one of the best moments of our life.

The car stopped at the Geneus laboratory. Almost everyone had left so extracting the viral-vector from its protective coating wasn't going to be too difficult. Under a biological hood, I depolymerized it, neutralized the base, and ran it through a syringe filter to sterilize it. I sucked the final solution up into a sterile needle and covered it, ready for application.

Just as I was leaving, I went down to the monkey lab to look in on our macaques. I'd been missing them.

Vanessa, one of our lab workers, was there. She looked upset.

"What's wrong?" I asked.

"They're going to terminate them." She nodded towards the monkey cages.

"What do you mean? They're supposed to be retired."

"Not any more. Apparently it's too costly. They've decided to euthanize them."

"When?"

"Saturday morning."

"What? Why wasn't I told about this?"

"I have no idea. Anthony just told me this afternoon. Is there something we can do?" Vanessa held her hands out like a school girl.

"I don't know. Who's going to be doing it?"

"I have to. I'm supposed to inject them and take them down to the city crematorium."

I went across to the cages and pushed some grapes through for Sika and Toby, my favorites. They squawked happily.

"I'll see if there's something we can do and call you. If I can find somewhere for them, will you help me get them out of here? I doubt Anthony will be too pleased with me undermining his authority."

"Of course."

When I arrived home, Annie was preparing a meal. I went over to her and we hugged for a long time. We had been in constant contact since I left, so in some ways it seemed like we hadn't been apart. Hugging her, though, was something my body had been craving for weeks.

"I've made your favorite. Farmed barramundi with fried rice and vegetables."

"Thanks."

"Glass of wine?"

"Please."

Annie stood in front of me and ran her fingers through my hair.

"You really have aged so much more gracefully than I have. Look at all this hair. It's getting a little long, though, don't you think? Maybe I should cut it for you, like I used to."

"I like it long."

"You're not going to become a hippy in your old age, are you?"

"Maybe." I smiled. The feeling of Annie's hands on my skull was calming and I closed my eyes for a second.

I wondered how I could ever live without her. We had loved each other and been best friends for over twenty years. She had been my companion in everything. We had made it through the poorest and the hardest times in our lives and come through them together, changed and hardened, but still hopeful.

She poured some red wine and handed a glass to me and removed the tray of fish from the oven. We sat down and I ate my fish slowly, savoring each mouthful as if this were the last meal I'd ever enjoy with my wife. This life, this togetherness which I'd always nurtured, this feeling of safety and warmth and love, was too much to lose. We'd never had children but we'd always had each other, and Annie was everything to me.

After dinner we slipped back onto the lounge. I put some Japanese flute music on the stereo and the gentle sound went whispering into the house. It was mournful but joyful also, the notes starting low then building and rising in yearning, then falling and rising again.

"There's something I have to tell you," I said.

"What's that?" She looked concerned.

"We managed to create a bio-vector containing our somatic immune system modification."

"Really?" She stared at me.

"Yes. I've got the solution here. We just need to find someone to test it on. Is there someone at your clinic who's got HIV-4 and is close to dying?"

"I told you before. I want you to test it on me."

"I think we should find someone else. What if something goes wrong?"

"Then it should be me."

"I have to return to the lab next week. I'm not going to be here to monitor you."

"How much have you got?"

"Just enough for one person. It wasn't easy to get out of

the lab."

"What form is it in? Liquid?"

"Yes. I depolymerized it at Geneus and put it into a syringe. It's in my briefcase."

"Give it to me, then."

"No. Let's think about it for a day."

"I don't want to think about it. I'm ready."

"We've got another problem." I wanted to distract her and give myself time to prepare for this. I told her about the monkeys.

"Is there anywhere we can put them?" she said.

"I don't know. I suppose we could release them into the wild. But I don't even know where. In the de-reg zone they'd probably get eaten. I thought about asking Dylan. Maybe they'd allow us to put them on one of the islands."

"Let's invite him and Sophie around for dinner tomorrow," Annie said, then she pushed up close to me.

An hour later I took a shower, and when I came out I found Annie sitting on our bed with my briefcase open and the syringe next to her — empty.

"What are you doing?"

"It was the only way, Michael. You know it and I know it. There wasn't any point arguing about it." Her voice was perfectly calm, and I sat down next to her on the bed and put my face in my hands. Annie put her hand on my back.

"It's okay," I said. "I'm okay."

It would be days before the bio-vectors started having any effect on Annie, and weeks before we knew if they'd been successful or not.

The following evening, Dylan and Sophie came over for

dinner. I told them about how the monkeys were going to be terminated and asked them if they knew where we could take them.

"I thought they weren't allowed to terminate them," Dylan said.

"The regulations have changed," I replied. "I don't know what to do."

"Is there any way you can get them out of there?"

"Yes. Vanessa's supposed to put them down and then take them to a local crematorium. She could just sedate them instead."

"Well, we could take them out to one of the islands. They could live in the forest there. They will survive in the wild, won't they?"

"They should be okay. Don't you think the people there might be upset, though?"

"I'm sure we can work something out. The kids would love them. And besides, if they ever get hungry they can always eat them." He smiled.

"Dylan," Sophie said, hitting him.

The next morning, Dylan and I drove into the car park of the Geneus lab and helped Vanessa load fifteen supposedly dead macaques into the back of our car.

"What are you going to take to the crematorium instead?" Dylan asked her.

"Rabbits," Vanessa replied. She'd been down to the market that morning and purchased fifteen dead rabbits, whose body mass wasn't that different from our macaques.

Dylan and I drove out to the airport and we put each of the macaques, still sedated, into cages that Annie and

Sophie had picked up for us. We loaded them all into the back of the Cessna.

"Where's the pilot?" I said.

"You're looking at him," Dylan replied.

"You're flying?"

"Yep."

"I'm not trusting the lives of these monkeys to you."

"It's either me or Sophie, and I can tell you who I'd choose," Dylan said, and we laughed.

Once we were on board, Dylan maneuvered the plane easily out to the beginning of the runway, and in just a few minutes, we were floating up over the city. I looked down to where the green grass ended and the shanty towns of the de-reg zone started. We were low enough that I could see the clusters of army vehicles and tents about five kilometers from the fence line.

There had been news in the last few weeks of melees between the government forces and the rebels who were trying to penetrate the regulated zone. If the rebels managed to get through, a full scale attack on the city itself was possible.

For a while, I'd naively thought the country might be better run under rebel control, but these weren't benevolent dictators: they were the most power-hungry, aggressive opportunists that had been relegated to the de-reg zone. Biker gangs and mafia groups who didn't hesitate to kill people who got in their way and who weren't at all interested in establishing any kind of democratic government. Not that the current government was very democratic, but at least they maintained vestiges of decency that these new leaders wouldn't bother with.

Half an hour later, Dylan banked left and we were above the water, and then it was blue all the way to the horizon.

After a couple of hours flying time, we glided down to a small island which rose up on steep cliffs from the blue water. The plane bumped along a grassy landing strip surrounded by forest. At the end of the landing strip was a tin shed and armed guards came out to meet us.

Dylan and Sophie got out of the plane first, and I saw Dylan hugging the two men.

"Do you think they're really going to want your monkeys?" Annie said, poking her finger through Toby's cage and scratching him behind a sedated ear. He opened a sleepy eye and looked at her, dribble coming out the side of his mouth.

"I hope so."

Dylan came back and opened up the plane door for us. "Let's go and talk to the chief and ask him what to do."

"You didn't ask him beforehand?" I stepped down out of the plane onto the dry grass.

"It would have taken too long. Trust me. This way's best."

Annie looked at Dylan skeptically.

The guards told us we could use their jeep and we climbed aboard and drove down a bumpy road between thick forest. The leaves of the trees beside the road were covered with dust, and more dust billowed up behind us. The sun was shining and a warm breeze brought with it the smell of salt and the musty tropical forest.

After about twenty minutes the forest thinned out and then cleared entirely. Here, people moved up and down between rows of vegetables, weeding and watering and harvesting. Rows of earthen houses stood between date and coconut palms. People waved; dogs and chickens scampered out of our way.

In the centre of town were some larger buildings, and we pulled up outside one of these.

"Welcome to Government House." Dylan turned to us and smiled.

The building in front of us had a small patch of green lawn out the front, palm trees shading it. A verandah surrounded the building and a man was lying in a hammock there, smoking. Dylan greeted him as we went past.

Inside was a large open room with rustic furniture and a thatched ceiling.

"Is Putuk free?" Dylan asked the man at the front desk, who was fanning himself lazily.

"Just a minute," the man replied. He had a brief conversation on an old-style telephone and we were ushered down the corridor.

A large, Polynesian man was working behind a desk and when he saw Dylan a smile spread across his face. He stood up and the two men hugged and Sophie greeted him as well.

"Putuk, these are my friends, Michael and Annie."

Putuk greeted us with enthusiastic handshakes.

"Sit down, sit down," Putuk said, motioning to some cane lounges. "Can I get you something to drink? Kava? Tea?"

"Kava sounds good," Dylan said.

Putuk went out and a few minutes later came back with a tray of cups and a large pot of tea which he served for us.

"You like Kava?" Putuk said to Annie.

"I've never tried it," Annie said.

"Very relaxing," Putuk assured her, nodding happily as if he'd already had quite a bit himself that day.

We sipped the tea while Dylan explained the situation with the macaques. He proposed that they either let them free in the forest, or that they construct a small shelter for them, like a zoo.

"Hmm," Putuk said when Dylan had finished. "I think we'll have to get a consensus."

"What does that mean?" I asked.

"We'll send a message out to everyone. Everyone gets to vote."

"Everyone on the island?"

"Yes. They'll have twenty four hours to decide," Dylan said.

"The island is everyone's. If we're going to let the monkeys stay here, then everyone must decide," Putuk said.

"How does that get done?"

"Software," Dylan said. "People don't have to vote if they don't want to. Or many have pre-opted for someone else to vote for them — their local representative, or someone else who they trust."

"You have v-space out here?"

"No," Putuk responded. "Just a very simple form of network using the simplest of computers. In case they ever break down."

"What if the people say no?"

"We'll cross that bridge when we come to it," Dylan said.

"You mean we might have brought them all the way out here for nothing?"

"It's okay." Dylan waved his hand at me. "Don't worry. Something will work out."

Dylan always had a carefree attitude and it was one of the things that annoyed me most about him. Still, he generally seemed to get what he wanted, so all I could do was hope that this occasion was no different. Why hadn't he worked all this out before we left? I knew Annie, who loved order and discipline, would be getting upset, and one look at her told me I wasn't wrong.

"So, will we be seeing you at the gathering tonight?" Putuk said to us, just as my body was starting to feel the warm glow of the Kava and my concerns over the monkeys were starting to fade. Everything would work out. There was no need to worry.

"Absolutely," Dylan said, and I turned to him, hoping he wasn't speaking for all of us. "Of course, you don't have to participate in all the ceremonies." He looked at Annie and I, smiling.

Putuk laughed.

We left Putuk and drove to a house that had been prepared for us.

"What about the macaques?" Annie said.

"I'll ask someone to take them to the animal pens," Dylan said. "I'm sure they'll have a chicken coop at least where they can keep them for the night."

"I'd like to go with them."

"Okay. We'll go and get them if you like."

We left our bags at the house, which was small but comfortable, with the same cane lounges I'd seen at Putuk's and thick rugs on the earthen floor. Then we drove back out to the landing strip to pick up the monkeys. They were still dopey and greeted us with droopy eyes.

Just as we were unloading them from the plane, a truck arrived. Two lithe black men jumped out and we all loaded them onto the back.

We followed the men into town and then out to a farm where chickens and cows roamed the fields.

A woman came out to greet us, and we told her what we needed.

"We've got an old shed out the back we can put them in," she said. She took us around to what looked like a food storage shed that was empty apart from a few bales of hay.

"This will be perfect," Dylan said.

We unleashed the macaques, and immediately they started playing. Annie and I took one another's hands.

"Maybe they'll be alright here," Annie said.

"I think so," I said. "Much better off than they were at the lab, anyway."

The woman, Liza, gave us some fruit for them, and we left them feeding noisily and rubbing themselves against one another.

That afternoon, I went for a walk by myself along the path which led down to the ocean. I thought about all that had happened over the past year, and then I started wondering if the bio-vectors that Annie had injected herself with were going to work. If they did, maybe we should move here. I looked out across the blue ocean to the waves rolling in steadily, curling gently into white foam from one end to the other, catching the low afternoon sunlight in their crests and along their smooth faces. I sat down on the sand for a while, and then I stood up and walked back to the house.

Inside the living area the others were relaxing on the couches. Dylan was just opening a bottle of sparkling wine that he must have brought with him and Sophie, who had slipped into a sarong, was rolling up a joint.

"I haven't smoked in years!" Annie said. She seemed happy.

I sat down in an empty seat.

"Did Michael ever tell you about our university years?" Dylan said to Annie, sitting across from her and lining up the champagne flutes, winking at me.

"I don't know. What are you referring to exactly?" Annie said.

Sophie lit up the joint, took a few puffs, then passed it to me, letting her hand brush against mine slowly as she let it go.

"I don't know. If he hasn't told you, maybe I shouldn't say anything," Dylan said, looking over at me.

"Well, I haven't told her everything, I suppose. It was before we started going out."

"I've told you things about my life before we started going out!" Annie said. "What is it that you haven't told me?"

"Thanks, Dylan!" I said. But because I was getting stoned for the first time in about twenty years, and Annie's sweet pheromones were wafting off her like an apple tree in spring, I couldn't summon up too much conviction.

It must have been good weed, as my mind was suddenly going a million miles an hour. The situation had taken a strange turn, and I noticed a subtle tension in the room that I hadn't felt before.

"Well, are you going to tell me?" Annie said. Sophie moved over next to Annie on the couch, casually picked up one of her hands, told her how much she liked her wedding ring, then started gently massaging her.

"You're my summertime," an old Rachel Grey song, came on the sound system. The light outside was softening as the afternoon came slowly to an end. Light dropped down through the windows and covered everything with a soft glow. Little specks of brightness glittered from shiny surfaces. Outside, the tops of bushes and trees were basted in orange.

"Michael?" Dylan said.

"Well, it's a bit late now," I said.

"Are you going to tell her or should I?" Dylan said.

"About what exactly?" Annie asked, looking from one to the other of us.

"I don't know... Julia?" Dylan said, looking my way.

"Who's Julia?" Annie said.

"Yes, who's Julia?" Sophie repeated.

"She was this girl who Michael introduced me to at university. Michael was in love with her, but I didn't know that at the time. Because Michael didn't tell me, did he?" Dylan said.

I felt my whole body start to produce hormones that made my head spin as if I were drunk. I hadn't thought about Julia in years. Images of some of the long sex sessions Dylan, Julia, and another girl called Ingrid and I had had when we were younger flashed through my mind. I remembered one night especially when we'd all taken some ecstasy and LSD and gone out to a club together and then gone back to the apartment where Julia lived, subsidized by her parents, and spent the whole next day listening to music and dropping more ecstasy and snorting coke and drinking and fucking each other's brains out. It had been one of the most intense days of my life, a day when I really thought that I was in love with Dylan, Julia and Ingrid all at the same time, and that maybe we'd end up living together, the four of us, for the rest of our lives.

"Well, if I'd known that about a week after I introduced you to her that you were going to start sleeping with her, then I probably never would have," I said, trying to keep my cool.

"Typical Dylan," Sophie said. "So you've always been like this, have you?" I noticed she was still working away at Annie's hand, which along with the pot and alcohol were sending Annie into what looked like a pleasant torpor.

"So, what happened?" Annie groaned as Sophie hit a nerve.

"Well, being the nice guy I am, I asked him if he wanted to join us," Dylan said.

"Of course," Sophie said, shaking her head at him.

Annie sat up straight, pulling her hand away from Sophie. "What do you mean?"

"Well, you know, asked him if he wanted to have a foursome with Julia and I and another girl I was seeing."

"And did you?" She looked at me.

I looked sheepishly down.

"He did," Dylan said. "We became a regular little family for a while there."

"Why haven't you ever told me about this?" Annie asked me.

"It was a long time ago."

"Long time ago or not. Don't you think that's the sort of thing you might like to tell your wife?"

"You always seemed so against that sort of thing that I didn't want to bring it up."

"I'm not against that sort of thing at all. You're making me out to be some kind of prude. I didn't complain for example when you and Sophie here almost slept with one another at that gathering you went to, did I?" Annie pulled away from Sophie and sat with her back tight against the sofa like a cornered animal.

I felt paralyzed. I wanted to go across to Annie and put my arm around her, but the weed was making everything weirder than it already was. It was like all of us had stopped breathing and there was some poisonous gas in the air that was going to kill us if we did breathe.

"Come on, you've never done anything like that?" Dylan said to Annie, breaking the tension.

"No, never!" Annie said. "It doesn't mean I wouldn't, though. Or that I'm against it in any way."

"You seem like a fairly liberal woman. I'm sure you got up to some pretty crazy things in your younger years," Dylan said, and I admired the way he was bringing her out of herself, relaxing her.

"Well, there were a few things, I suppose, that looking back on did seem a little crazy." Annie laughed, and I breathed a sigh of relief.

"Such as?" Sophie prodded.

"Well, nothing like that, of course." She was still looking at me in a way which frightened me. Like she didn't know me any more. Maybe it was just the pot. "I did steal a car once."

"What!" I said, trying to act outraged.

"Tell us more," Dylan said.

"Well, not exactly stole. It was my friend's car." Annie went on to tell us a story, about how they'd driven it across town when they were only fourteen and picked up two boys.

"You little rebel," Dylan said. "At least we were of age, weren't we, Michael?"

We all laughed, and I felt a warm glow of love stretch out for this, my only family.

Just before dinner, I followed Annie into our room as she went looking for a sweater.

"So, are you enjoying yourself?" I asked.

"Yes, I am, actually."

"I'm sorry about all that back there. I should have told you years ago. It was just one of those things that I was kind of embarrassed about, and then as time went by it became harder and harder, and then I kind of forgot about it."

"Forgot about it, or put it out of your mind?"

"The latter, I guess."

"Is it still something you're interested in doing? Dylan and Sophie look like they're up for it." She giggled.

"Not really. You?"

"No, probably not," she agreed, and then we both laughed and hugged each other with what felt like relief. "Maybe I am a bit of a prude."

"I like you being a prude," I said, and we kissed.

The night was warm and a breeze blew off the ocean. We

sat amongst a couple of hundred people around a large circular space where people were dancing, drumming, clapping with sticks or their hands, playing tambourines, triangles, flutes and recorders, or just adding to the general cacophony with their voices. After a few more cups of Kava and another couple of joints, I felt myself getting swept up in the euphoria and started clapping along myself.

Slowly, the party died down and people started huddling together in groups or going off together through the trees, and Annie and I walked along the dusty road together in the moonlight, leaning against one another and just enjoying for once the beauty of the moment.

The next afternoon we went back to visit Putuk, and he informed us that the people had agreed to let the monkeys free. There weren't any natural predators on the island, and the monkeys would be able to live a happy life amongst the trees of the island, which provided plenty of wild fruit.

Before we left the island, we went to visit them. They were feeding noisily in a wild mango tree. Toby came running across to us and climbed up onto my shoulder. I took him down and held him tightly in my arms.

"You're going to be okay here, Tobes," I said to him. "You're going to be happy. We'll come back and visit you soon. I promise."

CHAPTER SEVENTEEN

OVER THE NEXT few days, we monitored Annie carefully, but nothing changed.

And then I had to return to the base.

Annie came out to the airport with me and we gave each other a painful goodbye.

"Let me know the second anything changes," I said. "I'll come back immediately."

"I'll be fine," she replied, but her smile was forced and I let her go with a heavy heart.

That evening I went to find Justin. He was still in his lab, working on testing the immune systems of our patients to the Rebola virus. Thanks to the latest *in vitro* assay technology, we were able to do the testing outside the human body with a ninety percent certainty.

"How is Annie?" Justin burst out. I had sent him an encrypted message letting him know that we'd started testing the bio-vectors.

"No change, yet."

"Penny's in hospital. I really don't think she has long left."

"I'll let you know as soon as anything changes."

"Thanks," he said.

"How is everything going here?"

"The results vary. Some of them seem to be working perfectly, while others are not working at all." He went on to explain to me the reasons why. We had managed to increase the number and variety of antibodies, but in some cases the attack by the natural killer cells still wasn't fast enough. And with Rebola, that was crucial.

Three days later, just as I was sitting over a plate of rice and vegetables after hardly eating all day, I got a call from Annie.

"Michael, something's wrong."

"What? What is it?" I almost choked on my food.

"I don't know. I'm having some kind of a reaction to the new cells."

"Where are you?"

"I'm at the clinic."

I stood up and left my plate where it was, heading for the lab to find Justin.

"Okay, listen," I said as I ran. "Send me all the test results once you've got them. I'll go over them and we'll see what's wrong."

"Okay."

"Good. Just hold on. You're going to be fine."

Justin was in the lab, where I knew he'd be, working with a number of other people. I was in such a panic it was hard to focus. My heart rate, according to my com, was over a hundred.

"Annie's having a negative reaction to the bio-vectors," I whispered to Justin.

"What's wrong?"

"I don't know. Come with me."

We went into my office and accessed the results that Annie had just sent me. Thankfully she'd been at the clinic where they had an AutoAnalyzer.

"It looks like the engineered T-cells are killing too many cells too rapidly," I said. "She's having a shock response."

"How is that possible? Our trials with the macaques were perfect."

"I have no idea, but we have to stop it."

"We should give it another day. It might just be a period of adjustment."

"My wife could die." I knew that Justin was even more desperate for this to work than I was.

"If we don't get this to work, Penny is going to die." Justin stood there and shook his head.

I held onto him for a few moments, but then I needed to call Annie. Justin slumped down into the chair.

On the third ring, Annie answered and I could hear the panic but also the exhaustion in her voice.

"What should I do, Michael?"

"You're going to have to disable the new genes as we discussed."

"So that's it, then? It's not going to work?"

"No." I was frightened but angry too. Angry at myself. Angry at life itself for allowing this to happen. Then I realized how irrational that was and my mind started working away on other possible solutions, my heart racing and my chest tight as I wondered what to do next. This couldn't be the end of it. There was no way. Maybe if we could germline modify some children as we were trying to do before the military bought us out then we could use them to culture natural killer cells and also clone out genes for antibodies which would recognize HIV-4 more quickly. But that was going to take years.

"What are we going to do now, then?" Annie said.

"I don't know."

"I'd better go. I'll call you back in a few minutes."

"Is there anyone there with you?"

"Yes. Simone and Derek are here."

"Okay, let me know as soon as anything changes."

"I will. I love you."

"I love you too."

Twenty minutes later, the longest twenty minutes of my life, Annie called me back and told me they had administered the failsafe inducer. It would be hours before we knew what the outcome would be. I wanted to be there with her, but by the time I got there it would all be over: for better or for worse.

I went back to my room, and Annie and I spent the next few hours talking to one another. Neither wanted to hang up, in case it was the last conversation we had. I felt as if by staying on the line with her I was somehow keeping her alive.

Around 3am, she told me that Derek had come in to run some more tests on her. Half an hour later she called again and told me it appeared they'd gotten to her in time. The chemical trigger had shut down the new genes, and her immune system was starting to function normally again.

The only problem was: normal wasn't enough to cure her.

The next day I watched a report on the Indonesian situation. Indonesian troops were moving into the north of Australia. The military was there trying to stop more boats from landing, but there were too many of them and the area was too large.

Would the Indonesians really go to the extent of releasing the virus? It would be the end of civilization as we knew it. The start of a whole new era of total mistrust between countries and territories. It was almost inevitable, though. There simply wasn't enough food left to feed everybody. People were going to die. Lots of people. It was only a matter of who.

One night, around 3am, I heard a soft knock on my door and got up quickly to open it. Justin was standing there with his nose red and his eyes bloodshot.

"What's wrong?"

"Penny died," he said.

I put my arms around him and pulled him to me while he cried. Then I invited him in and he spent the night telling me all about their childhood together, how she'd always been the strong one and had stood up for him in school. They hadn't seen each other much in the last few years, as he had been so busy trying to find a cure for her.

The following day Justin left for the city to be with his family. I told him to take as long as he wanted, but he told me he'd be back by the end of the week. Penny was the only member of his family he really loved.

We continued our testing of the immune systems of the prisoners but the results still weren't conclusive.

"How are things going?" Savage came into the lab one afternoon.

"From everything we can gather, it seems all bar two of our test subjects would survive the virus," Kate said.

"What does that mean?" Savage said.

"It means that some people's systems respond better to the modifications than others'. We're trying to work out what the factors are, but it could take us weeks if not months. This is the human body we're dealing with here, not some kind of mechanical toy."

"So what are our options? Modify all our men and hope for the best, knowing that there's a chance twenty percent of them will die?"

"With such a small sample size it's impossible to know what the overall result is going to be," Kate said. "You can't just snap your fingers and make this stuff work, you know?"

"Well, I guess it's a hell of a lot better than nothing." Savage smiled in a way that didn't mean he thought this was funny.

Over the next few weeks we made some minor adjustments to our modifications and conducted more tests on them. Things improved, but still weren't perfect, so we adjusted again until eventually we decided we were about as close as we were going to get.

More and more reports came in about the Indonesian invasion of northern Australia. It wasn't only Australia they were attacking — they'd already taken over parts of Malaysia and Thailand too. And this only added to all the other wars that were already going on around the world. The company that now owned most of California, Glocome, was invading Mexico and Guatemala, and a Japanese multinational had recently declared war on south eastern Brazil, which was now its own territory run by a right-wing dictator. England and France were under attack by a North African alliance, and eastern Europe was slowly being eaten up by the Middle East. Apart from that, in almost every country, civil wars were raging, or gangs were fighting other gangs for what remained of resources.

One day I came into the clinic and all of the patients had gone.

"What happened to them?" I said to Kate.

"They've been moved," Kate said.

"Moved to where?"

"Bio-safety level four."

My heart almost stopped. "What for?" I said, although I already knew the answer.

"We're going to infect them with Rebola."

I stood there and stared at her, gripping onto the bench top by my side to stop myself from collapsing.

"That's illegal."

"They're classifying it as capital punishment," Kate said. "They are terrorists after all." There was a cynical tone to her voice that sickened me. Did she really not care?

"I can't allow it."

Kate stared at me with a blank expression. Then she furrowed her eyebrows, shook her head, and went back to her work. "There's nothing we can do, Michael. If you say anything you'll be arrested."

My heart was pounding by now and suddenly the feeling that I had always lived with, that I was in a country with a fair and reasonable government who would do the best by its citizens, was completely undermined. They were now our enemy. Not to be trusted, but not to be messed with either. Like some medieval king, they had complete and utter power. The organizations that once kept them under control — the United Nations, Amnesty International — hardly even existed any more.

At that moment, Savage came into the room.

"What the hell's going on?" I said to him.

"We need your cooperation on this, Michael. This virus is about to be released in our country and we have to find out right now exactly how good our modifications are."

"We've already told you. The tests are very accurate."

"Ninety percent isn't enough. That's ten percent of the population we're talking about, Michael. Do you want ten percent of the population to die because your tests weren't accurate enough?"

"No, of course not. We can continue testing, though. Improve the process. Get a better picture." Inside I was ready to break down and plead with him but I knew that wouldn't help anybody. The General was a man of war. Killing for him was a way of life. He did it with the same ease a butcher slaughtered animals.

"I can't be a part of this," I said.

"The military does not take lightly to traitors," Savage said.

I closed my eyes for a minute and suddenly realized

that the world had gone mad and that there was almost nothing I could do about it. Refusing to help would only make things worse. The best I could do was continue on and hope that either our modifications saved those men or there was something else we could do to help them if they didn't.

So, this was what war was like? People who were completely unprepared, either psychologically, emotionally, or spiritually, were forced to go out and kill other people who were equally unprepared.

I wondered if I would reach a point where it all just became more of the same. I remembered a pig farmer who'd once told me that the first kill was the worst, but that after that you got numb to it, even started to enjoy it. He'd made me sick at the time, but I wondered if maybe he was right. I'd become immune to killing mice, even monkeys sometimes. Maybe I could do the same with humans.

Every year over two hundred thousand animals were used in medical trials. People liked to think that their medicines came cruelty-free, but the truth was that a lot of suffering was caused by the research that went into them. Testing on humans still felt wrong, but why should we value human life over animal life? Was there really any difference? What was the difference between a human being and a fully grown adult chimpanzee? Thousands of whom had died or suffered in captivity in medical trials.

Kate led me through to bio-safety level four. We suited up and went into a long room where all of the men were inside quarantine bubbles. Thankfully they were sedated. Each bubble had an external IV line and a colostomy bag coming out of it.

Kate put the virus into the first man's drip, Adam. I stood there, my heart running a marathon, and hoped to hell it was going to work. Kate infected all of the men in the same way, including Ghanim, and then her and I and about ten nurses monitored them constantly.

Apart from the IV bags going in we had lines coming out so we could collect constant blood samples. We ran their blood through the AutoAnalyzer and after four hours our immune system modifications seemed to be doing their job. The rate of spread of the virus within the bloodstream was minimal.

Then, just as I was starting to relax and breathe normally again, believing that everything was going to be okay, a nurse called me over to Ghanim's bed. He was struggling to breathe and blood was dripping from his mouth and nose. There was nothing I could do but stand there and watch as his body twitched and strained against the fate before it. I felt as if my own body were dying. I felt myself struggling inside, twisting and wanting to wrench myself apart.

And then, finally, he lay still.

I started trembling, and I knew I wasn't going to be able to control myself. I went outside, through the washer, and then struggled to get out of my suit. I ran down the corridor, my fists clenched and ready to smash into anything, smash into my own body if they had to. I pushed open the door of the bathroom with so much force it crashed against the wall behind it. The sound reverberated down the empty corridor.

I locked myself in a stall and knelt down on the floor. I started pummeling the wall with both of my fists. I wanted to smash my head too and only just managed to stop myself from doing so. I hit the walls, the floor, the hard porcelain bowl of the toilet. When I couldn't take the pain any longer I thudded my fists against my own thighs, and then I kept on bashing; my right hand, thud, thud, thud, leaving red stains on the wall; my left hand over my face, which was half-blinded by tears.

All my life, I had hated those people who had killed my father, and now here I was, having done exactly the same. Although Ghanim was a convicted terrorist, what he was trying to do to our country was nothing worse than what our country and its allies had been doing to his for decades. My father had always had a love-hate relationship with the West. Although he supported the idea of a capitalist democracy, he said that too often it was propped up by exploitation of other countries like his own.

I thought back to how I had felt after my parents' death, so scared and so angry. I had hated myself. The day before they had disappeared, I had fought with them, screaming at them from my room because I had wanted to continue playing with my cousin, Salim, but they had forced me to come inside and do my homework instead. That morning, the morning they had died, I had been surly and had hardly spoken to them. If I hadn't been like that, I thought at the time, they might have taken me to school like they sometimes did instead of making me take the bus. And if they had taken me to school, they might not have been in the same place as that missile.

I realized now, for the first time, that it wasn't my fault. That it was someone else's fault. Someone like me, right this minute, making a conscious decision which had killed somebody. I felt so sick then that I started vomiting. I emptied the contents of my stomach into the toilet and then I kept dry retching until I could hardly breathe. I stood up and went to the sink and blew vomit out of my nose and wiped it away from my mouth and chin. I looked at myself in the mirror but I could hardly recognize the person looking back at me. That was somebody else. Somebody I used to be. It certainly wasn't the person I was now.

A few weeks later, the news that we'd been dreading came through. In the space of a few days, almost half of Darwin was wiped out by the Rebola virus.

That night, I called Annie.

"I think you should come and live on the base here with me," I said. "Things are getting too dangerous out there."

"I don't think it was the Indonesians who set that virus off," Annie said.

"What do you mean?"

"I think it was us. I think it was Australian forces."

"What makes you think that?"

"I have a friend in Jakarta. They're claiming it was the Australians who released it. Most of the Indonesian troops were wiped out, and it was only the Australian soldiers who survived."

Chapter Eighteen

THE NEXT MORNING, I switched the audio recorder on my com on, in case I ever needed a recording of this, and stormed in to General Savage's office.

"That virus was ours, wasn't it?" I said to him.

Savage looked at me out of deep blue eyes, unwavering, and said nothing.

"Why didn't you tell us?"

"Close the door, Michael. Sit down."

I stood there for a minute, hesitating, and then I realized I had no choice.

"Michael, I'm going to get right to the point." Savage folded his hands in front of him. "Things are bad out there. Way worse than they tell you. And it's going to get worse. Much worse. No holds barred. Whoever wins this one is going to do whatever the hell they like to the people living in the countries they conquer. Releasing that virus was our only option."

"So it was ours, then?"

"Yes."

"Why weren't we informed?"

"It was classified information, Michael, and if any part of this conversation finds its way out of this room then you're going to be arrested, do you understand me?"

I nodded, wondering if there was any way he could detect my recorder.

"The Indonesians are better armed than us, Michael, and there are a hell of a lot more of them. If this had gone on any longer they would have taken over the whole God damn country. Is that what you want? Indonesia taking over our country?"

"No, obviously not." I wondered if any of what he was saying was true.

"Good. Now, while you're here, I might as well share a little bit more classified information with you. Part of the reason we tested the virus out in Darwin was because we needed to know how well it would work and how well your vaccine worked."

My chest ached. I couldn't believe that I had been a part of what had happened. How many innocent civilians had been killed?

"And the good news," Savage continued, "is that on both fronts we were fairly successful."

"How many civilians were killed?" I said, not really wanting to know the answer but needing to anyway.

"None. Most of them were evacuated before Indonesia even attacked, and the rest got out shortly afterwards. Which is why it was the perfect test site. Combined with the fact that it's so remote, and that the virus works so quickly, means — touch wood — that it hasn't escaped."

I looked down at the floor. I realized now I couldn't trust a word he was saying, but what choice did I have? Obviously the media was being far more controlled than I had ever believed possible. There were no doubt a few dark-net forums that were still telling the truth, but even they would be shut down faster than new ones could pop up again. It wasn't easy staying alive these days — it was in very few people's moral fibre to make it even harder for themselves.

"Are you okay, Michael? Because this is a war here, son, and in war people die. Lots of people. There's not much we can do about that."

"Yes," I said, wondering what would happen if I said I wasn't. No doubt some high security prison awaited me where I'd never see the light of day.

"Good. Because we need to move quickly onto phase two."

"Phase two?" I looked up at him, dizzy and nauseous, wondering if I would faint or throw up, but trying to keep my composure. People like Savage were usually paranoid. If I showed too much disgust at what was happening he'd find a replacement for me.

"Phase two involves dealing with this rebel situation. Your vaccine worked well, but not well enough. We need to make it work perfectly."

"What do you mean, deal with the rebel situation?"

"We're going to do the same thing to those bastards that we did to the Indonesians. They're about to launch a full-scale attack on our city."

"There'll be contamination. It'll get into the regulated zone. And what about those living in the de-reg zone who aren't working for the rebels?"

"Have you been out there lately, Michael? Most of them are dying of starvation anyway. Pretty soon they all will be. There's just not enough food left to feed us all."

"What about the regulated zone?"

"That's why we need to improve your vaccination. Initial statistics show that there was a ninety-five percent survival rate amongst those vaccinated, even better than your lab tests here. We need to get that up to a hundred."

"Have you ever thought of creating a virus that doesn't actually kill people?" I needed to stall him, to get as much information out of him as I could. Was there any way I could stop this?

"You mean incapacitates them in some way?" Savage looked confused.

"Something like that. Not exactly incapacitates — just makes them unwilling to continue fighting." I was thinking about how my cooperation research findings could be applied to warfare.

Savage looked taken aback, and he scrunched his thick eyelashes down at me and stared out of cold blue eyes. "I'm not quite sure I get your drift."

"Imagine something like this: a virus that makes anyone who has been infected with it so friendly and empathetic that they have zero inclination to kill people."

"This is war, Michael. People get killed."

"They wouldn't have to, though. They could just be rendered incapable of warfare. To the point where they'd lay down their weapons in peace. Imagine a whole lot of hippies. We could give them the viral equivalent of LSD."

"Are you sure *you* haven't been taking any LSD?"

"Before the military contract with Geneus we were working on a process which could do this."

"And how long would these effects last?"

"They could be made to last forever."

Savage looked like he'd just eaten something disagreeable. "I'm afraid that's not really what we're after here, Michael. We're after something which kills people. Puts them out of action. Permanently. These are not nice people we're talking about. These are the enemy."

"It's not just the enemy, though, is it? Many of them are civilians. Do we really need to kill them all?"

"It's the most efficient way to achieve our goals. What the hell are we going to do with thousands of happy hippies running around? We can't lock them all up. We'd have to feed them, house them, clothe them... We can't even manage that with our own population. It would be a total disaster. I'm sorry, Michael, but that's just not what we're after here. Too inefficient. What if they come up with a way to reverse its effects? We need to win this war and we need to win it quickly."

I didn't know how to respond. There was no way I could tell him I wouldn't be involved, he'd already made that clear.

There must be ten million people out there at least. We couldn't kill off ten million people, whatever the situation. I thought about Sam and his family, and the other people I'd gotten to know in the de-reg zone. Good people. Humble people. People who didn't deserve to be wiped out like a rabbit population.

That night I went back to my room where Annie, who had

just arrived at the base, was waiting for me.

Once I finished telling her everything, she just sat there and shook her head. Then she looked up at me with tears in her eyes.

"What are we going to do, Michael?"

"I have no idea." The weight of the situation was so huge that I was having trouble comprehending it. How could I have been involved in something like this?

I disgusted myself. My desire to save Annie and Justin's sister and others with their disease, my arrogance that I could actually do something to help, my gullibility in believing what the military had told us — that we needed to protect our country from Rebola — had led me to be part of the greatest crime against humanity in this country since white people had wiped out the aboriginal population nearly three hundred years ago.

"What about Sam and his family?" Annie said.

"When was the last time you heard from them?"

"I saw Gilda a few weeks ago. She came in with an infection. We didn't have any antibiotics left but I was able to get to it before it got too bad."

"They'll be wiped out with the rest of them."

"Surely we can try to save some people at least. If they're going to be inoculating people in the regulated zone, can't they do it in the de-reg as well?"

"I don't think they will. I don't think they want to save people."

"Then we have to. We have to try."

"I'll see if Gendigm can help."

I contacted Bruno through an encrypted line to to tell him what was happening and ask for his help. I'd been in touch with him on a number of occasions since working for the military and had come to trust Gendigm and their motives.

"We need to vaccinate innocent people living in the de-reg zone," I told him.

"How are you planning on manufacturing a vaccine?"

"I'm not sure yet."

"Why don't you just tell people to stay inside?"

"It'll get to them anyway. It's airborne and can be carried by the wind. There's no way they could avoid it."

"I'll put it to the board," Bruno said. "They might say yes to helping with the manufacturing, but not with the distribution. And they might want something in return."

"What can I give them?"

"We're still interested in taking over Geneus. While they've got this military contract that's obviously not possible, but maybe once it's finished... We want to continue with your germline modification project."

"So do I," I said, thinking that was now our only chance of saving Annie.

"I'll get back to you."

"Well?" Annie said, when I hung up.

"He's going to try. If we try to inoculate people, though, then there's a good chance we'll get caught. The military probably has spy networks all through the de-reg, keeping an eye on the rebels. Someone will say something. The best we can do is vaccinate a small group of people without them even realizing."

"If we manage to vaccinate everyone first, though, it won't matter if we get caught."

"The chances of us doing that are unlikely, and if they

want those people dead, they're going to kill them whatever we do. This isn't some Hollywood movie, Annie. We're not going to be able to save everyone."

Annie started crying, and she went and lay down on the bed in our room, face down on the pillow. I felt horrible for letting my anger overflow, and I followed her in and sat down beside her. I put my hand on her back, patting her gently as she howled. I ran my fingers through her hair.

Suddenly I hated every single human being alive. Only humans were sick enough to try to wipe out members of their own species, and had the brains and the weapons to do it. The military was evil, but no more evil than all those people in the regulated zone like myself who had believed their bullshit, believed that we needed to defend ourselves.

All we really cared about was keeping ourselves safe, keeping ourselves comfortable. The world outside could go to hell and as long as we could turn a blind eye to it, pretend to ourselves that it wasn't really happening, that it was no more real than anything else we saw on the net, distract ourselves with banalities like sport or famous people or cheap entertainment, then we went about our daily lives and did nothing.

"There must be something more we can do," I said.

"Can't you stop the project from working? If they need one hundred percent reliability in their vaccine before releasing the virus, then make sure they don't get it."

"I can try to delay for as long as possible. Buy us some time. Too long, though, and they'll get suspicious. Besides, I'm not the only one working on the project. They'll just get someone else to do it."

"We obviously can't go to the media," Annie said.

"What about another country? Is there someone who could stop this?"

"I don't think any other countries really care at the moment. They're all too busy with their own problems."

"Then we're fucked."

"Yes. We are."

The next day I went to see Savage.

"I don't want to tell you how to do your job, General, but I think it might be a good idea if you either vaccinate people in the de-reg zone, or at the very least give them a placebo."

Annie and I had realized that if we could convince the military to give people in the de-reg zones blank vaccines then our own vaccination program there might go unnoticed.

"Why's that, Michael?" The General obviously didn't take too well to being told how to do his job.

"Once you start vaccinating people in the regulated zone, people in the de-reg are going to find out about it pretty quickly. If the rebels already suspect that we might use a bio-weapon against them, which they might well, then they'll be a lot more cautious."

"You're probably right. You're a real credit to the military, you know that? If this works out I'll personally make sure you're awarded a medal."

Over the next two months, we perfected our somatic modification to the immune system to make anyone who received it totally immune to Rebola. I delayed my part of the process as long as I possibly could, but there was only so much I could do without looking suspicious. If they realized I was delaying on purpose, I'd either be arrested, or at the very least fired, and our plan would be ruined.

Every day felt like a death sentence, not just for myself but for all those living in the de-reg zone. I imagined their faces, the effect that the virus would have on them all. Whole families, whole neighborhoods, whole towns of dying people.

Each night Annie and I tried to work out what more we could do, but apart from getting locked up ourselves, which no longer worried us, there was the larger problem: if this failed, the military would simply find another way. We were sure this wasn't their only option — just the best one they had at the moment. They could blame it on the Indonesians, protect everyone in the regulated zone, and protect the infrastructure in the de-reg zone. It was the perfect weapon. A bomb would be much too messy, and far too inaccurate, and ground combat would take too long and cost too many soldier's lives. A virus was perfect. But in the end — replaceable.

When the code was ready, the vaccines for all those who lived in the regulated zones were going to be produced at a factory outside Sydney, and I passed on this piece of information to Bruno.

A few days later, he got back to me and told me they'd managed to hack into the factory's automated system and place an order for an extra ten thousand doses of the bio-vector which would be delivered to a warehouse in the de-reg zone. It was the most we could do without causing suspicion.

Annie and I debated whether we should go ourselves, but by then it was almost as if we had a death wish.

CHAPTER NINETEEN

ANNIE AND I arrived back in Melbourne on a Wednesday evening. Over the last two months, the government had created twenty million doses of the vaccine to be spread throughout all the regulated zones of Australia, telling people they were protection against bio-weapons like the one the Indonesians had used in Darwin. Not only that, but they'd created ten million blank doses of the vaccine and were distributing them to clinics in the de-reg zone, telling them the same thing. They'd done a huge advertising campaign about how Australia was finally going to be united again, and how this was the first step of goodwill on the part of the government.

As soon as we arrived back, Annie and I drove out to the de-reg zone. We were stopped at the gate by guards but when they asked us what our purpose was we told them we were part of the vaccination program. They looked up Annie's credentials and let us through.

After picking up the vaccines, our vehicle found a place

to park as close as possible to Gilda and Sam's street, which was now crowded with so much temporary housing our vehicle couldn't get through. Dogs scattered at the sight of us, presumably hanging around the streets for food but afraid they might become food themselves. Malnourished humans, who didn't look much healthier than the dogs, walked as if all purpose had been drained out of them. I looked at their faces and imagined what their lives had been like before the flooding and the rest of the environmental devastation and over-population problems — probably not too different from my own. We came across a whole group of people sitting in what was once a park. They looked up at us with gaunt eyes. A few of them held up their hands but neither Annie nor I had any cash. A couple of people were dragging away what looked to be a dead body wrapped in a blanket.

Then I saw a group of men coming towards us, laughing loudly. There was no time to turn off or around.

"What should we do?" I said to Annie.

"Just keep walking."

We moved over so the gang could pass, but they blocked our passage.

"That's a nice looking pair of shoes you've got there, mate," one of them said.

I looked up at him. He was around twenty-two, with a set jaw and a glare in his eyes that was beyond his years.

"Yeah. What size are they?" another one said.

"Pretty nice looking pants as well," a third man put in.

"What's in that box there?" another said, referring to the vaccines I was carrying.

"We're friends of the Mendoza family. Please, leave us

alone," Annie said. I was shaking inside, ready to fly into attack even though I knew I would be taken down in seconds. I could hear my breathing getting louder and faster. My hands were clenched and I scanned the ground for a weapon: a rock or a stick. I worked for the military — why hadn't I brought a gun? Not that I would have known how to use it. And against so many assailants, it probably would have been turned against us anyway.

"And who gave you permission to be here?" An older man stepped forward. He had a tattoo down the side of his neck and his arms were scarred. His skin hung slightly loose around what was once muscle. He had a gold band around one arm — a luxury that very few could afford in this area and even fewer would dare to wear in public even if they could.

"We didn't have time to get permission," Annie said. "This is a medical matter." We had tried to contact Gilda before leaving but we hadn't been able to. It seemed the government had already started jamming communications.

"I recognize you." A younger man stepped forward, and the man who had just spoken glared at him. "She works at the clinic," the younger man explained. "She was the one who fixed my broken arm."

"David, isn't it?" Annie said.

"Yes," the man said.

"What are you going to see the Mendoza's for?" the leader said.

"I treated Sam for rabies last year. He hasn't been into the clinic for a while. I need to check on him."

The man stood there and looked at us for a minute longer, then finally said, "Come on boys. We've got work to do."

Before we knew it they were flowing around us and kicking stones and laughing down the street behind us.

I took Annie's hand. "Are you okay?"

She nodded, and we continued on.

We arrived at Sam and Gilda's house to find Gilda stirring a pot of stew on a small gas stove out the back. She was happy to see us and hugged us both.

"Where's Sam?" Annie said.

"He's with some friends," Gilda replied, and I was surprised that even amongst the turmoil of the de-reg zone children could still lead normal lives.

"I need you to bring him home," Annie said.

"Why?"

"Come inside. We need to talk."

Gilda looked up at Annie and was obviously about to ask her to wait, but then turned off the gas and followed us in.

"What we're about to tell you must not leave this house," Annie said. "We're going to try to help people, but if word of what we're doing gets out then all hell will break loose."

Gilda sat down at her wobbly kitchen table and crossed her arms in front of her. "What's wrong?" she said, her voice suddenly hard.

We explained everything to her, and she looked more afraid than I'd ever seen her before.

"They can't do that," she kept saying.

"They can and they will," Annie said. "They think the rebels present too much of a threat to the regulated zone."

"But that's not true at all." Gilda put her hands up to her

hair and pulled at it gently.

"What do you know?" Annie said.

Gilda shook her head. "It's just not." But she wouldn't say any more.

"We have to start vaccinating people," Annie said. "We'll tell people it's the same vaccine as the ones that are being given out at the clinics. That way we won't cause any panic and word won't get back to the military or the government that something's amiss. I'm going to go to my old clinic tomorrow and start working from there, but we should start here, tonight, by vaccinating the locals."

"How many doses do you have?" Gilda said.

"Ten thousand."

"Why don't we take some over to the clinic in Lilydale? And some more up to Belgrave? We can get it done faster if we spread out."

"Do you know anyone there who you trust? We can't let people find out what we're doing."

"Yes, I have contacts at both those clinics," Gilda said.

I wondered for a moment how Gilda was so well connected, but then Annie said, "Let's get to work."

"I'm going for Sam," Gilda said. "I'll start telling people to come here."

"Don't forget. You have to tell them that it's the same vaccine the rest of the clinics are giving out."

Gilda looked at her with a flash of fear and then turned around and left, the curtain over the doorway swinging behind her.

Annie and I started preparing the syringes, putting needles on them. Twenty minutes later Gilda returned with Sam. He ran over and hugged us both and I clung on to his thin but lively body, spinning him around for a minute before putting him back down.

Gilda asked Sam to sit down, but just as Annie was about to inject him a tall, heavy set man in torn khakis came through the door, a gun in his hand.

"Get away from the boy," the man said.

"Boon, it's okay, they're friends. This is Michael and Annie." Gilda stepped between him and us.

"Do you know what these people are trying to do?" Boon said.

"They're here to help us," Gilda said.

"Help us my fucking ass." Boon stepped passed Gilda with his pistol still pointed at Annie. "Now get the fuck away from him before I blow you both away." He waved the gun between the two of us.

"Boon, calm down." Gilda put a hand on the arm holding the gun, but it didn't sway.

"Do you know what this shit is? Do you?" Boon picked up a syringe and turned to her.

"It's a vaccine. These people are my friends. They're here to help us."

"This is a fucking virus," Boon said, pushing Gilda out of the way and coming towards Annie and I.

"It's a benign virus designed to modify the immune system," I said. "It works like a vaccine."

"Bull shit," Boon said, dividing the word in two. "We've had our people run tests on this shit. We don't know what the fuck it does, but we're pretty sure it's not going to be very nice."

Annie and I looked at each other. What was he talking about? He obviously thought this was the same vaccine they were handing out at the clinics, but what did he mean by it being a virus? The blanks they were delivering to the clinics shouldn't have contained a virus, and surely they weren't handing out the actual vaccines.

And then it clicked. They were using the "vaccines" to spread Rebola.

By now Boon was over next to Annie, holding his gun at her and taking the syringe from her hand.

"Stop," I said. "Look, you have to believe us. We're here to help. I'll show you." I picked up one of the syringes from the table, took the cap off and injected myself with it.

I watched Boon's tense body relax and the gun waver, but then suddenly it was pointing at me again.

"You've probably vaccinated yourselves," Boon said. "Of course you wouldn't be so stupid as to risk your own lives."

"Is this true?" Gilda looked at Annie and I with anger in her eyes.

"Gilda, of course it's not true," Annie said. "Why would we have told you what we did? Why would we even be here if this was the truth?"

Gilda looked at her and then she lowered her guard. "Boon, they're telling the truth. Sit down. Listen to what they have to say."

Annie and I repeated to Boon what we'd told Gilda and then I told them all about how the virus worked and how the military was spreading it.

"How do you know all this?" Boon said.

"I work for a company who works for the military," I said, not wanting to tell him everything.

"How long have we got?"

"A couple of days at most. Once people are injected they'll be dead within twenty-four hours. And within a few days pretty much everyone within a hundred kilometers of here will have it."

"Why didn't you come earlier?"

"They only just came up with the vaccine."

"We could have gotten away."

"There's no escaping this thing," I said. "It's airborne, and can last outside of the body for days."

"Why only ten thousand vaccines?"

"That was all we could get without being noticed. And if too many people survive, the military will just find another way to wipe them out."

Just then another woman came through the doorway. She looked at Annie and at me suspiciously.

"What is it, Macy?" Gilda said.

"Does anyone know why the gates have been shut?" she said, obviously referring to the gates leading back to the regulated zone.

"Since when have they been shut?" Annie looked at me with panic in her eyes. We had thought we had another few days at least.

"Since about an hour ago. Nobody's going in or out."

I tried to check the net, but there was no signal.

"You know this has absolutely nothing to do with the rebel situation, don't you?" Boon turned to Annie and I.

"What do you mean?" Annie said.

"They know there's no longer enough food left for everyone and most of the food growing regions are in the de-reg zone," Boon said. "That is the real reason they want to get rid of us."

"What do you mean they're going to get rid of us?" Macy said.

"Macy, go and get your children," Gilda said. "Bring them over here. There's a nasty bug going around. We need to vaccinate them against it."

"What's vaccinate?"

"It means protect against."

"And who's trying to get rid of us?"

"Nobody. It's just Boon talking crazy again. You know what he's like?" Gilda went over and put her hands on Macy.

Macy looked doubtful, but then Gilda said, "Go and get your children." And Macy left.

"I'll be back in a few minutes," Boon said to Gilda. "We have to start getting people in here. If this is a real vaccine." He shot one more questioning glance at me.

"It is." I nodded.

Boon and Gilda hugged in a way which told me their relationship ran deeper than just acquaintances, and then Boon strode away.

"Who is he?" Annie said.

"He's Sam's uncle," Gilda said. "My late husband's brother. You probably saw him at the funeral."

"I don't remember him. Are you sure you can trust him?"

"I'd trust him with my life."

"Do you think that's true? What he said?" Annie said.

"Yes. The rebels are only trying to protect the people here. They're not trying to take over the regulated zone."

Annie looked at her and shook her head. "Okay, here's what we do. You stay here with half the vaccines, try to spread them around as much as you can. Make sure whoever's doing the vaccinating has vaccinated themselves first. We'll go down to my old clinic and start vaccinating people from there. It'll be the quickest way."

Half an hour later, Boon came back with two other men.

"Let's go," Annie said.

"Will we be able to carry the vaccines between us?" Boon asked.

"Yes," I said.

The five of us went out into the night and headed for our vehicle, moonlight paving our way.

"What are we going to do?" I whispered to Annie.

"These people are going to need our help," she said. "The government isn't going to let people back in for weeks and once the virus goes through there's going to be so much that needs to be done. Getting rid of the bodies, for one thing. Without a good cleanup this place is going to become an infested swamp of disease, and even the ones we do vaccinate are going to die."

My heart and stomach ached as I thought about the deaths of all these people from a virus that I had helped the military make useful by creating a vaccine for. Even if I hadn't, it wouldn't have mattered. They had my research. Others knew how to use it. There was nothing I could have done to stop them. I suddenly understood how those who had been working on the Manhattan project felt when they heard the atom bomb had been detonated over Nagasaki and Hiroshima.

We got back to the car and Gilda and the two men loaded up with vaccines.

"I'll stay with you two," Boon said.

"Okay." I was glad to have a gun on our side.

The car drove us towards the clinic and on the way we stopped at a few people's houses and told them they needed to come to the clinic immediately. We told them to tell others, and for those others to do the same.

We arrived and started setting up. Instead of using the consulting rooms, which would only slow down the flow of people, we set up small tables in the waiting room, a box of vaccines on each with accompanying needles and syringes. If only we had more. The five thousand we'd kept were not going to last very long.

People started arriving fairly soon after we got there, and Boon directed them to form a line outside while Annie and I called them in one by one. We sat them down, gave them a quick shot, and told them to tell their friends and families to get down here quickly. I looked at each one as they went through: old people, young people, small children, families. People from all over the world — Australia had always been multicultural. It was early in the morning and they seemed surprised to be there, as if they weren't quite sure what they were doing.

By 8am, there was a line halfway down the block but we hadn't done more than a couple of hundred people. The nurses who lived in the de-reg zone came in with confused looks on their faces, and we told them what was going on and set up more tables for them. Doctors should have been arriving from the regulated zone by then but with the gates shut there would be no way for them to get through.

There were six of us injecting people but the line outside was still growing. We were running out of time. If they'd started giving out shots containing Rebola at the other clinics, it would only be a matter of hours before people started getting sick.

We worked all that day and into the night, taking shifts and sleeping in short spurts on the beds in the consulting rooms. By the next morning, the line at the door had only gotten longer, and we were down to our last fifteen hundred doses.

I was injecting a young family, three children and their parents, when I heard a screaming at the door.

"Get away. Get the fuck away from us."

A man had come in, blood running from his nose and mouth. He was having trouble breathing and with each breath more blood came up. People around the man were moving away from him, but instead of getting out of there, like they should have, they just stood there, watching.

The man started coughing, with his hand over his mouth. Blood ran between his fingers and down his arm.

"Help me," was all he could say before he crouched down on the floor, desperately trying to get enough air into his lungs. He was around thirty-five, with worn but clean clothes, and I imagined him as someone's husband or father. Annie rushed over to him and lay him on his side to clear his airways but I knew there was nothing we could do for him.

"This way, quick," I said to the family who I'd been working with. I'd done two of the children but hadn't yet done the third child, the oldest, or the parents.

There was a back door to the clinic and I showed them out it.

"Here, take these," I said to the mother, pressing a

syringe and three doses into her hands. "Do yourselves. Immediately." Both her and her husband, who had their youngest in one arm and their daughter by her hand, looked up at me like animals stunned by a car headlight.

"What the hell just happened in there?" the father said.

"You'll be fine. Just go," I said.

I went back inside and the infected man was now lying face down on the floor in his own blood, smears of bloody handprints around him. Annie was trying to herd people out, but those who had been near the door had rushed inside and there was a struggle over the remaining vaccines. Three people were trying to inject themselves, while others had taken doses and were heading for the back door. One woman had the remainder of my box.

"You can't take all of those," I said. "There are people who have been waiting here all night."

"I have a family." the woman looked at me out of dark eyes from between matted hair, and clutched them to her breast.

Just then there was a commotion at the door. Word had obviously spread back through the line about what had happened to the man inside, who Boon was now dragging towards the back door by his arms. Shouting started as a whole crowd of people tried to push into the clinic, unaware it was probably the worst thing they could do. They would have been better off waiting outside for us to inject them there.

Then I heard screaming.

"Everybody get outside," I called, but nobody was listening to me. I let the woman go and grabbed the box of vaccines from Annie's table. People were still stuffing them into their pockets along with syringes and needles. With a stampede at the door, the ones inside couldn't get out, and now Boon was trying to direct everybody towards the back. I wondered where he'd left the body, and wanted to tell him that people shouldn't go anywhere near it or the trail of blood he'd left behind. We needed to clean up. But then a man and a woman were trying to grab the remaining vaccines from me. I pulled two out and handed them to them.

"Where are the needles?" the man said.

"Over there," I said, pointing to a table.

They rushed off but then another man came at me and I felt a hand being stuffed in my face and the box being ripped away.

Outside it was complete mayhem. People were fighting one another, tearing at each other's clothes and pushing their way past one another to be first in the door of the clinic. People were bleeding and I wasn't sure if it was from fighting or if they were already sick. A couple of young men had pieces of wood and were beating their way through the crowds with them.

Just then a shot went off. I looked around and saw Boon standing there with his pistol in the air. For a moment everyone froze.

"Okay," he said. "Everybody just stop. You need to get out of here. This place is now contam—"

But that was all he could say. Another shot had rung out, from a man by the door who was pointing a gun at him.

Suddenly Annie was by my side together with the three nurses.

"This way," she said. "Quick."

Annie ducked down and pulled me along a corridor and we heard more shots going off and people started screaming and glass started breaking and then Annie opened up a door with a key and pushed us all inside and slammed the door shut behind us. Inside the room, which was lit with a single fluorescent globe, were racks of medicines.

"The drug room," Annie said. "The door's solid steel. We'll be safe in here."

I only nodded. I was in complete shock. Apart from the fact that my heart was racing I felt strangely detached from everything that had just happened, almost as if I hadn't actually been there.

We heard people bashing on the door and screaming out for us to let them in.

"Do you think the same thing is happening at Gilda's?" Annie said.

"Probably." I slumped down on the floor against the wall.

"We had enough, too," one of the nurses said. "If only they'd waited, we probably could have gotten to everyone. At least the ones who were waiting."

For another two hours the screams and yelling continued and then, as quickly as it had started, it quietened. There was no way that everyone had died so quickly, so I could only presume that there were no more vaccines left and that people had abandoned the place.

"What should we do?" one of the nurses said to Annie.

"I think we'd better stay here for a while."

The next morning, we tried the door. Something was blocking it and it took both one of the nurses and I pushing hard against it to remove whatever it was and create enough space for us all to get through. There were two bodies behind it, dried blood around their mouths. Down the corridor were another three, and in the main room of the clinic there were many more. Some of them looked like they'd died from the virus, but most of them looked like they'd either been shot or beaten to death. I saw fractured skulls and broken fingers. Crude weapons were still in hands but anything valuable, including shoes and even a pair of pants, had been taken. What sickened me most was a young girl, around four, with her eyes still open and blood dripping slowly from her mouth. I felt nauseous but looked around for Boon, but he wasn't there.

Outside, at least another thirty people lay dead, scattered along the dirt road. All the windows of our vehicle had been smashed in, but when I activated it with a voice command it still started. We had to drag four bodies away from the road to get out and it was then that I vomited. I hadn't eaten in nearly a day so there wasn't much to come up, but I dry retched and spat against the side of the car until the dizziness and nausea left me and I could see again.

"Where are you three going?" Annie asked the nurses.

One of them looked at her as if the question meant nothing.

"Home, I suppose," another one said.

We dropped the three nurses off at their houses and then drove as close as we could to Gilda's house. Bodies were all over the place and I had to put the car in manual and swerve from one side of the road to the other to avoid them, bumping over arms or legs. Crows, rats, dogs and cats were already feeding on them and ran or flew off as our car approached.

We parked and walked as quickly as we could towards Gilda and Sam's, afraid of what we might find there. As we got closer, the number of bodies on the street increased. We turned a corner into their street and found people carrying bodies away. Those doing the carrying didn't look much more alive than those being carried. We went inside the house and found Gilda and about five other people out the back sitting around on the rotting lounges and old camp chairs.

"Thank God you're okay." Gilda stood up when she saw us and hugged us.

"Where's Sam?" Annie said.

"Inside, sleeping," Gilda said, and I felt my insides slump and a tiredness the likes of no other come over me.

"Where's Boon?" Gilda said.

"I don't know," Annie said. "We got separated. I was hoping he had come back here."

"No," Gilda said. "Not yet."

Annie and I decided to try to get back through the gates and go home. We were both exhausted, Annie especially, and she was starting to cough in a way which frightened me. She wanted to stay and help clean up, but I insisted we leave.

As we neared the gates, we were stopped by an army squad about a kilometer out.

"You can't go any further," one of them said to us

through our broken window, holding a rifle at the ready.

"We live in the regulated zone," I said. "We got caught here."

"I'm sorry sir, but nobody's going in or out for a week at least."

"I work for the military," I said. "Contact General Savage and ask him if you should let me through."

"I'm sorry sir, I have my orders."

"Listen, you can either let me through, or you can explain to the General how you were responsible for the death of one of his top scientists, Michael Khan."

He looked at me. "Just a moment, sir." He walked across to his group commander.

The commander came across to me with a retina scanner.

"Michael Khan?" he said.

"Yes."

"Just look in here please." He held the scanner up to my eye and waited a moment for the results, then said, "We're very sorry sir, please go on through. I'll let the guys up ahead know you're on your way."

"Thank you," I said.

"You're lucky," he said.

"Why's that?"

"They're about to napalm the whole place."

"What?"

"Yes. The Indonesians made a real mess of things. They're going to napalm it before the rats start spreading."

Annie gripped onto my arm. "We have to go back for Gilda and Sam," she whispered.

"When is it going to start?" I said.

"In about an hour," the officer replied. "You'd better get moving."

Chapter Twenty

ON THE DRIVE back into the city my whole body was raw and shaking. I felt as if I personally was responsible for the deaths of all those people. Annie was in the seat next to me, coughing, breathing with difficulty. If it hadn't been for her, I would have wanted to kill myself. I no longer deserved to live. I imagined myself dying from Rebola, blood pouring out of my nose and mouth, choking me. That is what I deserved. That is what I wanted to happen. How could I be alive when all those people were dead or about to die?

When we got into the city, Annie was coughing so much we went straight to the hospital.

"You've got pneumonia," the doctor told us when she came in with the results. "Due to your HIV-4, you'll have to be admitted."

Visiting hours were over so they didn't let me stay. I climbed back into the car and asked it to take me home.

It felt strange to open the door and walk into our empty

house alone, and I felt a shiver run down my back as I closed the door onto the dark hallway. I curled up on our sofa. The sky outside was dark with smoke and the horizon glowed orange like sunset. Ashes started raining down upon the windows. I imagined the inferno that was choking, suffocating, scorching everything and everybody in its path. I thought about Gilda and Sam, how despite all they'd been through they had still been still strong, hopeful... I could only hope that they died quickly, but I knew that probably wasn't going to be the case. They were going to die in agony, like everyone else we had tried to save.

For a long time I just sat there, my body turned to a lump of flesh, every nerve exposed as if I'd been flayed. My mind fell into a dark abyss of depression, thoughts barely registering. I imagined fire coming in through the windows, the intensity of the heat, the pain as my skin and hair seared. I tried to cover myself, put my arms over my head to protect myself, but I couldn't breathe. For a few minutes I held my breath, hoping that I could end it, that it would stop, that I would faint and never wake up, but my body fought against me.

The next morning when I walked into the hospital, I felt as if I was a passenger inside my own body, watching it go about its routine but having no control over or connection to it. I said hello to the nurses on Annie's ward but it was as if someone else were saying hello to them. And the way they greeted me back, their eyes and smiles huge and distorted, frightened me. They seemed totally unaware of what had just happened. I felt like I'd walked into a different reality — one in which a third of the population hadn't just been annihilated. For a moment I wondered if I was going crazy, if maybe it hadn't actually happened.

Then I walked in to Annie's room. She opened her eyes briefly and looked at me, but neither of us said anything. There was nothing we could say. I sat down on the bed beside her and took her hand, but she closed her eyes and within seconds she was back asleep; her mind unable to bear it. I stared at a poster on the wall of Annie's room that said "A smile a day keeps the doctor away" with a yellow smiley face on it, but it meant absolutely nothing. Anything human that had once existed inside me, anything nice or beautiful or happy, had been erased. The only thing I could feel was a total contempt for all things human, and a strong desire to revenge myself against those who had been responsible for what had happened. I hated myself, I hated the military, the government, and I hated every other person in the regulated zone — either for their stupidity, like mine, at not knowing what their government was capable of, or for their complicity if they did know.

There were only two things that kept me going: my wife, who I still cared about, and the overriding thought that I was going to change humanity. We had destroyed our environment and now we had turned our destructive nature upon ourselves. What would be left when we had finished? The same thing that was left on Easter Island after they'd chopped down every last tree and eaten every last bird and mammal — the mauled bones of each other?

The next few days were a blur of going in and out of the hospital. Then finally, Annie was able to come home, and I picked her up.

I was sitting in my office that night when Annie came in.

"Gilda and Sam are alive!" she said to me.

"What? How?"

"I just got a call from Gilda. Apparently Boon went for them. He was given warning, and the rebels had bunkers in case the army attacked. A couple of hundred people survived."

Tears of happiness welled up inside of me. I couldn't believe it, and when my shock passed I stood up and hugged Annie tightly.

That night I lay in bed staring up at the ceiling, Annie by my side. It was 3am but I was unable to sleep. The thought of Gilda, Sam, Boon and the others all being alive cut through to my cold, empty heart like a scalpel. Not everything was hopeless. Not everything was lost.

I thought back to a time before my parents had died, when we'd gone to the beach for the first time in my life. Iraq was almost entirely land-locked, so we'd gone over to Turkey for a holiday. We'd arrived at night, and my parents had gotten me up early the next morning to walk down to the water with them.

The sun still hadn't risen as we crunched across the sand and watched the gentle waves breaking. We took off our shoes and played the game of trying to chase the ocean, running after it when it retreated and then running for our lives when it came after us again.

Then the sun came over the horizon, turning the entire ocean into a glittering, golden sheet, and my father lifted me up onto his shoulders. My mother was next to him and she took his hand and together the three of us stared at the transcendent beauty, and I was filled in that moment with such a feeling of love and togetherness that I couldn't have imagined a more perfect world.

"I have to go back to the base," I said to Annie the next morning. "I have to try to convince the Prime Minister to fund Geneus so we can continue on with our germline trials."

"Okay," she said.

I put a call through to Bruno.

"If I can convince the government and Geneus to support a continuation of our original project, do you think Gendigm would consider investing even if they don't get a controlling share?" I said to him.

"What are you planning?" Bruno said.

"We now have everything we need to complete the germline modifications. I might be able to convince the Prime Minister to allow us to continue with the project and maybe even get funding from the government."

"How?"

"They trust me now. They think I'm one of them. I'll tell them that germline modifications are the only way we can guarantee survival of our population. The somatic modifications are just a bandaid — they're never going to be able to protect people from the broad spectrum of modified viruses we're going to be facing. We need to get to the core of the immune system and that can only be done from birth. If they want their precious population to survive long term, which I presume they do, that's what they're going to have to focus on."

"Do you think they'll go for it?" Bruno said.

"I don't know. They might."

"Can you convince them to accept the cooperative side effects?"

"Who said I'm going to mention them?"

"Okay. I'll put it to the board."

When I got back to the military base I was informed that the official story about the attack on the de-reg zone was that it had been carried out by the Indonesians. Our own planes had dropped the napalm, as by then everybody was dead anyway and we had to get rid of the bodies, but that was apparently as far as our government's involvement had gone.

The Indonesian government presumably knew that it was us who had released the virus, just like we did in Darwin, and realized that if they weren't careful we'd release something very similar in their country. It was the perfect story, and as General Savage put it to me, drunk and slobbering one night, "That'll keep the bastards at bay for a while!"

The morning after this Savage called me into his office.

"Sit down, Michael."

"How can I help you?"

"I've been sent a memo, and it says that just before the napalm drop on the de-reg zone you and your wife were caught leaving there."

"That's right."

"Would you care to explain that?"

"We were saying goodbye to friends." I looked at him without turning away.

The General stared at me for a few moments and then

nodded and lit a cigar.

"Would you like one?" He held the box out to me.

"No thanks. I don't smoke. There's something we need to discuss, though."

"What's that?"

"It's only a matter of time before Indonesia or some other country comes up with a virus just as nasty as the one that was deployed in this country."

"What are you saying?"

"I would like you to organize a meeting with the PM for me."

"What for?"

"I think we need a broader protection for our population. We need to convince the PM to provide us with the resources to come up with not only a somatic but a germline modification that will ensure the safety of our newborn children, that will make them stronger and fitter and more resistant to future attacks."

The General looked at me for a while, then stubbed out his cigar.

"I'll see what I can organize."

How could he be so calm? Did he really believe that they'd done the right thing? It was like staring into the face of a serial killer and getting absolutely no reaction.

As I left the office, I took deep breaths and walked down the corridor as fast as I could. I started shaking and went into my own office and shut the door behind me. I could only imagine what would have happened if the General had decided to investigate my trip to the de-reg zone further. Maybe I had become so useful to them they were prepared to ignore this one little indiscretion.

Everyone had died after all. Wasn't that what they wanted?

"Mr Khan, nice to see you again." The Prime Minister came over and shook my hand in v-space, and I put my avatar on autopilot, shaking her hand confidently.

"Thank you for seeing me," I said.

"Please, sit." She motioned to a chair and sat down opposite me. "The General explained a little bit of your idea to me, but I would like to hear more about it from you."

"As you know, Geneus's main project, before we started this job with the military, was to develop both a germline and a somatic gene modification that would greatly improve our overall immune system. I would like to propose that we are allowed to continue with that research and that the government helps us to fund it."

"I don't know if we've got the resources, Michael."

"Just think about the consequences if we're attacked with a biological weapon. Look, I don't want to frighten you, but the viruses we've been working on are only the beginning. A can of worms has been opened and there are some pretty nasty worms in there. We can't just react to each one, trying to find a somatic modification that will protect against it. What we need is a broad spectrum modification that will protect ourselves and our children far into the future."

"Won't our enemies be able to find a way around that?"

"I don't think so. We can enhance the ability of the body to respond to new viruses by improving the innate immune response. We can also make the response more vigorous so that it is more easily able to tackle new viruses."

"That sounds incredibly impressive, but it's a very long term strategy."

"Wouldn't you like your grand children and your great-grand children to be able to survive, whatever happens to this world?"

"Of course I would. Everybody would."

"What if Geneus invested half the funds?"

"It was my understanding that Geneus was running low on cash reserves of its own."

"I think we might be able to get some more investment on board. Especially if we have the government behind us on this."

"Let me run it by the health department and see where we're at with the budget. If there's a chance we can move forward with this I'll be in touch."

We both stood up and shook hands as if we were really there.

"Thank you for an interesting proposal, Mr Khan. I'll have my staff be in touch with you."

"Just one question," I said to Susan before logging out.

"Yes?" she replied.

"Why keep up the pretence of democracy? Surely you could keep people under control without it?"

"This keeps them happy as well," Susan said, with a completely deadpan look.

If we hadn't been in v-space, I might have tried right then and there to strangle her. I needed to keep my cool, though. I needed their resources. For the problem wouldn't end here. Susan Green was not the first leader to order millions killed, and she would not be the last.

Then I realized it probably wasn't her anyway. She was just a puppet for whoever was really calling the shots. Some military dictator. Some weapons manufacturer. Some group of incredibly rich and powerful people who didn't really give a fuck about anybody. Then again — who knew? Maybe it really was the only way to continue feeding people.

Three days later, I got a message from the Prime Minister's office saying Susan wanted another meeting with me along with a number of other members of her cabinet and staff.

The following morning, I ran through the whole proposal again for everybody's benefit. There were a lot of questions and a number of objections, but by the end of the meeting they had agreed that if Geneus was willing to fund half of the project, the government might be able to fund the rest.

That afternoon, I had a v-space meeting with the directors back at Geneus. Anthony in particular was not looking very happy. I'd managed to turn around what had been his triumph and use it to get my germline modification project back on track.

"I don't think we should be investing any more money in this," Anthony said. "I thought we'd finished with this project once and for all."

"With the government helping to fund it, and HGM industries putting in some money as well, the amount of money needed to get it finished is far lower than it was," I said.

I'd spoken to Bruno before the meeting and gotten the go ahead from Gendigm, on the proviso I would help them take over Geneus given the right opportunity.

"I like it," John said. "Government funding is always fickle. If there's a change of leadership, we could just as easily lose our military contract. This will give us some long term stability, providing we can get it to work."

"We can," I said. "We've already been successful using the bio-vectors, and if we integrate that technology then I don't think it'll be long before we have a viable human baby with an extremely resilient immune system."

"I like it," Klaus said. "We've spent so long on this project, I admire your tenacity, Michael. And it seems like all the pieces have fallen into place. How much money's required?"

"Without doing the exact figures, I'd imagine somewhere in the ballpark of a eight hundred million, a third of which will come from the government and a third from HGM."

"How are we looking, Zhao?" Klaus turned to him.

"It's pretty much all we've got," Zhao said.

"Tell me honestly, Michael, how sure about this are you?" Klaus said.

"About ninety-five percent," I said.

Klaus sat there thinking for a little while.

"What if it fails?" Anthony said. "What then? The company will be left with nothing."

"We'll still have our military contract," I said.

A week later, Klaus and I met with both Jan from HGM and a woman named Sarah from a government funding body assigned to us by the Prime Minister. After a six hour meeting we organized the creation of an entirely new entity that would be controlled fifty-one percent by Geneus, but that would be funded by both HGM and the government. All the necessary patents relating to the project would either be transferred or licensed to the new company, but if anything went wrong, or the company went bankrupt, or could no longer continue to operate, then Geneus would be protected.

The only caveat, Jan insisted, before agreeing to everything, was that HGM had first rights to purchase the company if Geneus was no longer able to continue to run it. Klaus wasn't happy about establishing a pre-set price for this, but he finally conceded.

CHAPTER TWENTY-ONE

SIX MONTHS LATER, I sat in the boardroom of our new company, EidoGenesis.

"So, do you think we're ready?" Klaus said.

"Yes I do," I replied.

Over the last six months we had modified hundreds of batches of SCID-hu mice. The first few batches hadn't produced the desired results, but then slowly, using everything we'd learned during our military trials, we managed to create mice that were resistant to first one disease and then another, and eventually we created one that was resistant to absolutely everything we threw at it.

From there we moved on to trials with macaques, and our success was replicated. We decided to call the first one Lucy, in homage to the *Australopithecus afarensis* who was once thought to be the oldest living relative of the *Homo sapiens* lineage. Not only was Lucy's immune system excellent, but she was extremely friendly and cooperative as well.

Lucy had been born just in time. Ever since the annihilation of the inhabitants of the de-reg zone, Annie's health had been rapidly deteriorating. First it was pneumonia and then bronchitis and lately it was simply exhaustion and depression. After the failure of our somatic modifications to cure her, my only hope now was that a germline modified child might be able to provide us with the antibodies and the natural killer cells that were required to treat her.

Three months later, Masanori and I drove through the area where, just a year before, tens of thousands of people had lived. After the napalming, I had assumed that the fence would be taken down, but all that had happened was that more people in the regulated zone had been made redundant and had been forced to move out there. New shacks and shanty towns were going up in place of the old and it was as bad as ever. The government had sectioned off any arable land, though, and food shortages in the regulated zone, which had been getting worse before the release of Rebola, were no longer a problem.

Annie and I had been in contact with Gilda on a number of occasions and had provided her and Sam with the necessary means to move out to one of the New Church havens, and they'd been living there for the last few months. I wasn't sure what had happened to Boon, but Gilda said the survivors were all lying low. All up there'd been nearly five hundred of them.

Because we required a lot of space for our new clinic and wanted to avoid any potential viral contamination to the general population, we chose an old hospital in a deserted rural town about three hours drive from the city. We'd had it completely remodeled and fully fenced off, and that afternoon, Masanori and I walked into the foyer. With over thirty rooms, there would be plenty of space for the new mothers to be comfortable for the duration of their pregnancies, and once the children were born, there would be enough space to house them as well. When the children reached the age of five, we had plans to reintegrate them back into normal society, but until that age they would be carefully monitored and tested to judge the exact extent of our modifications.

Today, though, we were here to interview and run physical exams on potential mothers. It wasn't just enough for these women to be fit. For the next five years they would be required to live in this facility and raise their children here, almost totally isolated from the rest of society. They needed to be sound of mind as well as of body.

Beatrice, the head doctor on the project, met Masanori and I, and we headed down to a meeting room together to interview the short-listed applicants who had just finished taking a tour of the facility.

First on the list was a woman called Mabel, and once we were all seated she was shown into the room.

"So, who's the father?" Mabel said as she sat down, her curly hair bobbing around her wide, smiling face.

"The father's genes will come from a random selection of men with IQ's over one hundred and twenty," Beatrice said, obviously not getting Mabel's joke.

"Well, I'm not the brightest cookie on the planet, but I'm pretty sure I'll be able to give them a good education, however smart they are."

"Can you tell us a little bit about why it is you want this job?" Beatrice said.

"My parents are getting old, and neither of my two brothers is any use for anything. We've managed to survive, but it's getting harder and harder to find work these days, and the last thing we want is to move to the de-reg zone."

"And who will look after your parents while you're here?"

"I'll send the money back. Food and board are included here, aren't they?"

"Yes, they are," Beatrice said. "Have you ever had any children of your own?"

"I've always wanted to. I guess I just haven't found the right man yet." Mabel smiled, dimples creasing inwards.

"No medical problems that you know of preventing it?"

"None that I know of. But I guess you never know until you try, do you? Although maybe I shouldn't say that." Mabel covered her mouth.

Beatrice smiled. "It's okay. That's fine."

Beatrice continued through the long list of questions and then Mabel was shown out.

"What do you think?" Beatrice said.

"I liked her," I said, thinking she'd be a lot easier to get along with than Beatrice would be.

"Me too," Masanori said.

"Okay, next," Beatrice called to her assistant.

All together one hundred women were interviewed over the next five days. I didn't sit in on all of the interviews but took turns with Masanori. When I wasn't there, I made myself familiar with the labs and took long walks in the surrounding desert. A forest had once grown around here, but now only dry shrubs grew in the eroded soil.

A month later, twenty women had been chosen and were living on-site at the clinic, and we were ready to impregnate them with modified embryos.

"Are you sure you don't want to come with me?" I said to Annie as I was packing my bags.

"Yes. I'll meet you there in a few weeks."

Annie had decided she wanted to stay and spend some time with friends and family before moving out to the clinic. It might be the last chance she got to see them. I didn't want to leave her behind, but I knew I was going to have no time for anything but work over the next few weeks anyway.

"I'm going to miss you." I wrapped my arms around her neck.

"I'm going to miss you, too."

That evening, I ran across from my room at the clinic to the main concrete building which housed the labs and the offices. An afternoon storm had broken around six and everything smelled sweet and fresh. A breeze sent tingles of cold through me as it evaporated the water on my skin, but it wasn't really cold, and I knew as soon as the rain stopped it would be a warm, humid night.

I walked down an empty corridor past some offices and took a seat in the small conference room next to Yolanda. Justin, Masanori and Beatrice were also there. Richard came in a moment later and sat down on the other side of

Yolanda, looking at her in a way which made me think his feelings for her ran deeper than just collegial affection.

"Well, all the bio-vectors are ready," Richard said, rubbing his hands together, referring to the vectors into which we had inserted the DNA to make the required changes to the embryos.

"What about the surrogates?" Masanori said.

"All ready," Beatrice said.

"We need them in top physical condition," Masanori said. "We'll need daily monitoring as well, rather than bi-weekly."

"That will be fine," Beatrice said. "It's already been taken care of."

Over the next few days we began the process of harvesting eggs from the women who were ovulating. Before I had arrived they had all been on a treatment of reproductive hormones to encourage several eggs to develop in their ovaries at the same time. We gave them trigger shots of chorionic gonadotropin to induce final maturation before Beatrice punctured their abdominal walls and sucked the eggs out of their ovaries.

The sperm we had chosen were from a variety of donors and the first step was to thaw it and mix it with the eggs. The newly fertilized eggs were then transferred to a growth medium at the right temperature until, forty eight hours later, each blastocyst consisted of six to eight cells.

Once they'd reached the right size, the developing embryonic stem cells were then separated into two groups: one to be modified and the other to be used as the control group. The cells of the group to be modified were exposed to our bio-vectors, which added the new DNA to the genome. The other group were put aside to be introduced as they were.

Once our modified cells had continued to reproduce, we ran tests on them to check for the integration of the new genes. Beatrice and Richard then removed the nucleuses of our remaining egg cells, allowing us to insert our stem cells into them: modified for some and un-modified for others. From these two groups, twins would be born — one child modified and the other not.

Each morning, after the women had been impregnated, I did the rounds with Yolanda, Beatrice and the nurses to check on them.

Out of all of the mothers my favorite was the woman called Mabel who we'd interviewed first. She had a smile so wide and quick that almost anything could set it off.

One day, Mabel grabbed my hand and put it against her stomach. "Do you think my babies are growing yet?" she said. Her bright eyes stared up at me.

"All the tests look positive," I said.

"My babies are going to be just like Jesus," she said.

"Why's that?" I looked at Beatrice for a hint but she was checking Mabel's charts. I thought maybe Mabel was referring to the modifications we'd done which were going to not only make the children resistant to disease but more cooperative and empathetic as well.

"A virgin birth," Mabel said, upset that I hadn't seen and realized the importance of this. "Except there'll be lots of them. And they'll bring much happiness to the world, like Jesus did."

"Yes," I said. "They will."

Then, on another day, Mabel looked up at me imploringly. "I'm going to be alright, aren't I, doctor?"

"You're going to be fine," I said.

"Do you promise? Because they made me sign all these forms…"

"I promise." I put my hand on her arm.

"Thank you."

Yolanda and I were working in the lab one day when my com beeped.

"You'll have to excuse me for a moment," I said.

Yolanda nodded without looking up. I walked outside into the corridor.

It was Annie.

"Why haven't you called me?" she said.

"What do you mean?"

"I haven't heard from you in two days."

"I'm sorry, I've been busy."

"You've forgotten about me already, haven't you?" she said, half jokingly and half seriously.

"Of course not. We've just been flat out. Is everything okay?"

"Pretty much the same." She tried to sound upbeat but I could detect her underlying depression. Despite the new medication she'd been on, Annie's sickness had gotten progressively worse. Doctor Baxter had told her she probably had less than a year to live.

"Don't give up hope. Please. I'm trying to do all I can for you. If these modifications work, and these children survive, then I'm sure we are going to be able to use them."

"You've been saying the same thing for years, Michael. Maybe you should just come home. Let's go away, like we've always said we would. Spend my last year together."

"I don't want to spend the next year with you. I want to spend the next fifty years with you."

"I really can't see that happening."

"Well, I can. Please. Trust me."

One Saturday night, all of the adults in the compound, except for the new mothers, got drunk together around a bonfire, and as I looked at each of them in the firelight, smelling the smoke and the warm desert night, I finally felt that what we were doing was right, that this was something that generations of humans from this moment on would be thankful for.

At the end of the night, there were just six of us left: Justin, Masanori, Beatrice, Yolanda, Richard, and I.

"What if it works?" I suddenly pondered the very real possibility.

"What do you mean, what if it works?" Richard said. "We'll help humanity and all become exceedingly rich in the process. What more do you want?"

"Will we, though? Won't we just be helping rich people? Geneus is never going to make this freely or even cheaply available. They've spent too much money on it."

"Well, at the very least," Justin said, "if our cooperation modifications work, then we'll be creating nicer rich people."

CHAPTER TWENTY-TWO

AFTER A FEW weeks, Annie came to join me at the lab, and she settled into life at the clinic easily. Despite the fact that she was tired a lot of the time, she was able to help monitor the mothers-to-be, and now that everything was progressing according to plan there actually wasn't that much to do.

Each evening, Annie and I would take a walk out into the desert, watching as the sun went down across the red, green and gray plain, admiring how the desert floor and plants seemed to hold within them a gentle glow even after the sun had gone.

Often, after dinner, the staff and the expectant mothers would get together in the lounge and watch movies, read books, play games or chat. Mabel and a few others became friends, and we'd frequently sit with them at mealtimes and play rounds of cards afterwards. Although Mabel hadn't had much of an education, she had a street shrewdness and an amazing memory that helped her win almost every card game she played.

"So, what do you think you'll do once all of this is over?" Annie asked Mabel one night as we were playing a game of bridge.

"I think I'll take my children and my parents and go and live by the beach somewhere. I'd like to run my own little business, maybe a bed and breakfast. Something that allows me to work from home. How about you two? What are your plans for the future?"

Annie and I looked at each other, and Annie took my hand.

"We might do just the same," Annie said, smiling at me.

Very early one morning I got a call from Yolanda.

"Michael, come quickly." Her voice was full of fear.

"What's wrong?"

"It's the mothers. Some of them are sick."

I dressed quickly, without waking Annie, and ran to meet Yolanda and Masanori at the nurses' station.

"How many are sick?" Masanori said.

"Four so far," Yolanda said.

"And the other sixteen?"

"They seem fine."

Yolanda and I shared a glance of mutual fear and then she led us down a passage to one of the rooms. My heart almost stopped. It was Mabel's room, and inside Mabel was lying down with monitors by her side and electrodes attached to her skin. Beatrice was putting a drip in her arm. Mabel's face looked thin and exhausted and her eyes were shut. The room smelled of sweat and disinfectant.

"Mabel's doing the worst so far," Beatrice said. "We've

just run the first set of tests on her."

I remembered back to how Mabel had looked just a few days earlier, when we'd played a game of cards with her: relaxed and smiling.

"What do they show" I said.

"She's showing every sign of being under attack but there's no obvious cause. We thought it was pre-eclampsia to begin with, but it's gone beyond that. The symptoms are similar to auto-immune diseases, but all the mothers test negative for those as well."

"Maybe the fetuses' immune systems are attacking them," I said. "Or the mother's immune systems have rejected them, and have attacked them. Or a combination of both."

"The syncoblasts could be failing," Masanori said, referring to the cells in the placenta responsible for regulating the flow of nutrients between the mothers and the fetuses and for stopping their immune systems reacting to one another.

"That could certainly make sense," Beatrice said. "Fetal immune systems aren't designed to attack anything, though. In the developmental stage they're designed to accept foreign cells, or they'd end up attacking their own organs."

"Maybe if the mothers' immune systems are attacking them, they've gone into a different mode of operation," I said.

"That's possible I suppose. The question is — what to do about it?"

As much as I wanted this project to work, as it was my last chance to save Annie, I could not have the death of any

235

more people on my hands. "I think the first step should be to induce abortion as soon as possible. The mothers should be our first priority."

"We can't do that," Masanori said. "We promised Klaus we'd make this work. This is our last chance."

"There's absolutely no point in it working if they kill their mothers in the process," I said.

"We have to contact Klaus and tell him what is happening," Beatrice said.

We put a conference call through to Klaus's com.

"Yes." His voice came on the line after a long wait.

We explained the situation to him.

"You can't let this project fail. You know that, don't you?"

"We understand, but these women are going to die," I said.

"They knew that was going to be a risk. They agreed to it in their contracts."

"What do you want us to do?" Masanori said.

"Do whatever the fuck you can to make this work."

When I went back to my room that night, after spending the whole day running tests on the sick women, I felt nauseous. Since that morning, two more women had gotten sick, so now there were a total of six mothers and twelve babies at risk.

Annie, who had been helping run tests as well, spent that night with me going over the results. Maybe the only way to successfully bring to term a fetus which had been modified as much as these had was to have a mother who had been equally modified. Maybe there was no way for an ordinary human mother to give birth to one of these children. It was like trying to get a chimpanzee to give birth to a human child. Neither their reproductive systems nor their immune systems were ready for it. We'd skipped a couple of hundred thousand years of evolution.

The only way to do it might be to somatically modify the mothers. If we could find out why the syncoblasts were failing, and somatically modify them, then we might be able to stop the internal battle that was raging inside them. That was going to take time, though. Time that the women lying in that clinic didn't have.

The next morning, I hurried over to the lab. The weather outside was overcast and windy, and I looked across at the desert surrounding the lab and felt an overwhelming sense of futility and fear for the future of this planet and its inhabitants.

I tried to remind myself what this project meant to me. How I wanted to change humanity. How humans were a group of egotistic tyrants, greedy monsters who would do anything for their own personal gain, while at the same time justifying themselves and even convincing themselves they were good people. Just like I did. I tried to summon up all my dislike of humanity and apply it to the women who were dying in the clinic so that I could feel numb to the pain of their imminent deaths, but what worked on an impersonal level couldn't be put into practice when faced with a dying pregnant woman. Especially not Mabel.

As I walked into the cool, white space of the lab, an environment I knew so well and felt so comfortable in, my mind and tumultuous emotions settled and I felt focussed and in control. Laboratories were as welcoming to me as my own home. In fact, they were my home in many ways

— I'd probably spent more hours in them than I had at home. There was something refreshingly impersonal about them, something so separated from the everyday mess of humanity that I felt elevated to another plane by them.

Everyone was working overtime trying to find out exactly what the problem was. In the meantime, we were trying to keep the sick women alive as long as possible, at least until we could safely extract their children and have some hope of them surviving. The most premature baby to ever survive was eighteen weeks old, and these babies were sixteen, so it was only a matter of a few weeks.

"What about if we disarm both their immune systems?" I suggested. "How about those new mRNA decay drugs, developed for auto-immune diseases?"

"It might work," Beatrice said. "At the very least it will buy us some time."

"We can't do that," Masanori said.

"Why not?"

"It'll interfere with our testing. We have to find out what's causing this, or we'll never be able to fix it. Besides, who's going to accept a modification that requires the mothers to go on immuno-suppressants?"

Over the next twenty-four hours, we were eventually able to find the cause of the problem. The receptors that usually responded to proteins produced by the placenta to down-regulate the immune response by the mothers were not doing their job properly due to the high levels of modification in the fetuses' DNA. This had launched an attack on the part of the mothers' immune systems and a counter-attack by the fetuses. We thought the fetuses themselves might be affected, but it seemed that in all but two of the cases they were in fact winning the battle, and it was the mothers only who were suffering.

Based on the tests we'd run, we decided the best way to tackle the problem was to use a somatic therapy application that would modify the mothers' immune systems and stop them from attacking the fetuses. This would stop the cytotoxic t-cell reaction from the fetuses, and both sides would call a cease-fire. But it was going to take weeks if not months.

Masanori and I had a conference call with Klaus and explained the situation to him.

"We have to make this work," Klaus said. "That is our priority. Start the somatic modification trials."

"If we do that the women will possibly die," I said. "I think we need to either administer immuno-suppressants or abort. Either way, the decision should lie with the mothers."

"We can't afford to start a whole new round of trials. I agree with Masanori — people will never accept having to go on immuno-suppressants, but if we can find a somatic modification they might accept that. Especially if it helps them in other ways. We might be able to throw in a few extras for them, like improving their own immune systems. If the immuno-suppressants interfere with the testing then we can't do it. I'm sorry, Michael. Find out what the problem is and fix it. If you can't get it working this time, the project is over."

After the meeting, I went into the room where Mabel was lying on the bed with a battery of medical equipment hooked up to her. Her round stomach protruded under the sheet like a tumor, slowly killing her.

"Doctor?" she said to me, her voice woozy. "Have you

got a cure for me yet?"

"Not yet. How are you feeling?"

"I'm okay, I suppose. I don't want to lose my babies, but I don't want to die."

"I know. I understand." I took her hand. "We might have to make a choice, though."

"What choice is that?"

"We might have to abort your babies in order to save you."

"No, please," she said, clasping her stomach. "Isn't there something you can do to save them?"

"There is, but it's riskier."

"How much riskier?"

"We really don't know." I was optimistic it would work, but I didn't want to give her false hope.

She looked at me for a minute, then looked down at her belly, rubbing it gently. "I'm prepared to take the risk," she said.

"Please don't mention this to anyone else."

"Why not?"

"They are prepared to let your babies die." I didn't want to tell her the whole truth — that they were prepared to let her die.

"I won't. How are the others?"

"They're okay."

"If I do die, my family will get the money, won't they?"

"Yes," I said.

"That's okay, then."

I went out of Mabel's room, and into the rooms of all the other mothers and asked them the same question. All the mothers said they were willing to risk their lives to save their babies.

I went up the stairs of the clinic and out onto the rooftop. The sky was dark and moonless and a whole universe of stars shone down upon me, gleaming like tiny diamonds in the black rock of a cave. If I was going to do something, I had to do it soon.

I stood at the edge of the concrete parapet and looked down to the paving below. For a moment I imagined myself falling through the air, crashing into the ground. The feeling of relief was immense.

I sent a message to Annie, who was doing the rounds of the sick women, and asked her to meet me.

Ten minutes later, she came up the stairs.

"What is it, Michael?"

"We have two options. We can force the mothers to miscarry, which will protect them, given it's the fetuses which are causing the problem, or we can try to administer immuno-suppressants that will potentially save them both. All of the mothers have said they'd prefer to try the immuno-suppressants. Either option will probably get me fired and maybe arrested. "

"What do you think the chances of them working are?"

"I think they're pretty good, as long as we can do it soon."

"Let's do it then. I'll help you."

"Okay, but I think it's better if you're not involved."

"Why not?"

"You're sick. We need to cure you. This is our last chance, and if we're both arrested that'll never happen."

She took my hands and we squeezed one another tightly.

CHAPTER TWENTY-THREE

AT 2AM, THE immuno-suppressant drugs I'd ordered arrived by helicopter. I met the courier a kilometer away from the clinic so that nobody would hear the helicopter landing. By now all of the women were sick, so I was going to have to administer the drugs to all of them.

After driving back to the clinic, I hid the drugs in a storeroom and went into the lab where Masanori, Yolanda, Justin, Beatrice and Richard were working, along with the rest of the team.

"Where have you been?" Richard asked me.

"Getting some rest. Why don't you all go and do the same? Justin and I can handle it from here, and the rest of you can take over from us at seven."

"We'll see you at six-thirty," Masanori said.

I knew that when Masanori said six-thirty, he would be there not a second earlier or later.

Justin was just as worried about the mothers as I was, and I explained to him what I was going to do, knowing I could trust him.

"You're crazy. Klaus will have you charged."

"That's a risk I'm willing to take. I can't be responsible for any more deaths."

"Let's get to work then," he said.

"No. You have to let me do this. I can't have you implicated."

"I don't care. Let me help you."

"No. If they put me in prison or fire me I might need you."

"What for?"

I explained to him how I hoped to be able to use the babies' blood samples, once they were born, to clone out genes for useful antibodies and culture natural killer cells to cure HIV-4.

"Okay Michael. Just be careful. Promise me." He put his hands on my shoulders, and I felt for the first time that our roles had been reversed: that now he was protecting me.

"I will."

The drugs couldn't be administered directly or the patients risked going into anaphylactic shock. There was a range of other drugs that needed to be given first, and I went about hooking them up to their IV lines.

I wondered whether or not to try to inject some of the immuno-suppressant drugs straight into the fetuses, but decided that it would be too much of a shock for them and that they'd be better receiving a smaller dose through the umbilical cord.

Once the first round of drugs had been set up, I asked Justin to keep an eye on the mothers and went back to the storeroom. From the fridge I took the vials of immuno-suppressants and set them out on the bench top. I took twenty syringes from the cupboard, carefully drawing one milliliter of the drug concoction into each of them. My heart was thumping, and every few seconds I thought I heard something and stared around me, but it was nothing. Just the wind outside which had started whipping across the dry plain of the desert, tearing at the leaves of the eucalypts in the compound. I slipped the syringes into the pockets of my lab coat.

By the time I was ready it was nearly six.

"Are you alright?" Justin said. "You look a little pale."

"Yeah, I'm fine. How are the mothers?"

"They're okay. None of them seem to have gotten any worse, at least."

"That's a relief. Why don't you go and get some rest? I'll wait for the others. They'll be here soon."

"Let me help you. You haven't got much time left."

"No. Please, Justin. You can't."

"Okay," he said. "Wake me when you need me."

"I will."

I waited until Justin pattered off down the corridor and then I went over to the station where Christina, one of the nurses, was entering some information into her com.

"How are they going?" I said.

"They seem okay." She looked up at me.

"You can probably cut the rounds back to every hour. Give them a chance to rest."

"I'll let Tania know."

"Where is Tania?"

"I think she's down with Mabel."

I walked down to Mabel's room. Tania was taking her blood pressure.

"How's it looking?" I said.

"No higher than it has been."

"Good. How are you feeling, Mabel?"

"I just want to sleep," she said.

"I know, I know."

I waited until Tania had gone out of the room and Mabel had closed her eyes again and fallen back to sleep. I took the first of the syringes out of my pocket and took the cap off the needle.

I injected the contents of the syringe into Mabel's IV bag then slipped it back into my pocket. I stroked Mabel briefly on the head and went out to follow Tania.

Tania was just finishing up with another of the mothers, Chloe, and I pretended to look over Chloe's chart while she did so. Once Tania had left the room, I emptied the next syringe into her IV bag and moved on.

I checked my watch. It was six-fifteen. I still had fifteen minutes. I did eleven more mothers in the same way. Just as I was onto the fourteenth one, Juliette, I heard someone coming towards me.

"Morning Michael," Richard said, coming into the room.

"Morning," I said.

"How's Juliette doing?"

"She seems to be fine."

"Would you mind coming with me?" Richard said.

My body flooded with anxiety.

"What is it?" I said, following Richard into the corridor.

"It's Jane's blood results. I'm a bit worried about them.

What do you think?" Richard sent the results to my public overlay.

"They look okay to me." I scanned them briefly. "I don't think it's anything serious."

"You sure?"

"I'm not really sure about anything at this stage. Maybe you should get Beatrice to have a look."

"Okay. Will do."

Then I realized that Beatrice might order another round of bloods, and the drug I'd just administered to Jane might come up, and Beatrice would be sure to investigate.

"You know what, it's okay. I think she'll be fine. Beatrice has got enough on her plate."

"Really?" Richard said.

"Yes, it's fine. If she shows any other signs let me know. Otherwise leave it. Beatrice needs to sleep."

By this time Masanori had arrived, so I had one more person to dodge, and I still had seven more mothers to do.

I went back into Juliette's room but Masanori was in there.

"Everything okay?" I said, glancing up at the IV bag. It was running out.

"Yes, seems to be," Masanori said.

I stood there.

"Are you okay?" Masanori said, looking up from Juliette's charts.

"Yes, fine," I said. I decided to do Samantha first, and then come back to Juliette. If I did that, though, there was a good chance Juliette's IV bag would be finished.

I ran down the corridor, but Tania was in Samantha's room.

I came out and saw Masanori coming out of Juliette's room. I slipped in after him and ran over to the IV bag with my syringe at the ready and injected it into the last hundred milliliters of fluid.

Just then I heard Tania outside, and before I knew it she was in the room staring at me.

"Is everything okay?" she said.

"Yes, fine," I said. "The bag's almost finished. I was going to disconnect it."

"You need to disconnect it at this end first, you know that, don't you?" she said, reaching for the catheter going into Juliette's arm.

"Yes, of course," I said, my heart pounding as I watched the last of the fluid along with the drug I'd injected into it run down into Juliette's veins just before Tania pulled the line out.

I eventually managed to do the remaining mothers, and then told Masanori that I was going to get some sleep.

I walked back to my room in a state of sleepless shock. As I rounded the concrete corner of the building and walked up a small path to the covered walkway outside the accommodation wing, nothing seemed real anymore. I opened my door, went inside and lay down on the bed next to Annie, who was asleep, and imbibed her warm smell.

"How'd you go last night?" Annie said to me when I woke up.

"Okay, I think. I've got to get back."

I dressed quickly, kissed Annie on the lips, and ran over to the clinic.

"How are all the mothers going?" I asked Yolanda, who was the first person I ran into.

"They seem fine so far."

"Do you know where Beatrice is?"

"No."

I pinged Beatrice's com. She was by the bedside of Juliette.

"How's everything looking?" I said.

"They actually seem a bit better this morning. By the way, Mabel asked to see you."

"Okay."

I walked down the corridor to Mabel's room.

She had her eyes closed but as I came in she opened them.

"Hello Doctor," she said.

"Hi Mabel. How are you feeling?"

"I'm okay. And my babies? Are they okay?"

"They should be."

"I don't want to lose my babies." Mabel clutched at her protruding stomach.

I sat down on the side of the bed and took her hand. "I know. We're going to do the best we can."

Suddenly, a loud, high-pitched scream filled the clinic passageways.

"Heart rates on both babies are dropping rapidly," Beatrice said when I ran into Juliette's room. "We have to deliver these babies, now. Let's get them down to the operating theatre."

Juliette was rushed down to the theatre and wheeled in. One of the nurses hauled up Juliette's robe and slathered her stomach with iodine. Another passed Beatrice a scalpel.

Within minutes they had sliced Juliette open, the hiss of the vacuum sucking up her blood. They removed the dying fetuses and tried to resuscitate them, intubating them and using the paddles, but it was no use, they were too small. Both of them died on the table.

I stayed in the clinic all day but thankfully none of the other fetuses were affected, and by that night almost all the mothers had improved. I couldn't help thinking that if I had gotten to Juliette a little bit earlier, and if Tania hadn't interrupted me, then we might have saved her babies as well.

I went back to my room exhausted. Annie was there, lying on the bed, motionless, and for a moment I thought something was wrong.

"Annie?"

She groaned but didn't open her eyes.

"Are you okay?" I said, going over to her and putting my hand on her.

She looked up at me. "Yes, I'm fine. How did it go?"

"Juliette lost her babies." I slumped down next to her.

"And the rest?"

"They're all fine."

She sat up and wrapped her arms around me.

A few days later, back in Melbourne, I took the elevator to the thirtieth floor of the Geneus building. My hands sweated. Klaus had asked me to come and see him. What was I going to tell him? When they'd done an autopsy on the dead fetuses, Beatrice had discovered the immuno-suppressants in their blood and I'd had to admit it was me. I thought back to the support Klaus had always given me, and how more than anyone he had been like a father figure to me.

I walked down the corridor to the glass door of Klaus' corner office and tapped lightly.

"Come in," I heard his voice.

I pushed the door open, and found Klaus with one arm flat on his desk and the other supporting his chin. I stood there with my hands behind my back.

"Sit down," Klaus said, not offering me his hand.

I sat in the leather and stainless steel visitors chair in front of his large black desk. Behind Klaus was a view across the city. A new residential tower was going up; cranes were hauling concrete into place.

Klaus leant back in his chair and crossed his arms over his chest. He shook his head.

"What the hell were you thinking, Michael?"

"I'm sorry. I just couldn't let those mothers die. Too many people have died already from projects that this company has been involved in."

"What are you talking about?"

"You know what I'm talking about."

"No, I don't. Enlighten me." He sat back and put his hands out.

"You really don't know?"

"About what?" He slapped his hands on the desk in front of him.

"What happened in the de-reg zone?"

"What do you mean? If it hadn't been for us the Indonesians would have wiped us all out."

"That was us. We did that. Our own government released that virus." I stood up. How could he not know that?

Klaus looked taken aback as if he'd just been stung.

"Have you gone out of your mind, Michael? Sabotaging our project, coming up with conspiracy theories. What the fuck is wrong with you?" He stood up as well.

"Klaus, please, you have to believe me. It was all our own military. The Indonesians had nothing to do with it. General Savage admitted it to me himself."

"They never said anything to me."

"Of course they wouldn't. It was classified information."

"Why didn't you tell someone? Me? Go to the press?"

"They threatened to have me arrested."

"I just can't believe this, Michael. This is outrageous. Why would they even want to do that?"

Just then I remembered the audio I'd recorded at my meeting with Savage. I had it on my com and sent it across to Klaus. "Listen to that."

As Klaus listened he sat down slowly, dumbfounded, shaking his head. He didn't say anything for a minute and then he said, "Michael, I'm sorry. I had no idea."

"Now do you understand why I couldn't risk those mothers lives?"

Klaus stared at me and I watched his whole face change.

"Yes. I suppose I can."

"I had no option. I just couldn't go through that again."

"I'm sorry, Michael. I really am. I don't know what's happened to me. I don't know what I've become. Trying to protect this company has made me into someone that I never wanted to be. I don't even know why I do it any more."

"If we can somatically modify the mothers before

pregnancy, I'm sure the next round of trials will work."

"I don't think I can afford to keep going. I've spoken to Jan over at HGM and they're not going to invest any more without taking a controlling share in the company."

"What are you going to do?"

"Maybe I should give it all away. I simply can't afford to invest any more money in this." His face was starting to go red. His hands clenched up in a ball in front of him. I wasn't sure if he wanted to hit me or cry. He slumped down onto his desk, but I couldn't bring myself to feel sorry for him. If it hadn't been for him and his greed we never would have gotten involved in the project with the military, and I wouldn't still be living with the guilt and the nightmares of having been responsible for the deaths of millions of people, including people I had loved.

Over the next few months, arrangements were made, as per the original contract, for HGM industries to take over the management of the entire project.

During this time I had a meeting with Gendigm.

"How long do you think it will take?" Bruno said.

"A year at the most," I said. "We know what the problem is now, and it won't take long to fix."

Four months later, thirty-eight healthy babies were born.

Annie and I went into Mabel's room and found her lying in bed with a tiny baby on either side of her wrapped in a blanket.

"I've decided to call them Rhonda and Rose," Mabel said, a smile of pure pleasure on her face. "After my mother and my grandmother."

That night, I went across to the serology lab. Everything was dark and quiet and I switched on the lights with a feeling of trepidation. I took a sample of Annie's blood from one of the fridges that we had tested just a few days earlier. I held it up for a moment, looking at the blood behind the glass and thinking how fragile we really were. And then I took samples of the blood that we'd taken from all of our newborn babies.

Over the next few hours, I isolated natural killer cells from the babies' blood. I thought about extracting antibodies as well, to see if any of them would have a higher level of affinity for HIV-4 infected cells, but it would take a long time and the chances were unlikely. They had never been exposed to HIV-4.

I purified Annie's blood sample to remove the infected T-cells and then divided it into twenty samples. Using the lab's AutoAnalyzer I added the enriched natural killer cells to the virally infected cells and assayed for a natural killer cell response using cytokine production.

In almost every case, the result was the same or less than Annie's own natural killer cell response. In one case, though, there was a slightly higher level of death amongst the HIV-4 infected cells. It was only small, probably not enough to cure her, but it might just give her the boost she needed to stay alive until the next round of children was born.

I put the cells in culture, knowing that within a few weeks I'd have tens of thousands of them, and I went back to my room and lay down beside the warm body of my wife.

"Where have you been?" she said.

"Nowhere," I replied. "Go back to sleep." I put my arm around her and pulled her in close.

A week after that, my natural killer cell colony was ready, and I injected Annie. Within hours her viral load was down. I monitored her for days, continuing to inject her with the cultured cells. For a while I almost let myself believe that this would cure her — but all I managed to do was to reduce the severity of her illness and hopefully give her a few more years of life.

Chapter Twenty-four

OVER THE NEXT three years, under the governance of our new company, now run exclusively by Gendigm, we were able to bring to term children that were resistant to everything from the common cold to HIV.

In the last few months I had been extracting a range of antibodies and natural killer cells from the latest childrens' blood and testing them for their effect on HIV-4. I had found a combination that seemed to not only attack the virus but kill it, even when it mutated, and we were almost ready to start Annie, who was now sicker than ever, on the treatment. The cells that I'd extracted from the modified children in the first round of trials had kept her alive this long, but her illness continued to advance and I knew if we didn't do something soon she'd be dead within months. If we were successful — not only her but tens of thousands of people around the world would be cured.

In the last few hours, though, Annie had started to develop a fever and we weren't quite sure what was causing it.

"How's her temperature?" I said to Beatrice. We had Annie in one of the beds in the clinic.

"It's thirty-nine," Beatrice said.

I kissed Annie on the forehead. "I'll be back straight after my talk. Are you going to be alright?"

Today we were hosting a small conference. Politicians, NGO reps, doctors and medical company executives had flown in from all over the world to hear first-hand about our success.

"I'll be fine." Annie smiled up at me out of serene eyes. The news that we might finally have a treatment for her had lifted her spirits in a way I hadn't seen for years.

I walked over to the cafeteria and made my way through the groups of people milling around, talking, drinking and eating. A number of them approached me and tried to ask questions, but I excused myself and headed for the podium where Rebecca, our PR officer, was setting up a microphone.

"There you are," she said.

"Sorry I'm late."

"All ready?"

"I hope so."

Just then I got a call from Beatrice.

"Excuse me," I said to Rebecca, holding up a finger.

I answered Beatrice.

"We've just gotten the results on Annie. It's the flu."

"Any idea what type?"

"No. It's not one we've seen before."

"You don't think it's come from the kids, do you?" There were now over a hundred genetically modified children and a hundred unmodified children living at the compound. Annie loved the kids and spent a lot of her time with them despite her illness. Two of them, Harvey and Shy, whose mother had disappeared one night, were her particular favorites.

"We're hoping not. We're running more tests at the moment."

"Has anyone else got it?"

"Not so far. Not that we know of."

"Okay. Keep me informed."

"I will."

I called Justin. "Annie's got the flu. One they haven't seen before. It might be from the kids."

"I'll get over there right away," he replied.

"Cross check it with the most recent flu strains that we've been using in our testing. I'll be over as soon as I've finished here."

"Will do."

"Ladies and gentlemen," Rebecca was saying, "if I could have your attention please. Welcome to EidoGenesis!" There was a round of applause from the audience. I hardly even saw them, my eyes focussed on my message overlay, waiting for a message from Beatrice or Justin. Then I thought it best to turn the overlay off. There was no way I'd be able to give a coherent speech otherwise.

"Today is a momentous day for us all," Rebecca continued. "After nearly ten years of research, we here at EidoGenesis have finally reached our dream of creating children that are able to withstand diseases that up until now have been deadly to humans. Let me introduce you to Dr Michael Khan, one of the leading forces behind this project."

There was another round of applause, and I looked out across the sea of people in front of me. I went up and tried to smile. "Welcome," I said. "This has indeed been a long road. Much longer than we ever anticipated. But then, given the millions of years it took evolution to come up with its fairly average immune system, I think we've actually managed to do it fairly quickly." I was speaking from a speech I'd prepared on my com and people laughed.

I went on to describe all the recorded benefits of our modifications and many of the suspected future benefits that we hadn't been able to test for, such as protection against cancer.

Then Rebecca got up and spoke again, and after a long round of applause everyone went back to the food and wine.

I jogged quickly back over to the lab. Justin was running the data that Beatrice had sent him, searching for matches between the DNA of the last flu virus we'd used in our testing and the one Annie was now suffering from.

"Just as we suspected," Justin said.

"Really?"

"Yes. A mutation of one of our flu viruses. The question is, what to do about it?"

"We need to modify our somatic processes, see if we can develop an appropriate response from the immune system."

"I don't know if we've got time to do that. Maybe we should inject her with the antibodies and natural killer cells you've been working on, and see if that works."

"They're not quite ready," I said. "And they're only

really tailored to HIV-4."

"If we can fix her immune system, it might be strong enough to fight this. Either way, we have to put her in isolation. If this thing spreads who knows what it'll do."

I put a call through to Beatrice and told her we were going to need one of the isolation bubbles, then I went back to Annie's room and told her what had happened and what we were going to have to do.

"Don't come too close," Annie said.

I wanted to go over to her and hold her but stopped myself.

Nurses came in with masks on and wheeled Annie out. I followed them down the hall. They put the bed inside the plastic bubble that had just been prepared and sealed it off.

I went over to Annie, slipped my hands inside the thin plastic gloves and took her hand. "My love. You're going to be alright."

She opened her eyes under a sweaty forehead and looked out at me through the plastic.

"I'm sorry. I'm so sorry," I said.

"Don't blame yourself, Michael. Even if I do die, which I don't plan on doing, being with you has been the most amazing thing in my life. I wouldn't have had it any other way." She smiled again, and my heart felt like it was being constricted into a tiny ball and I wanted to wrap my arms around her and protect her. I felt tears coming to my eyes.

"Why are you crying?" she said.

"I love you, you know that, don't you?"

"Yes. Of course I do."

My body was exhausted and lethargic, but adrenaline was flowing into me like the saline in Annie's drip. "I'm going to go and help Beatrice and Justin. We're going to have to inject you with the antibodies and natural killer cells that we've prepared and see if that helps."

"You need to develop a vaccine first, to protect others."

"We'll work on that, too."

"It's a pity I haven't been modified like the children," she said sleepily. "Imagine how strong they're going to be."

"Yes." I gripped her hand. "But you're strong, too. And you're not going to die. Promise me that, Annie. You're not going to die."

She smiled, almost blissfully. "Okay," she said.

When I got to the lab, Justin and Richard were examining blood cells under a microscope. On the public overlay was a genetic and molecular representation of the cells.

"It's in here," Richard said, pointing to a place on the overlay. "This is the virus. You can see how it's mutated from the original. These are the genes here."

"Why is it so much stronger?"

"The immunogenic epitopes have varied dramatically relative to the last several flu strains," he said, referring to the parts of the virus which elicit immune reactions.

"How is it replicating? Like a normal flu?"

"Yes."

"Annie's already been given the somatic modification, though."

"Yes."

"And it's not working?"

"Doesn't seem to be. At least not well enough. Maybe it's because of her already compromised immune system."

I lost myself in the work. It was all I could do to stop

my mind from tearing itself to pieces, but I had to focus.

In the afternoon, I went over the hospital again and sat by Annie's side.

"Tell me a story," she said.

"What kind of story?"

"I don't know. Tell me about the future. About what earth is going to be like when finally all of this is over."

"Well, to start with, there won't be so many humans on it. Maybe a billion at the most. I mean, do we really need so many people?"

She struggled to laugh.

"There'll be more room for other species. Maybe we'll even invent some. Not too smart of course, we don't want them threatening us. How about an animal with a habit of collecting garbage and piling it up in plastic rubbish bins? It could be their mating ritual — the fuller the garbage bin the better chances of finding a mate."

She smiled at me and I squeezed her hand.

"And trees and plants of course will be everywhere again. The whole world will be like one big garden."

"But without spiders?" Annie had never liked spiders.

"Definitely without spiders. Well, maybe a few, to keep the insect populations down. But they'll never go anywhere near houses."

"Great."

"And of course, people will never get sick. They'll live until they're about a hundred and fifty and then, when they're ready, they'll go to their local doctor and ask to be put down in a civilized fashion. They'll have their friends and family around them. Many will even choose to die together, with their loved ones, so that nobody gets left behind."

"I like that idea," she said.

"And everyone will cooperate. Helping others will hold a higher value for them than helping themselves. Everyone will have everything they need: food, education, accommodation, healthcare if they need it, which of course they won't, thanks to us."

She smiled again, but her eyes were starting to close and I could see she needed rest. I stopped talking and just held her hand until I could see her pupils racing back and forth behind her eyelids.

All the modified children in the compound had been sealed away in the accommodation wing. In order to access them, to draw blood and isolate the antibodies, we had to wear hazmat suits, as did the parents and staff who were looking after them. The children ranged between two months and three years old, and many of them were scared by this new scenario.

We decided to divide the children up into groups. The youngest, who hadn't as yet been infected with the flu virus, were sent off-site with their mothers to an old office building close to the clinic. The older ones, who posed the greatest risk, were also split up. We put them into groups based on their exposure to various pathogens and then divided up the higher risk subjects and separated them from one another. The problem was that our modified children had an incredibly high tolerance to disease. Even at a high pathogen titer, they showed no symptoms. And then, in the time it took their immune system to eradicate it, the virus had already moved on, and possibly mutated, thus staying alive. Separating them all and quarantining them would stop that from happening.

Richard had the idea of sending everyone out into the desert. We hired portable toilets and some large mobile homes from a place in the regulated zone and set up a number of campsites a couple of kilometers from the clinic.

This obviously wasn't going to be a long term solution, and I thought about how we could separate the children and put them somewhere they were going to be safe. Permanent adoption was an option, but with people's resources stretched, I doubted there was much market for it. Then I thought about Dylan and wondered if there was any chance he'd accept the children on the New Church havens.

That afternoon, I went across to visit Annie.

"How are you feeling?" I said.

"I wish you'd let me out of this bubble. Or that you would come in here with me. It's very boring."

"I'm sorry."

"It's okay. How is the vaccine coming along?"

"Justin's re-visiting our old somatic modification codes, and seeing how we can adapt them for this new virus. It's going to take a while, though. In the meantime, we're separating and quarantining everyone."

"How are the kids taking it?"

"A bit scared I think."

"All this trouble just for one stupid flu virus. I'm sure I'll get over it anyway."

"We can't be too careful."

"We haven't been that worried up until now."

"We never expected it would mutate so quickly in such a low population density."

"Maybe all your work will be in vain. As soon as the modified children become resistant to one thing, another will evolve to take its place. You can't beat nature."

Her head flopped back onto the pillow and her eyes rolled up towards the ceiling before she closed them.

"Are you alright, Annie?"

"Yes, I'm fine. Just fine. It's so nice out here."

"Out where?"

"Out here."

"Annie. Wake up." I shook her arm.

"I'm okay." She opened her eyes and came back to me.

My heart pounded painfully in my chest.

"Don't do that to me," I said.

"Do what?"

"Go off like that."

"I'm sorry." She smiled. "But Michael, I want you to promise me something?"

"What's that?"

"That you'll take care of the children."

"Of course I'll take care of the children. We'll both take care of them. Together."

"Especially Harvey and Shy. I know I shouldn't pick favorites, but they are my favorites; even Harvey who hasn't been modified. I want you to adopt them."

"Why don't we talk about this when you're better, and we can adopt them together?"

"I want to talk about it now. In case I don't make it. I want you to promise me that you'll adopt them, and that you'll make sure nothing happens to them."

"Okay, I promise."

The antibodies and natural killer cells I'd been working

on were finally ready and we had nobody but Annie to test them on. Her defenses were so weak that I feared her body wouldn't be able to handle them.

"What do you want to do?" I asked her.

"Give them to me," she said. "If I die, I die. I'm ready."

Beatrice and I looked at each other.

"Let's do it," I said to Beatrice. "She's not going to survive otherwise."

We injected her with the mixture and then I sat down in the chair nearby to wait, my heart on edge. For a few hours nothing seemed to happen, and then slowly, one decimal point at a time, her temperature started dropping.

For the next four hours this continued, and by 1am the next morning her temperature was almost back to normal. I was so happy I wanted to wake her, but she looked so peaceful, a tiny smile in the side of her mouth as if she were having the most wonderful dream she'd ever had in her life.

I fell asleep in my chair, but a short time later I was woken by the screaming of her heart rate monitor.

Beatrice, Richard, Tania and a couple of other nurses came running in dressed in hazmat suits, and I was ushered quickly out of the room. I stood behind the second door of the airlock, just able to see through the two small windows to where they were tearing open the quarantine bubble and giving Annie CPR.

I remembered the time we'd ridden out to that lake together and she'd gone off with those boys and I thought I'd lost her forever. And then I thought about all the times we'd spent together since then. Her desire, like mine, to do something good with her life, something worthwhile, something which she would be remembered for, stronger than the fear of death.

After nearly five minutes of CPR, Annie's heart finally started responding. I wanted to rush into the room, but I didn't have a suit on and I didn't want to leave the window to find one. After a few more minutes, Beatrice and Richard came out and closed up her quarantine bubble. They went out through a side door into the rinsing off area, leaving the nurses to monitor her. I knew I should go and find a suit in case there was any residue virus in the room, but I rushed in anyway, going over to Annie and putting my hands through the plastic gloves to touch her.

"You shouldn't be in here," Tania said.

"Michael, is that you?" Annie opened her eyes and blinked.

"Yes. It's me. I'm here for you."

"My chest hurts. I feel like I've just been run over by a bus."

She drifted off again, a smile on her face, but her heart stayed strong.

The next morning Annie woke up and her temperature had nearly returned to normal. Not only was she over the flu but it seemed her viral load was dropping faster than it ever had before and her platelet and white blood cell count was on the rise.

"How am I looking?" she said to me when she woke.

"More beautiful than ever," I told her, and then without even caring I opened up the bubble and went inside to hold her.

CHAPTER TWENTY-FIVE

A WEEK LATER, Sophie and Dylan met Annie and me on the landing strip of the island we'd visited nearly three years earlier, and they drove us back to their house. It was very similar to the one we'd stayed in last time: earthen walls and wooden roof, brightly colored rugs on the floor and rough-hewn furniture made on the island itself. On the verandah a few hammocks swung in the sea breeze.

That night, Dylan prepared us a dinner of roast chicken and home-grown vegetables, and after dinner we retired to the lounge room where he opened a bottle of wine.

"Where'd you drag that up from?" I said.

"It's probably the only bottle left in the whole world," Dylan said, and we laughed.

We chatted for a while, and then I came to the purpose of our visit. I explained to them everything that had happened at the clinic.

"We need to quarantine the children," I said. "If the government finds out what happened they'll either destroy the children or they'll want to keep them for their own purposes."

"What are you asking me? If you can put them on the New Church havens?"

"Yes."

"What makes you think this won't happen again? That they won't keep breeding viruses?"

"If we separate them, it won't happen. It is only because of the close proximity of so many kids that it happened like that. With a few children on each haven, that wouldn't be a risk."

"I'll have to discuss it with Rowen and the other leaders. Now's a difficult time, though."

"Why?"

"Rowen's funeral's on Saturday."

"He died?" I was shocked. Why hadn't Dylan mentioned this?

"Not yet," Sophie said.

"What do you mean?"

"He's going to euthanize himself," Dylan said. "He wants to speak at his own funeral, and then he wants to die and for us to put his body in the ocean."

"Where? Here?"

"No. He's at our main military base. There's an aircraft carrier and a sea-stead about two hundred kilometers from here."

We talked about other things for a while, then Dylan said, "Enough of all this talk. We should dance." He got up and changed the moody jazz to some upbeat swing music.

"I can't dance," Annie said.

"Of course you can. Everybody can dance. Here."

Dylan took her hand and lifted her up off the ground, cupping her in his arms and spinning her around the floor.

Sophie and I looked at one another, and Sophie reached out her hand and I took it and we pulled each other up. We clasped on to one another and started jiving around the floor, and I could hear Annie laughing for the first time in months.

"See, told you you could dance," Dylan said.

"But you're doing everything," Annie said, laughing again as he spun her light body around in circles.

Then a waltz came on, and I could feel Sophie getting closer to me. At first I kept a respectable distance, but then I looked across and saw Annie swaying gently against Dylan, her chin nuzzled up against his neck, and I let my inhibitions go and felt the tingling pleasure of Sophie's body pressed into mine.

The next morning we all went down to the place where the land met the ocean, and swam. I watched and cried as Annie splashed in the waves, laughing and then screaming at them over the sound of their relentless onslaught.

Annie wanted to see the macaques, and we drove out to the small patch of forest where they usually hung out. There were a number of fruit trees there, and apparently the monkeys never ventured too far from them.

We got out of the car and it wasn't long before we could hear their playful screeching.

"Toby, Sika," I called out. "Sika, Toby."

The play in the branches continued and we could see a group of them up there swinging around, resting, or grooming one another. And then I saw Toby — looking down at me from one of the highest branches.

"Toby, it's me. Toby, come."

"Sika," Annie called out. "Sika."

Just as I thought he wasn't going to move, Toby swung down from the branches and slid down the nearest trunk and came running across to us. He leaped up onto my body and before I knew it he was sitting on my shoulder and had his arms wrapped tightly around my head.

"Toby!" I lifted him down and hugged him tightly against my chest.

Annie came over too and we both embraced him.

"Where's Sika?" Annie said, half to me and half to Toby. "I hope she's alright."

Just then we saw another set of eyes peering at us from a lower branch, and then Sika too was coming across to us and climbing up onto our bodies.

We spent the next few hours playing with them and enjoying being in the forest.

"A couple of local scientists have been out here observing them," Dylan said. "Apparently, they've been seen helping out their sick. A few months ago one of the older ones got some kind of a fever and wasn't able to move for a few days, and instead of leaving her alone the others took turns in bringing her food and sitting with her."

"Not only that," Sophie said, "but apparently they've been seen helping other animals as well. There was a dog out here that got caught in an old net a while ago and some of them helped free it."

A few days later, a small plane carrying twelve of us circled over an aircraft carrier and a sea-stead in the South Pacific ocean. I gripped my seat tightly as we swooped down and thudded gently into the runway, and the engines brought the plane to a grinding halt just meters from the railing.

Dylan climbed down from the pilot's seat and as we disembarked he held out his hand to Annie. The other passengers all seemed to know their way around, and they headed off in the direction of a swing bridge which connected the huge floating hulk of the aircraft carrier to what looked like a floating town.

I stared up at the gray metal turret of the ship's control tower. At the top was a row of windows and above them three radar dishes slowly circled. Along the sides of the landing strip fighter jets stood at the ready. Groups of soldiers were doing exercises in front of them.

"Training," Dylan said, following my gaze.

"You're expecting an attack?"

"You can never be too sure."

"A few soldiers are hardly going to be able to prevent an attack. You're pretty exposed out here." I looked out at the ocean surrounding us in every direction.

"There are two submarines equipped with long range tracker missiles and anti-aircraft launchers just a few kilometers away. And under the runway here are another twelve F-37 bombers."

"All for this platform?"

"This is the main hub. If this place goes then many of our key people would die. But there are other places like this a few hundred kilometers from here that our forces could get to easily enough if required."

"And governments allow this?"

"Most of them are too caught up in their own problems

271

right now to worry about us. Our main concern is if some dictator takes over a well-armed country and decides to invade us."

We crossed the long swing bridge between the aircraft carrier and the nearest floating platform, and I looked down at the waves below, crashing against the hull of the ship and the floating pylons under the town.

"So do these things move around?" I said.

"They're designed to be towed if necessary. If the climate gets much worse we'll probably need to move them further south to cooler waters."

On the other side of the bridge was a small park with a four-story office building overlooking it. Dylan led us over to a golf cart. The streets were just wide enough for two golf carts to pass one another.

We stopped outside an apartment building. Our room inside was barely twenty square meters, but it contained a bed, a desk, a small dining table, a kitchen and a bathroom.

"Space is limited, I'm afraid. But hopefully this will do."

"This will be perfect." I went over to a window that looked directly out onto the ocean. Waves were at a meter and a half but ran underneath us without causing any noticeable effect on the stability of the platform.

"Would you like to rest, or to have a look around?"

Annie stayed to rest, but I decided to have a look around and I followed Dylan and Sophie back down to the street. It was a warm, sunny, slightly humid day, but the sea breeze provided cool relief. Dylan had some business to attend to, so Sophie offered to be my guide.

The town was just like a miniature version of any

normal town. Most of the fresh produce was grown hydroponically, inside greenhouses, although they apparently got a shipment of dry foods once a month. Water was collected from roofs and stored in the pylons which held the platform aloft. Their main source of food was fish, which they got from floating fish farms. Sewerage was treated on board and then discharged into the sea. The whole place ran on solar, wind and wave power, and they had communications-dishes that linked them via satellite to the net. There was a school, a university and a hospital, as well as a small shopping centre where people could get food and essential household items.

The next day, nearly twenty thousand people stood on the decks of the aircraft carrier. People had been coming in by plane all night, and hundreds of boats floated in the ocean around both the sea-stead and the carrier itself.

"Welcome to my funeral," Rowen said over a loud speaker when the noise quietened down. "Thank you all very much for being here. I've always found it disturbing that the dead never get to hear the eulogies at their own funerals, or get to have a say themselves, so I thought I might change that!" People chuckled, and then Rowen's brother came on.

Over the next two hours he and nine other people all spoke passionately of Rowen's love for life and of his unlimited generosity and optimism. Finally, Rowen himself came on again, and people clapped and cheered.

"Thank you. My life would not have been the same without you, especially those close to me. There are too many of you to mention, but you know how much I love you all. I've had the most amazing life I could possibly imagine, and the thing that has struck me most is how my life turned out nearly exactly as I thought it would. Unfortunately, even the bad bits! So, keep a rein on your imaginations, people, but don't be afraid to use them. Don't be afraid to imagine that however bad things are, a time is coming which will be better for everyone and everything on this tiny planet. Be kind to your neighbors, to other species, to each other, love one another, and above all, try to have fun! You deserve to be happy. You deserve to live in peace. So please, celebrate not my death but my life, and celebrate your own lives at the same time."

With that, Rowen held up a glass of Nembutal, saluted us all, and drank it down.

Not long after, his body, lain to rest in a small canoe covered in flowers, was carried up over the water by a helicopter and set upon the waves.

That night and all the next day, an endless celebration took place.

On the third morning, Dylan came to visit for breakfast and told me that there was going to be a meeting of the chiefs of all the havens, and that they were going to decide the future of the organization. He asked me if I would come and speak to them and explain to them what I needed.

A few hours later, I stood in front of an audience of nearly a hundred men and women and gave my speech. Most of them seemed receptive, but whether or not they'd accept the idea was something Dylan told me was going to take days if not weeks of negotiations.

CHAPTER TWENTY-SIX

A WEEK LATER, I sat at a large boardroom table on the seventy-second floor of a serviced office building. Surrounding me on the black leather chairs were the other members of Gendigm. It was the first time I'd ever met any of them except for Bruno in person.

I looked around the room at these people who were possibly going to be responsible for the future of human life, and wondered if what we were doing was right. Desperate times required desperate solutions, though, and the world had become a desperate place.

"We need some way of making sure we can eventually wipe out any *Homo sapiens* who do manage to survive, or at least sterilize them, and if we're working on too large an area that'll be impossible," Frank was saying.

"Hopefully, if what just happened at our clinic continues to happen, the modified children will start to create superbugs that will wipe out *Homo sapiens* naturally," Zoe said.

"I personally don't think that's necessary," I said. "In fact, I think we should create a somatic modification for *Homo sapiens* to protect them against that happening. A few tweaks to some of the modifications we've already come up with and I think we could manage that."

"Why on earth would we want to do that?" Marianne said. "We need to get rid of *Homo sapiens*, not protect them."

"Whatever we do, we definitely need to put some kind of safety control into our genome, so that procreation isn't viable," Graeme said. "We don't want our gene pool to be sullied."

"I don't know if that'll be necessary either," I said. "Our new species will be so genetically superior that any infiltration into the gene pool will die out naturally."

"What are we going to call them, anyway?" Jonathan said.

"How about *Homo novus*?" Zoe suggested.

Everyone looked around and nodded in agreement.

"What about if we altered the expression of sperm-egg adhesion receptors in *Homo novus*?" Jonathan said. "GV9 might be a possibility. That way procreation with *Homo sapiens* would be impossible."

"Or we could alter their pheromone coding, so that the *Homo novus* are only attractive to one another," Zoe said. "We could, in fact, make it so that *Homo sapiens* pheromones are a complete turn off for them."

"Not a bad idea," Jonathan said.

"It could lead to some fairly nasty cases of unrequited love," Graeme put in.

"Okay, let's work out the details of this in the lab, shall

we?" Bruno said. "What other ideas have we got?"

"I think we need to find a way to allow the *Homo novus* to identify one another in a way that is invisible to *Homo sapiens,*" said a biologist whom my overlay informed me was called James Sterner, of MIT. "Maybe we should endow them with vision for an added spectrum, and do something to their skin which reflects that, so they stand out to one another."

"I'm not sure that's such a good idea," Colonel James, an ex-military officer, said. "We want them to be able to infiltrate the population as safely as possible. Any exterior marker which allows them to identify one another could easily be turned against them by *Homo sapiens* and used to weed them out."

"That's why I think we need to find a way to wipe out *Homo sapiens,*" Frank insisted. "What's the point of going to all this trouble if *Homo novus*, or whatever you want to call them, is just going to be killed by the more aggressive species? I mean, look at us. We're a bunch of brutish cannibals who'd eat our own friends if we had to."

"There's also the issue of making *Homo novus* prolific enough so that they do end up taking over," Jonathan said. "If we don't tip the odds in their favor by removing some of the competition, then their numbers will never reach that critical mass."

"Given half a chance, somebody will probably try to come up with a version of Michael's immune system which doesn't incorporate our cooperation and empathy modifications," Zoe said. "Which basically means *Homo novus* will lose all evolutionary advantage, and be lost to the world just as millions of other species have been."

I wondered where all this was going to end. I felt like I had gone crazy; lost all sense of what was right and wrong. The immensity of it helped in some ways to disassociate myself from it, to remove some of the personal guilt I felt; but sitting in this chair, listening to the way these people were talking, as if wiping out *Homo sapiens* entirely was a difficult but necessary step, was against everything I believed.

What else could we do, though? If humans continued on as we were, we'd end up wiping out ourselves and everything else out along with us. Global warming had already passed the tipping point, and as much as I believed in science, even scientists weren't going to be able to save the majority of the population now.

They could have: eighty years ago, at the start of the century, there was probably still just enough time to limit the population or make the massive transition from dirty energy to clean alternatives. But we hadn't been able to cooperate. Poor countries blamed rich countries for causing the problem, rich countries blamed poor countries for their over-population and rapid development, oil and coal barons went about happily selling their wares as they'd always done, and meanwhile the majority of the population was just too greedy or lazy or plain misinformed to do anything about it, despite the fact that they could have.

It was a pity, really, at the start of the 21st century we had gotten so close to creating heaven on earth. A place where even eight billion people could have lived in relative peace and prosperity.

"I have an idea," I said, thinking that these people were starting to become just as ruthless as the military. If there was anything I'd learnt in the last few years it was that if we were going to change humanity we had to do it for the right reasons. We couldn't change humanity because we hated ourselves, we had to change humanity because we loved ourselves. Because we were worth saving. Because, despite a few minor flaws in our genome which had led us down the wrong garden path, we were an incredible species. Probably the most incredible species to ever walk the planet. Not only that, we were the only species with the capacity to save both ourselves and all the others.

"What's your idea, Michael?" Bruno said.

"Well, up until now we've kept our somatic modification of the mothers and our germline modification of the embryos separate. I think it's time we joined the two. I also think that we could create a further somatic modification that would protect *Homo sapiens* from diseases that *Homo novus* might create."

"If we do that, how are we ever going to effect the changeover?" Frank said.

"By integrating the changes to the eggs and sperm into our modification. If the modification does everything: alters the sex cells that so that any offspring are *Homo novus*, provides the necessary modifications to the reproductive system so that women can survive pregnancy, and protects against any viruses that the modified children might breed, then everybody will be happy. *Homo novus* will take over within a generation, and no parents will die from disease before their kids are old enough to fend for themselves."

Everyone sat there and looked at me.

"I like it," Bruno said, looking at me and smiling.

"Why would people take it in the first place?" Frank

said.

"They'll have to," I said. "Their own desire for survival and procreation will be turned against them. They'll be so worried that other people will be taking it, and that if they don't take it then either they or their offspring will be wiped out by all the new diseases going around, that they'll be forced to."

A few days later, I received a call from Dylan. The New Church leaders had decided they were willing to accept a few children on each of the havens. In total there were over one hundred havens, so there would be plenty of room for all of them.

Annie and I decided to adopt Harvey and Shy and go with them to the same island that Dylan and Sophie were living on. Annie stayed in Melbourne to start preparations for selling our house and packing all of our belongings, and I headed to the desert to help the mothers and children prepare for the move.

CHAPTER TWENTY-SEVEN

THREE MONTHS AFTER first being taken by ASIO, I am transported to a regular prison. Although my cell here is not much larger than my last one, at least I am allowed into the yard during the day and into the dining quarters at meal times, and have exposure to the other prisoners. Not that this is always a good thing — I've already been roughed around by guys who do nothing else with their lives but work out. I have made a couple of friends, though, and those friends have friends who do nothing but work out. So it's not too bad.

Finally, after nearly three months without any contact, I am allowed to see Annie. I pace around my cell all morning, wondering what to say to her and how she is going to react. How could I have been so stupid as to get myself arrested? Why wasn't I more careful? I should never have gone back to the city.

I wonder how they even found out. I presume that someone at the clinic, one of the nurses, told them about the virus that Annie had caught from the children. Maybe even Savage had me under surveillance — ever since I was caught leaving the de-reg zone. I'll probably never know.

I wait eagerly with the other prisoners for access to the visitors' booths. I want to hug Annie, kiss her, spend weeks alone with her, but fifteen minutes is all we've got. How ironic, that after spending years trying to cure her, I may never be able to live with her again.

Finally, my name is called and I can see Annie through the glass, walking towards booth twelve. I run down, not wanting to miss even a second. She is there, as beautiful as ever, even more so as she looks younger than when I last saw her. I press my hands and then my face up to the glass and she does the same. I stare at her, trying to fill myself with her image, every detail of her face, to take back to my cell. It's lonely here, and I have been starting to forget the smaller details of her face.

I take hold of the phone and she does the same.

"My love!"

"My darling!" Her voice goes straight to my heart and I can't stop myself from crying.

"How are you?" I say, sitting down and clutching the phone as if it were her.

"I'm okay. I'm better now. For months I had no idea where you were. Thank God you're okay. Are you?" Despite her youthful appearance I see new lines in her face.

"Yes, I'm okay. I suppose. I've certainly been better." I smile. "How is your health? Are you better?"

"Yes. One hundred percent. Baxter can't believe it. We've started cloning antibodies and culturing natural killer cells to help others."

"What about the children?"

"They're okay. They're fine. Harvey and Shy are here, in Melbourne."

"With you?"

"No, of course not. They're safe. It's okay."

"Why didn't you let them go with the others?"

"They're smart kids, Michael. They need an education. A proper education. That's something they're only ever going to get here."

I look at her and shake my head. I want to ask her more about the other children, where they are, what has happened to them, but I can't risk it.

"What's happening now?" Annie says.

"I need you to get me a lawyer. The best you can find. They're trying to charge me for terrorism."

"But that's ridiculous. They're the fucking terrorists."

"Shh, Annie, calm down, it's okay. We're going to get through this. Just get me the best lawyer you can find. Please."

"Okay. I'll see what I can do."

Before I know it, our time is up and a guard comes to take me away. I press myself to the glass one last time and Annie puts her fingers up to meet mine.

Three days later, James Harrison, a tall, handsome lawyer, comes to visit me. We sit in an interview room together. James goes over my case and explains to me the charges. Dylan, apparently, is going to be one of the prosecutor's main witnesses, having made a plea bargain in return for a reduced sentence and the safety of the New Church havens. Although James doesn't yet know exactly what Dylan is going to say, we both presume it is not going to be good.

James asks me to tell him everything from the beginning, and I go over every detail of the last few years.

When I finish, he sits there staring, nodding his head.

"Well, what do you think?" I say.

"I think it's all going to come down to intent. The government believes you did this on purpose. Did you?"

"No, it was an accident." He is referring to the virus that was created by the children, and the potential for them to create even more virulent strains.

"Then why didn't you hand the children over to the government?"

"They would have killed them or else used them for their own purposes — to create more bio-weapons."

"Either way — that wasn't your choice to make."

"No, but I think it was the best one given the circumstances."

"What are our chances of getting the other members of Gendigm arrested? That's what the government really wants — to get to the larger organization behind this. I think that if you give them the information they want and it leads to their arrest then they will let you off or at the very least reduce your sentence."

"No. I'm not prepared to do that."

"Why not? You're their scapegoat, Michael."

"If there's any chance of saving my project then that's what I want to do."

I can only hope that by now Gendigm has completed my work. At that last meeting, we debated using a benign but contagious disease to spread the modifications, but decided on a pill that could be distributed through the black market instead.

"Okay, if you're not going to try for a plea bargain, I suggest we try to tell them that it was a mistake made under a lot of pressure. That you did what you had to do, which was to quarantine the children on the New Church islands, and that to the best of your knowledge nobody has died. In fact, you managed to come up with a cure for HIV-4 and potentially a lot of other diseases. They've got nothing else to go on, really."

"What will happen to Dylan? He can't claim it was a mistake caused by clouded judgement."

"That's not your concern."

"I imagine they probably threatened him in the same way they threatened me. If he hasn't given away the location of the children, then I don't want him going down for this."

"If you don't want to spend the rest of your life locked up in a small cell, Michael, I'm afraid that's a risk you're going to have to take."

The next day, a guard comes into my cell and tells me that I have another visitor. I am taken to the booths again and directed to booth number seven. On the other side of the glass sits Sophie.

She looks up when she sees me but she doesn't smile. I look a mess and I know it. Prison jumpsuit, unshaven, my hair long and unkempt. My eyes starting to retreat into their sockets as the world closes in around me.

I slump down into the chair and pick up the phone. I don't even know what to say to her.

"How are you?" She shakes her head.

I try hard to contain my tears. "I'm so sorry, Sophie."

She shakes her head again. "How could you let this happen?"

I put my head in my hands. "What have they told you?"

"That you're a terrorist. That you were planning to run a terrorist camp using the New Church islands. Is that true, Michael?"

"Of course it's not true. What has Dylan said? Have you spoken to him?"

"Yes. I spoke to him a few days ago. For the first time in months. I had no idea what was happening."

"I'm sorry."

"It was horrible." She wipes away a tear.

"And what has Dylan said? Has he given away the location of the children?"

"No. Not yet. They're trying to get him to give up the children in return for his release. They say that if he does then he will get off. They're acting like we're some kind of terrorist organization — a threat to the country. Other government and corporate run states, their allies, are supporting them."

"And is he going to give up the children?"

"No. He doesn't want to. They've been asking him about a group called Gendigm, though. They say you're working for them. That you're trying to destroy humanity. Is that true, Michael?"

"Of course it's not true."

"Well, apparently if you tell them what they want to know about Gendigm, they will let you both go."

"Yes, I know."

I am starting to wonder how much the government has

said to Sophie, and how much of what she is telling me is what they've told her to tell me. Are they listening in on everything we are saying? It hardly matters any more. I have to protect Gendigm. They have the code for the modifications. They are the only ones who can spread it around the world and make it freely available. Even if governments spread propaganda about how dangerous these children are, nobody will risk not modifying their children this way if they have a choice. Thousands of children like the ones we've already created are hopefully already being conceived. Within a single generation the whole of humanity will be different.

"Michael, please," Sophie says. "Dylan doesn't want to testify against you, and he doesn't want to give up the children, but if you won't tell them about Gendigm then he'll have to."

"He won't have to," I say.

"Yes, but if he doesn't they'll start a full scale war on the New Church."

"They're bluffing," I say. "I don't even think they have the resources."

"How can you be so sure?"

I don't know what to say to her, and while I'm trying to work it out our time is up.

CHAPTER TWENTY-EIGHT

I SIT AT a well worn wooden desk before a judge and jury. Due to the nature of the proceedings, the public has not been permitted to enter, but a row of eager, seagull-like reporters sits in the media stand. To my right sits James, my lawyer, Karen, James's legal assistant, and Barnaby, my trial lawyer.

"If it pleases your honor…" Danny Brown, the short, thick-necked, prosecutor is saying.

"Go ahead," says Justice Granger, a thin, bearded man. He waves his hand at Mr Brown.

"Ladies and gentlemen of the jury," Danny starts, "the evidence that I am going to be presenting before this court over the next few weeks will show beyond the shadow of a doubt that this man who sits before you today, Mr Michael Khan, is guilty of seven charges of terrorist activity.

"For eight years, Mr Khan has been involved in creating genetic modifications for the human immune system that will endow those born with them with far more resistance to diseases than normal. Now, you may think at first that such a modification would be wonderful, and no doubt Mr Khan's defense will try to convince you that Mr Khan had only the public's best interests at heart when he created this procedure. Until, however, you realize how such modified humans could quite easily be responsible for breeding strains of viruses that might be deadly to the rest of us.

"Not only has Mr Khan modified these individuals to be highly resistant to viruses, but he has also modified them to be extremely cooperative. So — a highly cooperative group of individuals who have a much higher than normal tolerance to disease... Mr Khan's defense will tell you that these modifications were being created for the benefit of humanity, but our evidence will clearly show how he was planning all along to use individuals modified in this way as weapons of destruction.

"Let's go back to the beginning, though. Over thirty years ago, Michael Khan met another student, Dylan Hume, at Melbourne University. Michael and Dylan were roommates and, as they were both studying genetics, they became friends. You may know of Dylan Hume — he is now one of the leaders of the organization known as the New Church. The New Church believes that a total collapse of society is upon us and, as such, owns many self-sufficient islands and sea-steads around the world. Now, when Mr Khan and those he was working with needed a safe place to raise and train their genetically enhanced children, what better place to use than self-sufficient sea-steads whose destination almost nobody knows about?"

As Danny Brown is speaking, I keep an eye on the

faces of the jury. Judging by their expressions, my chances of getting off are in free fall. I want to get up and explain to the jury and even the press, right then and there, why exactly I did what I did, how it was all their fault as much as mine, how I was only trying to do what was best for the planet as a whole. Not for the current generation of *Homo sapiens* maybe, but for the countless other species with whom we share this planet and even for the future of humanity itself.

Once Danny is finished the judge calls a short recess, and my team and I retire to a small, wood-paneled room off to the side of the courtroom.

I sit shaking my head. Karen puts a hand on my back.

"It's okay," she says. "They always make it sound ten times worse than it is. That's their job."

"Well, are you still ready to go ahead with our plan?" Barnaby says.

"I think it's the best hope we've got," I say.

Fifteen minutes later, Barnaby stands up in front of the judge and jury. He is young, only thirty-seven, but he has a reputation as one of the best trial lawyers in the country. I watch him walk up to the jury, tall and good-looking. Not good-looking in a swarthy, seductive sense, but in an innocent, kind-of-guy-you'd-like-to-marry-your-daughter sense, which makes almost everything he says seem like the truth.

"This shouldn't be a trial about my client, Michael Khan," Barnaby says to the judge and jury, holding out his hands, "and how he supposedly wanted to destroy the world through genetically modifying a highly-cooperative, highly disease-resistant army. That is just a paranoid hallucination on the part of our government. The true crime, ladies and gentlemen, committed by the government itself, as well as every single one of us, is what we are doing to this planet and to each other. And that is what this trial should really be about.

"Given that it isn't, though, and that instead we are here wasting our time trying to convict an innocent man — over the next several weeks we will show how, far from being a criminal who deserves to be locked away for the rest of his life, Michael Khan is a dedicated scientist who was using his intricate knowledge of science to create a better world for humanity. In case some of you, like the prosecution, haven't noticed, the world, ladies and gentlemen, is in a very sorry state.

"Now, my client here, understanding what is going on probably better than almost anybody else in the world, decided, along with a number of other scientists, to do something about this. They decided to genetically modify humans not to be smarter, or stronger, or better at sports as many other companies are doing, but to modify humanity to be more cooperative and empathetic and resistant to diseases. Does this sound like the work of an evil genius to you, ladies and gentlemen? Would any of you, upon meeting a person like this on the street, say "Oh my God, who in God's name created this terrible abomination?" If you were to meet a person who no longer got sick from AIDS, or cancer, or the flu, or malaria, or HIV-4, or almost any other disease, would you want them destroyed?"

"Over the next few weeks, we will introduce a wide range of scientific experts who will back up almost every aspect of Michael's world view, and we will prove how

Michael's plan, to create a more cooperative, more disease-resistant species, far from being part of a plan for world domination by a race of super-soldiers, is actually part of a very well thought-out scientific plan to save humanity from themselves and their very self-destructive habits, and to save what's left of the rest of this planet at the same time. Now, if that sounds like a good idea to you — then watch out. The government will probably try to lock you up too."

Some chuckles emanate from the jury and all of a sudden, far from living in fear as I have for last six months, my heart glimpses the tiniest possibility of hope.

"Now, the prosecution will try to convince you that everything Michael has been working on over the last ten years was guided by his over-riding desire to destroy humanity. Why, ladies and gentleman, would a man who wanted to destroy humanity, an extremely intelligent and capable man like Michael Khan, go about trying to destroy humanity by creating a cure for many known diseases? And why would he then try to bring up children from birth to use in fifteen or twenty years as biological agents? Wouldn't a man with the skills and knowledge that Michael obviously possesses, find it far quicker and more economical to simply develop one or two highly contagious diseases and create a vaccine for those diseases that could easily be applied to a select group of "soldiers", who Michael wished to keep alive, including, presumably, himself and his family members?"

We were warned before giving our case that any mention of the work I did for the military would land us all in prison without a trial. Barnaby wants to stretch that ruling as far as absolutely possible, but hopefully not to overstep it.

Barnaby continues: "It is my duty here to prove to you over the next few weeks that there are far easier ways to achieve what the government is accusing Michael of, and, that if someone like Michael wanted to do this, he could easily have done so in a much more efficient manner. Now, either Michael is stupid, which evidence will show he is clearly not, or he is not guilty of the crimes that he is being charged for."

Barnaby goes on for another fifteen minutes, and by the time he's finished Mr Brown's brow is furrowed and he is whispering urgently to one of his assistants.

"Thank you," I say, when we return to the small room off the side of the court again.

"Don't get too excited," Barnaby says. "We've still got a long way to go yet, and it's going to be an uphill battle."

"It's going to come down to whether or not the jury considers your actions terrorism," James says. "It's a very good thing you didn't talk to the government more than you did while you were locked up, or they might have tried to mount a different case against you."

That night, back in prison, I am taken to an interrogation room where Don is waiting for me with a cappuccino and a slice of what he tells me is his wife's best chocolate cake, although for all I know he could have bought it at the staff cafeteria. James is there with me.

"How can I help you?" I say to Don, stuffing my mouth with cake.

"We were wondering if you've reconsidered?" Don says. "And want to offer you one last chance to do so."

"Reconsidered what?" I say, although I know exactly

what he's talking about.

"Reconsidered disclosing everything you know about Gendigm. They're the ones really behind this, and we're pretty sure that even with you locked away they'll continue on with their plans. They're hardly going to care about one scientist, are they?"

"I'm really not sure."

"What is it you think they're trying to achieve, Michael? Why is it that you're so interested in protecting them? Do you really think they're doing the best thing for humanity, for purely altruistic purposes? Don't you think they might have a hidden agenda of their own?"

This is an option I've considered, and now Don makes me consider it again. "Such as?" I say.

"Such as controlling the world once everyone else on it has been modified to be more cooperative. You don't think that's a dangerous situation? One that will give whoever is in charge an unfair advantage, if they're not actually modified themselves?"

"And why would they want to do that?"

"Don't be naive, Michael. That's what humans have always wanted: power. You think something like this wouldn't give someone an almost unlimited amount of power?"

"I don't think you understand the way our modifications work. Those who are modified aren't just going to follow anyone. Just because they're more cooperative, doesn't make them stupid. It just means that instead of trying to take for themselves all the time they're just as concerned about the welfare of others. The welfare of the group, and of other groups."

"So you're prepared to sacrifice everything for these people, are you? Not only your own life but Dylan's life, the lives of the people in the New Church, and the lives of the children you've already modified?"

"I'm not the one threatening them."

"You leave us no choice, Michael."

"We always have a choice. And you're making yours."

"Listen, Michael, I know you're angry. I know some pretty bad things have happened to you, and that you think this government is responsible for them. But that doesn't mean you should give up on us. That doesn't mean you should become worse than the people you're trying to destroy. If you let that happen, you'll never forgive yourself."

"I'm never going to forgive myself for what I've done as it is." I think about all those people in the de-reg zone who were wiped out by the virus I helped create.

"Well think about those children then. Harvey and Shy, is it? The ones you wanted to adopt?"

"How do you know about them?"

"Wouldn't you like to protect them and all the other children? Wouldn't you like to protect your friend Dylan, and the New Church? The people who have done so much for you? Are you really prepared to give everything up? Because you know we'll go after them, don't you? If we can't get at Gendigm, we'll have no other option but to destroy the New Church. Someone has to pay, Michael. It's the way things work. You understand that, don't you?"

I nod.

"Well, have another think about it," Don says, and he leaves the room.

"What do you think?" I say to James.

"Let's hope he's bluffing," James says. "I'm sure the government has probably got a lot more important things on their plate than attacking the New Church just to kill a hundred children. Especially seeing as the code for the modifications is out there already anyway."

I breathe a sigh of relief. It's hard to think straight when you're locked up in a cell every day, and I depend on James for support.

The court room comes to life again at 10am the next morning.

Anthony Simons, my old nemesis from Geneus, is on the stand, and Mr Brown runs him through his history with me and our project.

"Did Dr Khan ever mention that his wife had HIV-4?" Danny says smugly.

"No, he didn't."

"Was it his duty to disclose this information to the company?"

"He wasn't required to, but it certainly would have made a difference in how we viewed the project. We believed that Dr Khan was carrying it out because he truly believed he could make it work, and not just because he was interested in finding a cure for his wife."

"And he kept this information hidden from everyone at Geneus the whole time?"

"Yes, as far as I know."

"Why do you think he did this?"

"Objection," Barnaby calls again. "This witness can't possibly know what was in the mind of my client."

296

"Overruled," the judge says. "I'll allow it."

I am starting to get the impression that the judge is on the side of the prosecution. I wonder how many strings have been pulled, although I am actually a little surprised that I am getting a trial at all. With the country as it is at the moment, nobody would really care too much if an obscure geneticist went missing. Then I wonder if all this isn't just an elaborate ploy to get me to disclose my knowledge of Gendigm, and to tell them everything I know. Surely torture would be more efficient. But maybe they're worried I've got contacts — and that torture of their own citizens would turn people against them. The whole thing is starting to feel like a farce.

"There were many times in the life of the project when we were about to shut it down," Anthony continues. "The project almost sent the company bankrupt, and it was only because Michael kept convincing our CEO, Klaus Hofferman, that he was so close to finding a solution, that we continued. On many of these occasions, it turned out Michael was no closer to finding a solution than he'd ever been. He was stringing us along, risking the entire company and the jobs of all its employees in the meantime. If we'd known that his wife had HIV-4, and that was his true motivation for wanting to keep the project alive, we would almost certainly have shut it down."

"Okay, thank you, Mr Simons. That's all for now," Mr Brown says.

"Mr Savoir, do you have anything you would like to ask Mr Simons?" The judge looks over at Barnaby without raising his head.

"Yes indeed, your honor, I have plenty of things I'd like

to ask the witness."

"Well, get on with it, then." The judge motions impatiently to the floor.

Barnaby takes his time, checking some last minute notes, and then just before it seems the judge might explode in anger, he glides on over to the stand.

"Mr Simons, thank you for taking the time to come in today," Barnaby says. Anthony nods, his face slightly twisted — whether out of displeasure or fear I'm not quite sure. "Well, first up, I'd like to ask you a bit more about why you think it was necessary for Michael to disclose that his wife had HIV-4 to Geneus."

"As I said, if he had told us that, we probably wouldn't have continued with the research."

"But what if Michael truly did believe he could make this project work? In fact, hasn't time proven that he could? Doesn't he now have a fully functional immune system modification that makes its bearers resistant to many diseases ordinary people aren't resistant to? Hasn't he cured his wife of HIV-4, and isn't that same treatment now being used on others?"

"Yes, but that's not the point. The point is, at what cost to the company? And how was that achieved?"

"Was Michael under any sort of legal obligation to disclose this information to the company?"

"No."

"Did you disclose to the company every detail of your life at the time?"

"Anything which might have been relevant to company decisions I would have."

"So did you disclose the fact that your father-in-law had

a fairly sizable investment in Geneus, no doubt at your suggestion, and that if the company went bankrupt due to Michael's immune-system project he would have lost a lot of money?"

Anthony looks worried and glances around the room for a moment. "I never suggested that he make that investment, and none of my dealings within the company had anything to do with it. Plenty of board members had shares in the company. I did myself. So did Michael."

"Not a fifteen percent share, though? Around two hundred million dollars at the time."

"Not that big a share, no. But again, that did not affect my behavior in the company in any way."

"But you think the fact that Michael's wife had HIV-4 did affect his behavior?"

"He was putting the whole company at risk."

"Yes or no please, Mr Simons."

"Yes."

"So, what you're saying, then, is that the only reason Michael was involved in this project was to save his wife?"

"Maybe not the only reason. But certainly one of the main reasons."

"So it wasn't, then, as the prosecution is suggesting, to wipe out humanity?"

Anthony is caught. He looks over towards the prosecution then turns back to Barnaby.

"Answer the question please, Mr Simons," the judge says, in what appears to be his first swing to my side.

"Well I don't know—"

"Yes or no please, Mr Simons," Barnaby says.

"No."

"Thank you, Mr Simons. That will be all."

Barnaby smiles as he comes back to our bench and I can't help smiling with him. No doubt Mr Brown was trying to use Anthony to shed doubt on the morality of my character, but Barnaby skillfully turned this against them. I wait to see if Danny will get up again to question Anthony further, but he doesn't.

Next up on the stand is Richard. I am not exactly sure why Richard has decided to turn against me. Maybe ASIO threatened him as well. Or maybe he was the one who turned me in in the first place.

Richard is sworn in and after going through the questions of how we met, Mr Brown says, "Mr Grant, can you please tell us about the first experiment you conducted using Mr Khan's immune system modifications?"

Richard tells them how the mothers of our first batch of modified embryos were attacked by the fetuses growing inside them, and how two of the fetuses died. Danny pulls some images up on the screen of the dead babies.

"Are these the babies in question?" Danny says.

"Yes," Richard replies.

"So what did you do when these problems started? Did you give them abortions?"

"No. We tried to keep the mothers alive."

"And were you risking the women's lives by doing so?"

"Yes, we were."

"So why didn't you give them abortions?"

"Michael said they were his instructions. I believe they came from Klaus Hofferman, the CEO of Geneus."

"But at the time Michael was in charge over there?"

"Yes."

"So he could have ordered them to be aborted?"

"He may have lost his job, but yes, he could have."

"Was there anything else that could have been done to better protect those women?" Danny says.

"Yes, I believe there was. I believe that we started the human trials too quickly. I think we should have conducted at least another year of animal trials first. In the animal trials that we did there were a number of deaths. I think this should have been investigated further."

"And why wasn't it?"

"I'm not sure. It was Michael's decision. He wanted to push ahead with the human trials as quickly as possible."

"Any idea why?"

"There could have been a number of reasons. Scientists like to make decisions based on the greater good, though. What will serve the greater good. And in this case maybe that's what Michael was doing — risking a few to save the many."

"Couldn't it have been to save his wife? Or for the financial state of the company?"

"Objection," cries Barnaby.

"Sustained," says the judge, but the question still hangs ominously in the air, and Danny leaves it there for a few moments.

"Well, on to more recent events," Danny says eventually. "Can you please describe to us in detail the events surrounding the recent problems at the EidoGenesis compound?"

Richard goes on to tell the court everything that happened.

"So, was this something which you think could have

been prevented?"

"We never believed it would be a risk," Richard says, referring to the viral outbreak and the need to quarantine the children.

"And how big a threat do you believe these children might pose — to the general population?"

"The virus that attacked Michael's wife was fairly benign, but given that it evolved so quickly in such a small group of modified children, I'd say the risk that they'll create something much more serious is quite high. Especially if there are more of them."

"If you had been in charge, what would have you done in the situation?"

"I would have alerted the authorities."

"Thank you. Your honor, that's all from me."

"Mr Savoir. Any questions?" the judge says, a weariness in his tone as if he is no longer happy with Barnaby and his choice of client.

"Yes, just a couple, your honor."

Barnaby goes and stands in front of Richard. "Wasn't it actually Michael who decided to inject the mothers with immuno-suppressants, defying his orders and helping to save both the mothers and the children?"

"Two of the children died," Richard says. "So he didn't save them all. And our instructions were to try to save the mothers using somatic modification. Something we might have been able to do, had we been given a chance. Due to Michael's intervention, we weren't given that chance."

"So it's your opinion that had Michael not done that, the women would have had just as high a chance of survival?"

"Yes. It is."

I look at Richard with anger. He knows as well as I do that injecting those mothers with immuno-suppressants was a much safer course of action, and probably stopped almost all of the mothers, and the fetuses, from dying. Why is he saying this? Maybe he really does believe I sabotaged the company for the sake of saving Annie. Not knowing about what really happened with the military — how could he possibly understand me?

"That's all, your honor." Barnaby has lost the playful demeanor he had with Anthony. I am not sure if he really is shocked, or if this is simply a display for the jury — remorse on his client's behalf.

"Aren't you going to ask him anything else?" I say to Barnaby as he comes back to the table. "He's lying through his teeth."

"No," Barnaby whispers. "The jury's sympathy is with those women and those babies right at the moment. If we go too hard on him, we'll get them offside. We have to admit this for the mistake it was and move on."

That night I go back to my cell despondent. Barnaby explained to me trials are more about manipulating emotions, provoking compassion and identification for the defendant in the hearts and minds of the jury, than who is right or wrong. In this case especially.

It is hard to identify with and have compassion for someone whose reckless actions could easily have caused the deaths of twenty women and their babies, and did actually kill two babies. However good a job I did, however much my work might help to save people, the jury will want to see me punished. And if the only way they can punish me is by calling me guilty for the crimes the government is laying on me, they will do just that.

That night, I am led once again into the interrogation room.

"Okay," Don says, "this is your last chance, Michael. We know you didn't mean for that flu to break out, and that you probably didn't create those children as a threat to the human race, but if you don't help us now we can only assume that you do mean for people to die."

"Why is it okay for the government to wipe out millions for their own suspect purposes, but not for me to do something for the greater good?"

"Governments are elected to make decisions for the greater good, Michael, you have not been. Have you gone completely mad? I hope you don't think you're going to get off on an insanity plea." Don starts to get angry, but then changes track and continues in a softer tone. "Look, Michael, I can understand your anger, I really can. But think about those people you love. Who have helped you. Do you really want them to suffer?"

I take a deep breath. Of course I don't want them to suffer. I don't want Dylan or Sophie or indeed anyone else to have to pay for this.

"Michael, think clearly. Think about what you're doing. You've had a difficult time, but do you really want to blame the world for that? Do you really want to take all your anger at this government out on the entire species?"

"And what if I do tell you what you want to know? What will happen then?"

Don smiles, and his body relaxes into the chair with exhaustion. "Then everything gets easier. Easier for you, for your wife, for Dylan, for Sophie, for your modified children, for the New Church populations, for everybody involved. Nobody has to get hurt. We can come to an arrangement. The children can be quarantined on the havens, where you put them so they can't do any harm. You and Dylan will be free to go and live there too if you like. You won't be able to stay in this country, but we won't stop you from living somewhere else. You can live a free life, Michael. You can put all of this behind you and enjoy your life a little. Spend time with your wife. Know what it's like not to live in fear all the time. Be at peace. Isn't that what you've always wanted?"

The next morning, Dylan is on the witness stand.

Danny Brown stands in front of the jury after Dylan has been sworn in. Dylan has avoided looking at me, but now he glances over at me, giving a tiny shake of his head as he does so, pleading me with his eyes to understand him.

Mr Brown leads Dylan through a range of questions, establishing his identity and his relationship to me. In just over two hours they cover the entire extent of our past, and every one of our conversations about my immune system project.

Finally Danny gets to the damaging part. "Mr Hume, can you describe for the court exactly what it was that Michael said to you on November the eleventh of last year, the last time you saw each other?"

"He asked me if he could use the New Church islands to put his modified children on."

"And did he tell you why he wanted to do this?"

"He said they posed a threat to society. That they had

been responsible for a viral outbreak at the compound they were being kept at, and that they shouldn't be so close to each other. He said if they were separated, then they'd be safe."

"Did he explain to you what his purpose was in bringing up these children?"

"He told me that as the world descended into barbarism over the next fifty or so years, following the total collapse of the eco-system, these children and their descendants would be better able to survive than unmodified humans."

"Did he tell you that it was his plan to try to spread the code for this modification around the world, so that others would be born with it too?"

I wonder where they got this piece of information from. Was Gendigm already spreading the modifications? They must be — or there is no way they could have found out about this. But why are they doing it now, while I'm on trial? Surely they must realize that it will threaten my chances?

Maybe they don't trust me to keep quiet. Or maybe they have to do it now. Once the trial is done, if the government doesn't manage to get the information they need here, every government and corporate run state in the world will be after them. If they start releasing the modifications now, while they've still got time, there's a chance they'll succeed.

"Yes," Dylan says.

"And did he mention what he thought might happen once these modified children reached a critical mass?"

"No, he didn't."

"Can you tell me what you think might happen? You're

a trained biologist, are you not?"

"Yes, I am."

"Then?"

"There is a chance that they would start to breed new viruses."

"That are deadly to unmodified humans?"

"Yes."

"So do you think it was Michael's plan for this to happen? That this wasn't just an accident caused by his work?"

"It wasn't his plan, no. That is why he wanted to separate and quarantine them — so that they wouldn't put anyone else at risk. Not only that, but Michael was working on a somatic modification that would protect *Homo sapiens* from any diseases that these children might breed."

"But what about as the children grow older? Won't they present an even greater threat? And how was he going to make sure that everyone on the planet received his somatic modification?"

"I'm really not sure."

Danny continues to grill Dylan even further about his knowledge of Gendigm, but Dylan doesn't know any more and gives nothing away.

By the time he is finished, Dylan looks exhausted.

And then it is Barnaby's turn.

"How long have you been one of the leaders of the New Church for?" Barnaby asks him.

"Approximately two years."

"And when you were agreeing to testify for the prosecution, were you under any duress?"

"What do you mean?"

"I mean, were you being threatened with any criminal charges involving this case?"

"I was told that I could be prosecuted as the leader of a terrorist organization, and that because I was involved with Michael, I was just as liable for everything that he was doing as he was."

"Were any other forms of coercion used?"

Dylan hesitates for a moment, and looks over at his lawyer. "What do you mean by coercion?"

"I mean apart from threatening to prosecute you for Michael's crimes, did they do anything else to force your testimony?"

Dylan hesitates again, and then looks directly at me. We stare at each other for a long time and I can feel something pass between us through the court room. I shake my head at him, but he answers anyway: "I was locked up for months in solitary confinement. I was told I had to cooperate or I would never get out. That they would charge both of us. They told me that Michael was giving evidence against me, that he was trying to claim the whole thing was funded by the New Church, and that he was willing to testify against me."

"Objection, your honor," Brown says. "This wasn't in the witness statement. This is completely new information."

"I'll allow it," the judge says.

I sit there shocked. An outpouring of love for Dylan pervades me. I know that Dylan is risking his own freedom, that if they think he is trying to sabotage their case they will go after him with everything they've got.

"Thank you very much, Mr Hume. That's all, your

honor." Barnaby walks back to the desk.

"Mr Brown, have you got any further questions?" the judge says.

"Yes, I do, your honor."

"Go ahead, then."

Danny stands up and walks towards Dylan like a bull. "Mr Hume, are you suggesting that your statement was falsely given? That everything you said was said only because you were being forced to?"

"I only said it because I was forced to, yes."

"Does that mean it's not true?"

Dylan looks across at me. I know this is the moment. If Dylan tells them that it wasn't true, there is a good chance that I will get off. Unable to prove their case, they will lose. If Dylan says that, though, there is a good chance that he himself will be convicted. The government will not take lightly to their key witness committing perjury. Dylan and I lock eyes once again, and I shake my head at him.

"Mr Hume, will you answer the question, please?"

"No," Dylan says.

"No what?"

"No, it doesn't mean it wasn't true."

"So, despite the way this information was extracted, you are still admitting that everything you told us was the truth?"

"Yes," Dylan says.

"Thank you, your honor." Mr Brown turns back to his desk and sits down as if he's just won the trial.

I feel my body collapsing under me.

Finally, it comes time for us to make our case.

"Michael, would you mind telling the court exactly what you were planning on doing with these modified children of yours?" Barnaby says.

"As you have heard, I have been involved in a project to modify the human immune system to make people more resistant to disease. Having seen my wife suffer from HIV-4, I know how terrifying and debilitating it can be for both the sufferer and the families of someone who has a life-threatening illness. Given that governments are now involved in bio-warfare, and that there are only going to be more diseases than ever in the future, I wanted to create an immune system which would protect future generations against this suffering."

"And have you succeeded in doing this?"

"Yes, I have."

"There have been some problems, though, haven't there?"

"Yes. The modified children have started to breed viruses that are a potential threat to normal, unmodified human beings. Because their tolerance levels to viruses are much higher, the viruses have a chance to mutate when the modified children are in close proximity to one another."

"Is this something you anticipated might happen?"

"No, it's not."

"Why not?"

"Nobody could have. There are always more precautions you can take in experimentation like this, but at some point you have to take a risk. If we didn't take that risk, cures for many of the world's diseases would never be found. Cures which save millions of lives."

"Now that you know it is a risk, why is it that the code

for this modification has been made freely available to the public?"

James informed me last night that pills containing our modifications had been discovered on the black market. They were starting to be spread around the world. There was also information available on the net as to exactly what those modifications would do for both you and your children, and the likely consequences of not taking them.

"I have no idea," I say. "I was arrested before that happened."

"So who is in charge in your organization, EidoGenesis?"

"I was, along with a number of others."

"Did you give the order for this modification to be released?"

"It was always our intention to release it once it was finished, but if I had had a choice I would not have released it so soon."

"And what did you imagine would happen once it was released?"

"The modification we were working on was designed to protect *Homo sapiens* as much as it was to protect their offspring. We imagined that eventually our new species, *Homo novus*, would begin to take over from *Homo sapiens*."

"So you imagined that *Homo novus* would wipe *Homo sapiens* out?"

"No. I believe that *Homo sapiens* are taking care of that themselves."

There is silence in the courtroom.

"Would you care to elaborate, Michael?"

"Science has proven that global warming has reached the point where, within the next fifty years, eighty percent of *Homo sapiens* on the planet will be wiped out. To stop themselves being part of that eighty percent, governments and corporate leaders around the world are resorting to bio-warfare, wiping each other out in the millions but protecting themselves. The problem is, this is a zero-sum game. We're all going to lose. So what I imagined happening was a slow replacement of the surviving *Homo sapiens* with *Homo novus*, much in the same way *Homo sapiens* took over from Neanderthals. *Homo novus* is not only better adapted for disease, but they are also, thanks to their augmented cooperation, much more likely to establish a fair and just society."

"So you did want *Homo novus* to take over from *Homo sapiens*?"

"Let's not talk about them as if they are two completely separate species. They are identical to humans, in fact they are humans. The only difference is, they are better adapted for the future. A future that we're creating."

After lunch, Danny Brown gets up to cross examine me. This has always been the risk with putting me on the stand, but it is one we thought was necessary to take.

"Michael, can you please explain to us why you didn't hand the modified children over to the government as soon as you realized they were a potential threat to the population?"

Without being able to say anything about the government's role in the mass-murder of those people once living in the de-reg zone, explaining this is going to be hard.

"Quarantining the children on the islands was the safest and quickest way of dealing with the situation."

"Do you really think you had the right to make that decision? To potentially put at risk the population of this country?"

"As I said, I believed it was the best thing we could do to protect the population, and to protect those children."

"And you didn't think it was necessary to report this incident?"

"We didn't have time. I was arrested before we'd even had time to finish dealing with it."

"Were you yourself not about to flee the country at the time of your arrest?"

"I wasn't fleeing the country. I was going where I was most needed — to help the modified children and their mothers settle on the New Church islands."

"Can you tell us exactly who was behind this project, Michael? Who was funding and supporting it?"

"You mean apart from the government? We did receive a fairly large grant from them."

"Yes. Apart from the government."

"The name of the company was HGM Industries. My original company, Geneus, was also involved, but they pulled out about two years ago for financial reasons."

"You said before that governments and corporations are resorting to bio-warfare, and that you did what you did to protect people from that, but weren't you yourself resorting to bio-warfare to help your new species survive?"

"That was never my intention. As I said, our modifications were also designed to help existing *Homo sapiens* survive. What would be the point of modifying children if they killed their own parents with diseases before they were even old enough to look after themselves?"

Barnaby and Danny give their closing statements and then for nearly three days, the jury deliberates. On the fourth morning, I once again sit in the courtroom. Once everyone is seated, the jury files slowly in.

"Has the jury made their decision?" the judge asks the foreman.

"Yes your honor, we have."

"And how find you?"

The woman stands up and looks across at me. "On the count of intent to release a bio-weapon on Australian soil, we find the defendant not guilty. On the count of organization of terrorist activities, we find the defendant not guilty. On the count of conspiracy against the Australian people, we find the defendant not guilty. On the count of reckless endangerment of human life, we find the defendant guilty. On the count of attempt to avoid prosecution, we find the defendant guilty. On the count of withholding information of terrorist activities, we find the defendant guilty. On the count of conspiring with a terrorist organization, we find the defendant guilty."

Two days later, I sit before the judge for sentencing.

"Michael Khan, given that you still refuse to disclose the names of the other members of the organization for whom you were working, I hereby sentence you to fifteen years in prison without parole."

EPILOGUE

I SPEND MOST of my time reading these days. Not many books are being written any more, as most people are just struggling to survive, so I read all the old classics.

It's taken me a good six months to adjust. Before I came here I was a scientist, a husband, a friend. Someone who was trying to do the best for the world in the only way I knew how. And now what am I? A prison inmate. No better or worse than the guy who killed three women who's locked up in the cell next to mine. It takes a while for one's ego to get used to that kind of change.

Now I have, though, I almost feel free. Funny that I should feel freer in here than I ever did outside, when I had all the freedom in the world. It's a freedom from myself. I've come to terms with my incarceration. And although I don't think I should be locked up for the things the government has locked me up for, I do think I should be locked up — for my part in what happened to the people in the de-reg zone.

I guess they call that karma.

Annie comes and visits me regularly and tells me about the lives of little Shy and Harvey, who she adopted out to two different families but keeps a close eye on. She never tells me who the families are, but I presume they're nice. She occasionally gets a call from Dylan, who managed to avoid prosecution, and apparently all the other children are growing up healthily as well.

Even Justin comes in to visit me occasionally and tells me about a new job he's working on: genetic modification of the digestive system so people can eat all the crap they want without ever getting fat. It's the best job he could find. At least he's happy with Shung, and they have two children of their own — both *Homo novus*.

Most importantly, though, our genetic modifications have gone viral. Now they're open source, people all around the world are taking them. For a while they were outlawed by governments and corporate states, but given that everyone else was using them even those laws were soon overturned.

We weren't the first species in this line of evolution, and we certainly won't be the last. We're nothing, after all, but perfectible animals.

DEAR READER,

IF you liked *Perfectible Animals*, please consider helping me out in 3 easy ways. I'm a self-published author and don't have a big publishing house behind me. Perfectible Animals took me nearly thirteen years to write, as many other things got in the way (mainly that annoying thing called reality). I hope to have the next part (yes, there will be a sequel) finished A LOT quicker and to one day make writing a full-time job, but I won't be able to do it without your help.

1. Please recommended my book to your friends!

2. Please leave a review on www.amazon.com or www.goodreads.com Reviews are one of the most important tools people use when deciding to purchase a book or not. If you could take just a few minutes to write a review (good or bad) I will be eternally grateful.

3. Visit www.thomasnorwood.com.au and sign up to my mailing list and you'll be the first to receive news of my next book release. You can also like my Facebook page or follow me on Twitter.

Thanks again for reading and I'll see you next time.

Thomas Norwood.

ACKNOWLEDGEMENTS:

I WOULD like to say a huge THANK YOU to the following people who helped in the development of this novel. Without you this novel would never have become what it has.

Iliana Hernandez (Manuscript assessment and life support), Allan Dyen-Shapiro (Science advisor and manuscript assessment), Ezra Lunel (Story development consultant), John Robert Marlow (Story development consultant) and Derek Broughton (line editor).

And my beta readers: Lucy Norwood, Zara Officer, Niyati Mavinkurve, Sara Marschand, Alysia Seymour, Derek Broughton, Catalina Perez, Chen Xi, Darlene Suber, Juliette Hughes-Norwood, Tristan King, and Kathleen Reagan.

ABOUT THE AUTHOR:

Thomas Norwood is an Australian novelist. He lives in the hills of the Yarra Valley with his wife Iliana and their two cats, Camila and Sawa. Perfectible Animals is his first novel.